# WHEN I KNEW YOU

# What Reviewers Say About KE Payne's Work

### 365 Days

"One of the most real books I've ever read. It frequently made me giggle out loud to myself while muttering, 'OMG, RIGHT?'"
—*AfterEllen.com*

"Payne captures Clemmie's voice—an engaging blend of teenage angst and saucy self-assurance—with full-throated style."—Richard Labonte, *Book Marks*

### me@you.com

"A fast-paced read [that] I found hard to put down."—*C-Spot Reviews*

"A wonderful, thought-provoking novel of a teenager discovering who she truly is."—*Fresh Fiction*

### Another 365 Days

"Funny, engaging, and accessible."—*Kirkus Reviews*

### The Road to Her

"A wonderful, heart-warming story of love, unrequited love, betrayal, self discovery and coming out."—*Terry's Lesfic Reviews*

### Because of Her

"A must-read."—*Lesbian Fiction Reviews*

### Once The Clouds Have Gone

"Delightful and heart-warming, this sweet romance was everything a good romance should be."—*Prism Book Alliance*

Visit us at www.boldstrokesbooks.com

# By the Author

365 Days

me@you.com

Another 365 Days

The Road to Her

Because of Her

Once The Clouds Have Gone

When I Knew You

# WHEN I KNEW YOU

*by*
KE Payne

2016

**WHEN I KNEW YOU**
© 2016 BY KE PAYNE. ALL RIGHTS RESERVED.

ISBN 13: 978-1-62639-562-6

THIS TRADE PAPERBACK ORIGINAL IS PUBLISHED BY
BOLD STROKES BOOKS, INC.
P.O. BOX 249
VALLEY FALLS, NY 12185

FIRST EDITION: MARCH 2016

**CREDITS**
EDITOR: RUTH STERNGLANTZ
PRODUCTION DESIGN: SUSAN RAMUNDO
COVER DESIGN BY SHERI (GRAPHICARTIST2020@HOTMAIL.COM)

# Acknowledgments

My sincere thanks to Ruth Sternglantz and Susan Ramundo for making all my books look so wonderful, and to Cindy Cresap, Connie Ward, Sandy Lowe, and all the other wonderful people at BSB who work so tirelessly behind the scenes for us all. Also to Sheri for taking my picture idea and turning it into the beautiful work of art you see on the front cover.

Thank you to Sarah Martin for being an amazing beta reader, and for explaining the finer details of shoulder dislocations to me! A big thanks to Mrs. D too for all her support and friendship.

To BJ for tirelessly reading and rereading endless drafts with me, but mostly for all the love, laughs, and support.

Finally, a massive thank you to all the readers who continue to buy my books and who take the time to contact me. I truly appreciate every email, Facebook comment, and Tweet that you send me. Your continued support is immensely important to me—thank you all so much.

## CHAPTER ONE

Ash hadn't seen her at first. But there she was, cutting through the crowd, the nausea of recognition hitting Ash when she spotted a brief glimpse of that familiar blond hair in amongst the throng of people. A dizziness of memories tightened the band across her chest when she heard a snippet of her adorable laugh filtering through the noise of the room, a laugh that Ash was once so at ease with, but which now reminded her of another time, bringing with it a thousand memories crashing around her.

Ash was glad she hadn't seen her at the funeral; it had been hard enough being there as it was, saying goodbye to Livvy, without having to cope with that as well. But now, here at the wake an hour after Livvy's funeral, it was clear the day had decided to throw her one last unpleasant thing before it was finally done with her.

Ash didn't want to approach her, let alone talk to her. How would she even begin to start a conversation with her, after all this time? *Hi, how are you? Remember me? The girl whose heart you broke all those years ago?*

Others in the room faded around her as Ash protectively cradled her glass in hands that were sweatier than they had been moments ago and watched as she chatted easily with an elderly man Ash didn't recognize. She hadn't changed, Ash noticed. Most people alter slightly over the years, subtle changes that prove time cannot—no matter how hard you try—be stemmed. Not her, though. Long black eyelashes still accentuated those beautiful cobalt-blue eyes that Ash once found herself lost in, while her perfect hair tumbled about her face, just as it used to do as a teenager. Despite her reservations, Ash couldn't tear her eyes away from her. Honey-coloured skin that Ash swore she could still taste, after all these years. Slightly upturned lips that always made her look as though she were smiling, those same lips that Ash had once kissed over and over again. The breath caught in Ash's throat as a vivid memory struck her, and she hastily looked away, choosing instead to stare resolutely down into her glass, astonished at how she still managed to make her feel. Dismayed that Natalie Braithwaite still had the power to elicit any kind of emotion from her after so many years.

"Ashley Wells!" A voice beside Ash dissolved her thoughts in a heartbeat. "My God, you're a blast from the past."

"Lisa…" Ash screwed up her eyes, remembering. "Saatchi. Right?"

"It's Turner now." Lisa lifted her left hand and waggled her ring finger, now clad in a wedding band and a ring with a stone in that Ash couldn't see quickly enough. "Boring, hey? Should have kept my maiden name."

Ash smiled.

"Good turnout." Lisa lifted her chin to the room.

Did that require an answer? Ash nodded, adding, "Mm," just in case it did.

"When was the last time you saw her?" Lisa asked. "I couldn't believe it when I heard."

Nat? No, of course not Nat. Ash stole another look across the room. She was still there.

"Livvy?" Ash's face clouded. "Six months or so? Not long."

"Hard to believe she's gone," Lisa said. She lifted a hand to someone standing some way from her. "Not quite thirty-five. Makes you think, doesn't it?"

Ash had done nothing *but* think since she'd taken the phone call two weeks before and heard news she never expected to have to hear. Hours turned into days, and still she hadn't been able to make sense of why a perfectly fit and healthy thirty-four-year-old should succumb to cancer, or why Livvy had decided to keep her illness to herself. It was inconceivable that it had even happened. Other people got cancer: smokers, drinkers. Not her best friend. Not Livvy.

"How's Chloe coping?" Lisa asked.

Ash followed Lisa's gaze over towards Livvy's daughter, standing with Livvy's mother Judy and two other people Ash didn't recognize.

"As well as you'd expect a fourteen-year-old to cope." Ash shrugged. According to Judy, Chloe had handled the situation with a maturity way beyond her years. At least as far as the outside world could see, anyway.

"You were as thick as thieves, you three." Lisa took a drink.

"Sorry?"

"You, Livvy, and…what was her name?"

"Nat." Ash's voice sounded thick to her. She cleared her throat. "Nat," she repeated, clearer this time.

"Natalie Braithwaite!" Lisa nodded enthusiastically. "That's right. Posh name for a posh girl. I remember now."

Nat's name burrowed into Ash's ears and buzzed around inside her brain, like an annoying bee. She'd refused to think it or speak it for years. If Ash pretended Nat didn't exist, it meant she was finally over her. Those were the rules, and always had been.

"We all used to be quite jealous of you three." Lisa laughed. "At school. You know? You were The Untouchables."

"Seriously?" Ash looked at Lisa, suddenly willing her to shut up. Or go. Either would do right now.

"You were all so close. It was sweet."

"It was a long time ago now." Ash smiled, her smile masking her increasing discomfort.

"Was it Nat that told you about Livvy?" Lisa asked. "She emailed Megan Fairweather. You remember her? Is that still her name? Anyway, she emailed her apparently, and then Megan emailed Sophie, and that's how I heard."

"Nat and I haven't been in touch for years." Ash peered down into her empty glass, wishing it still had something left in it to drink. Anything to wash down the lump in her throat. "I heard from someone else."

"You don't speak to Nat any more?" Lisa stared at Ash. "I'm astonished. You two were joined at the hip, weren't you?"

"Again"—Ash smiled tightly—"it was all a long time ago."

"But you went to university together?"

"We went our separate ways when we were eighteen." Ash glared at Lisa. Couldn't she take the hint? "No biggie."

"Well, I'm amazed." Lisa shook her head. "I always thought—"

"Like I said," Ash repeated, annoyance creeping into her tone, "it was no biggie. If you'll excuse me." She moved away, making a show of seeking out the drinks, leaving Lisa behind her. Once safely squirreled away in the corner of the room, Ash's breathing eased. She put down her glass and rubbed her sweaty palms down the sides of her trousers, adjusted the collar of her shirt, then pulled each cuff down tight through the arms of her suit, just for something to do. It was either that, Ash thought, or allow her irrational thoughts of Nat—brought to the fore thanks to Lisa—to engulf her.

Nat Braithwaite.

Ash closed her eyes. She had spoken her name in her head again, and the familiarity of it after years of silence was beautiful to her. Even after everything.

She forced herself to open her eyes, the knot of tension that had been steadily inching its way up her neck, threatening a headache all day, not yet ready to untie itself. If only she could leave now. Ash's mind took itself back to her hotel and imagined how good it would feel to sink down into her soft bed. Raid the minibar. Catch a few films on some obscure satellite channel. Forget today had ever happened.

Ash tuned out the chatter in the room and focused on Lisa's words to her. The Untouchables. Thick as thieves. Joined at the hip. They were all true. Seventeen years ago, Ash, Livvy, and Nat had had the world at their feet, and a great, yawning, fabulous future ahead of them all. They'd never be apart. Virtually from their very first day at school, as naive, wide-eyed eleven-year-olds, they'd forged a bond they knew would never be broken. Strangers to each other in the morning, they'd become firm friends by the time their first school day together had ended. Months later, they'd even sworn on the strength of their bond, one wet and windy day during afternoon break, hidden away from prying eyes behind the science block. Friends forever. Ash ran her thumb across the material of her suit, over the small scar on her forearm hidden underneath, high enough not to be seen under a sleeve, low enough to remind her of the vow they'd all taken. She blinked. So stupid. They'd been so stupid and immature back then. How could they have vowed never to be apart? How could they have known what the future would hold? How could Ash and Nat have ever foreseen that they'd eventually form a bond of their own, with a whole new set of secret vows that even Livvy wasn't party to?

As if by some force of their own, Ash's eyes sought out Nat again. Faces ebbed and flowed about her. Some strangers, some familiar. She dropped her gaze and melted back into the shadows before Nat had the chance to spot her. She'd know she was here, of course, but would she try and seek her out? Ash hoped not; she was here to remember Livvy. To reminisce, supposedly, with school friends. To mourn her oldest friend, rather than opening old wounds after years of trying to heal. Torturing herself over Nat, in the same way she'd done a hundred times in the immediate years after they'd parted.

Her gaze fell back to Nat. Some wounds, it seemed, still refused to heal.

"How's it going?"

"Boy, am I glad to talk to you at last." Ash sank a shoulder against the frame of the window, gaining comfort from Gabe's voice. She pulled back the curtain and peered outside. Afternoon had given way to early evening and the pace of the street outside her room was finally slowing down. Commuters had disappeared into the bowels of the Underground, tourists had trudged, weary, back to their respective hotels, shops had pulled down their shutters. The

West End of London could—albeit temporarily—breathe a sigh of relief. At least until the theatre-goers emerged in a few hours' time, anyway.

"So how was it?" Gabe asked.

"As expected." Ash watched a pigeon peck at some chewing gum down on the pavement, hopping from foot to foot as it dodged the odd pedestrian, before resuming its task. "Livvy's mother was in bits."

"Understandable," Gabe said. "And the daughter?"

"The same as her grandmother," Ash replied, "but holding it together." She paused. "Gabe?"

"Yuh-huh?"

"I wish you'd been with me." Ash let the curtain drop from her hands. The room darkened. "I know you couldn't come, so don't think I'm playing the guilt card on you." She laughed. "Just could have used some of that famous Gabriel Buchanan manly support."

"You're sweet." Ash heard Gabe make a kissing sound down the phone. "I did offer…"

"I know." Ash held her hand up, even though Gabe couldn't see. "But then you'd have had to cancel trips, and we'd have lost three days' profits…"

She looked back into the gloom of her room. To lose three days' profits, she knew, would be unthinkable. Her mind wandered back down to Cornwall. To home, and to her beloved boat. She'd started her tourist boat business ten years ago, starting slowly, unsure whether it was what she really wanted to do. It had been tough too, in those first few years but she'd dug in and persevered, turning it into the thriving business it was today. The three days away from it that Ash had taken off to come to London for Livvy's funeral had so far felt like forever.

"And Aston Grafton from the Preservation Trust would have kicked up a fuss," Gabe added.

"Aston Grafton can go screw himself." Ash walked from the window. "He still owes me some money for last month's trips."

"Good luck with getting that back," Gabe said.

"Nat was there today." Ash sat on the edge of her bed.

"*The* Nat?" Gabe laughed. "The same Nat that stole your heart all those years ago, and that you *still* talk about, even after all this time?"

"The very same."

"Did you talk to her?" Gabe asked.

"Jeez, no." Ash frowned. "I totally freaked if I'm honest. I sort of hid from her so I wouldn't have to speak to her."

"Weirdo."

"I didn't want to have to revisit my past," Ash said defensively. "Not there. Not at Livvy's send-off."

"I guess that *could* have been awkward..."

"Ugh. Exes." Ash shuddered. "Who'd have them, hey?"

"Chicken, sometimes in life we have to bump into exes," Gabe said gently. "It's in the official exes' handbook, so it must be true." He paused. "Granted, most people don't have to wait nearly seventeen years, but..."

"She'd hardly changed." God knows, Ash had thought about nothing else in the two hours since she'd left the wake. Her eyes. Her voice, the same but mellower with age. Her beautiful smile. All still had the same mesmerizing effect on Ash that they'd always had. "I kind of wanted her to have, you know?"

"She still looked eighteen?" Gabe gasped. "Ashley, my dear, I want whatever moisturizer this Nat girl uses."

"You know what I mean." Ash eased her shoes from her feet, shuffled back further onto her bed, and stared up at the light fitting in the middle of her ceiling.

Plans. There had been so many plans. The Untouchables would never be broken up. That was their vow. They'd all choose the same university, all achieve the goals they'd set themselves as they neared the end of their school years. Ash frowned, remembering the night she and Nat made their pledge to study medicine together, to become successful doctors together. Livvy would achieve her dream of becoming a lawyer. They'd even laughed about who would get the better final mark. Livvy was convinced she would. They'd find a house together too, Nat had said—Ash, Nat, and Livvy—and while Livvy would bore them with legal jargon, Ash and Nat would revolt her by bringing specimens from their lab home with them. It was going to be a blast. It was going to be perfect.

"You think you'll see her again?" Gabe's voice roused her.

"Doubt it." Ash hesitated. "Probably just as well."

"Because?"

"Because seeing her again lit this little spark inside me," Ash said. "Just…here." She pointed to her stomach.

"Honey, I can't see you."

"You know what I'm talking about."

"The little feeling inside that sometimes only an ex can set off?" Gabe offered.

"But not how you think." Ash fell back onto her pillow. "More a combination of memories and sadness than anything else."

"I know," Gabe said. He paused. "So when are you coming home?"

"Wednesday," Ash said. "I'm going over to Livvy's mother's house tomorrow." She frowned. "She has something to give me from Livvy, apparently."

"That's sweet."

"You're certain you can manage without me another day?"

"Ash, I already told you," Gabe said, "we'll be fine here."

"Sure?" Ash asked again. "And you can cope with Widgeon a bit longer?"

"Sure I'm sure," Gabe affirmed. "And looking after your dog is a doddle, you know that." He laughed. "Take all the time you need. You should make the most of London while you're there."

"There's no sea here though." Ash pulled a face. "I miss the sea."

"You left Cornwall, what? Twenty-four hours ago?" Gabe laughed. "How can you miss the sea already?"

"It's in my blood."

"Says the girl born in Surrey."

"Stop picking on me," Ash whined down the phone, making Gabe laugh again. "I miss you, I miss Doris—"

"And why you had to name your boat is still a mystery to me."

"I miss being outdoors." Ash looked around her room, trying to ignore the creeping suffocation. Her mind skittered down to the sea, to her boat, to the fresh air and the sense of freedom that always accompanied such thoughts. "London's so…grubby."

*And so full of reminders of Nat.*

"You'll be back before you know it," Gabe soothed. "In the meantime, take all the time you need."

"I will, thanks." Ash paused. "But I can guarantee I'll be on the first train home on Wednesday." She looked to the window and to the chink of dusky light filtering through the curtains, and shuddered. "Way too many memories around this city for my liking."

Nat rested her head back against her pillow and allowed the tensions of the day to ease slowly away from her neck. Her recently downed double brandy sat warm, but acidic, in her empty stomach. She rolled her head across the pillow and spied her unopened sandwich, still on her dresser where she'd tossed it down earlier. Nat extended her arm, knowing it would be too far away to reach, then let it flop to her side, the brandy turning her limbs to wool.

She'd seen Ash again. The same Ash she'd thought about day after day for years, and it hadn't been as weird as she'd often thought it might be. Nat closed her eyes. Ash had seen her too, Nat was sure of that, and even though she had so wanted to go to Ash, her feet had refused to comply. To talk to her, just to hear her voice again, would have been wonderful. So why hadn't she been able to make herself walk across the room to her?

It had been too long since she'd seen Ash. Flashbacks appeared to Nat in the darkness: the first time they met, aged eleven; the first time, a few months later, she and Ash had spent time alone when Livvy had been off school for a week with a cold.

Nat swallowed.

How old had she been when she'd first fallen for Ash? Thirteen? Fourteen? Of course, back then, Nat had assumed her feelings for Ash were simply because Ash was the cool kid in school and Nat had valued their close friendship. But then, Livvy had been cool too, and she'd never made Nat feel the way Ash had. She'd never made her insides flip over just with a look, or a laugh, or a friendly arm around her shoulder. Livvy had never been constantly in Nat's thoughts, had never made Nat feel ten feet tall. With Ash it had been different. Ash had felt it too, Nat had found out months later, although both had been too shy to admit it to the other.

Until netball.

Nat turned over and smiled into her pillow. Who'd have thought throwing balls into a hoop could have led to *that*?

Netball had been their thing. Nat's and Ash's. Livvy, being far too cool, had said she'd much rather spend her Wednesday afternoons watching the boys' football team than standing under a hoop with her arms in the air. Her words. That had been fair enough; they *were* fifteen, after all. The age where girls preferred sizing up the boys than getting sweaty with a whole bunch of other girls. Well, some girls did. Others were different.

Even now, the memory of her first kiss with Ash made her insides dance. Alone in the changing room one afternoon after netball, having hardly been able to take their eyes off each other during the game, they finally gave in to their feelings and forgot their shyness. They'd held hands—something they did often— but that day Nat had felt a difference in the way Ash's thumb had trailed over the back of her hand. Had felt a shift in the way Ash was looking at her.

"I've never kissed anyone before."

Ash's words to her were as clear today as they were then.

"Me neither," Nat had replied, the anticipation nearly killing her.

"We could…you know? If you want?"

Before Nat had even had time to answer, Ash pulled her closer. Thinking they must be mad, because at any moment someone might come back in and find them, Nat hadn't pushed her away and it had been as if she'd waited her whole fifteen years just for that moment. It had been perfect, even more so when Ash's mouth had found hers straight away again after that first kiss. Kissing Ash had been everything Nat had always imagined it would be. Soft. Sweet. Quite unlike the disastrous fumbling Nat had endured with Gareth Bates from her French class in the bandstand at the park a year before, when she'd used him in a vain attempt to try and forget that Ash was rapidly creeping into her every thought. It hadn't worked.

"Was it okay?"

Ash's concern had been touching. Nat had nodded, unable to keep the grin from her face or the fizz of excitement from her stomach.

"It was perfect."

After their netball kiss, Nat and Ash found they quite liked it. Kissing. Found they were pretty darned good at it too, so despite the guilt they both felt at hiding their fledgling relationship from Livvy, they carried on kissing. A lot.

A car horn blaring on the street outside stirred Nat from her memories. She rubbed at her eyes.

That first kiss was such a long time ago now.

She swung her legs over the side of the bed and padded across to the dresser, then scooped up the sandwich, opened it, and sniffed it. Nausea caught in her throat. She'd been dreading the funeral, knowing she'd probably have to see Ash again. Her nervousness had risen and deflated on an almost hourly basis as the days had crept closer, escalating to a peak that day. Nat had eaten hardly a thing over the last forty-eight hours or so. Surely she'd be hungry now it was all over. Nat sniffed the sandwich again. Perhaps not.

Despite everything, she had had a pinprick of hope that Ash would have forgiven her by now, rather than ignoring her. Would have sought her out, apologized for her silence for all those years, and laughed everything off as just being a run-of-the-mill teenage relationship and breakup. Nat frowned at her sandwich, annoyed at her own thought process. Of course Ash wouldn't have dismissed it so lightly. It had been so much more than that, and to call it a routine breakup was doing it an injustice. What she and Ash had shared had been the most wonderful romance, an all-consuming, roller coast of a ride. They were sixteen and in love, and Nat had flourished with Ash—almost as if she'd only been existing until their relationship.

Love had made her grow as a person; thanks to Ash, Nat realized she actually quite liked herself. She came out of her shell, found a sense of humour she didn't know existed, teased out by Ash. Became the person she always thought she might be, underneath the shyness. Comfortable in her own skin.

Nat tossed the sandwich back down.

Ash had been just what she'd needed. Girlfriend, best friend, confidant, soul mate. Ash would have done anything for her—and frequently had. Nat had been Ash's world.

Then Nat had let Ash's world fall apart.

# CHAPTER TWO

L ivvy's childhood home in Wimbledon looked exactly the same as Ash remembered it, bringing with it a fresh rash of memories. Even the avenue on which it sat—and which was now dappled in soft October shade from the large, still-leafy trees that lined it—didn't seem to have changed much since the last time Ash had walked down it from the train station, probably over fifteen years or more before.

The outside of number twenty-two Bartrim Avenue had always struck Ash as being a treat for the eyes: a classic Edwardian, it was set back a little way from the pavement with the most immaculate front lawn and impeccable borders lined with an array of flowers. It was typical suburbia, and always pleasantly quiet; you would never guess, Ash now thought as she strode down the road, that the centre of London, with all its noise and glitz and grime, sat just a few miles north.

Ash's gaze rested on the front door, the same front door she'd stood behind so many times in her teenage years, waiting for Livvy to answer, watching through the frosted glass to see her shadowy figure hurry down the hallway stairs inside. She had been lucky, Ash now thought, that she, Livvy, and Nat had all lived no more than a fifteen minute Tube ride from one another. Their childhood had been spent in and out of either one or the others' houses, long summers spent playing in one another's streets, Halloweens spent hanging around whoever's district had something cool going on, cosy Christmas Eves in either Ash's, Nat's, or Livvy's front rooms, depending on how they felt, or who had the best fire going. It had been idyllic.

Then the idyll had twisted into pain.

Ash frowned the thought away and rang the bell. She stepped back but couldn't stop herself from watching through the frosted glass, waiting to see a shadowy figure approach the door, even though she knew it wouldn't be Livvy this time. Old habits obviously died hard.

Livvy's mother, when she answered the door, looked as though she'd been crying.

Ashley hesitated on the threshold, unsure of her next move, relieved when Judy made the first move.

"Ashley." Judy approached her and pulled Ash into an embrace. "Thank you for coming over."

Ash accepted the embrace, feeling every inch a child again. Still shy in Livvy's mother's company, still too shy to tell her she preferred to be called Ash. To Judy Fancourt, Ash was, and always would be, Ashley.

"I've made tea." Judy pushed the door closed behind them and beckoned Ash to follow her. "And I've got cake. You still like cake, don't you? Victoria sponge. That was always your favourite, wasn't it? Do you still like it?" Judy's grieving energy shimmered off the walls of the hall.

"I love it." Ash followed Judy to the lounge. "Thank you."

The lounge was as Ash remembered too. Sublimely decorated in neutral colours with classy furniture—expensive, but not so expensive as to be pretentious—and possibly the comfiest sofa Ash had ever sat on. Old money, as Ash's mother had often said. There were cards everywhere too. Ash looked about her, to the multitude of sympathy cards lining every available space. A darkness approached as the reality hit her: Livvy really was gone. It had all been true. Ash sank down into the sofa as Judy took the chair next to her. Her best friend was gone, and Ash would never see her again.

Guilt tumbled over her. She should have made more of an effort to get up to London more often to see her, rather than hiding herself away in Cornwall pretending that it was the business keeping her there. It wasn't. In reality, she'd had no desire to return to London, the city of her worst heartbreak. What if she ever bumped into Nat? Ash's actions had been ridiculous, and she'd known it; the chances of her encountering Nat in a city as large as London were zero. But the nagging worry that an unknowing Livvy might have engineered a surprise meeting for them all still prevented her from returning too often. Emails and Skype calls to Livvy were all very well, but they weren't the same. Despite Ash's reluctance to meet up though, she and Livvy had remained friends to the end.

Then Livvy had died.

"Do you take sugar?" Judy's voice pulled Ash back. "The cake I remember," she said, laughing, "the sugar…" Judy shook her head.

"No." Ash smiled. "No sugar, thanks." She took her tea from Judy and watched as she cut her a slice of cake, holding her cup with one hand, and her saucer with the other, thanks to hands that had somehow developed a tremor the minute she'd entered the house. Was that the guilt again? Ash should have known about Livvy. Why had she never told her? If she'd known, Ash would have been on the first train up to London, despite everything.

"It's so good to see you again." Judy placed a plate with Ash's cake on it onto the table. She reached over and put her hand on Ash's knee. "You've grown into a lovely young woman. I only thought yesterday. At the…at Livvy's funeral."

Ash felt heat spread across her neck. "Thank you." She took a hasty sip from her tea.

"You were this shy teenager last time I saw you." Judy sat back in her chair. "I can picture you now, sitting on that sofa with Livvy and Nat, laughing at something that'd amused you." Judy lifted her head to where Ash now sat. "Giggling amongst yourselves, crowded around one of Livvy's music magazines."

A flicker of a smile passed Ash's lips. "It seems like a lifetime ago now."

"And then one day you stopped coming round." Judy studied Ash. "Just like that." She smiled. "Teenagers, hey?"

Ash smiled back. "Never understand them." She sipped at her tea, as if by doing so it might change the subject.

Perhaps not.

"We never knew why." Ash watched as Judy picked up a knife and cut herself a slice of cake. "Livvy would never tell me. She just said you rarely came up to London once you got into your twenties."

*Because coming back to the place where I'd once been so happy was too painful.*

"All she told me was that you failed your exams and decided to travel. Try a different path in life," Judy said. She tilted her head to one side. "You could have still done it, you know."

"Done what?" Ash picked up her cake and bit into it.

"Gone to medical school," Judy said. "Like you always planned."

Ash swallowed her cake. "No," she finally said. "I couldn't have."

"You could have retaken your exams," Judy pressed. "Gone a year later, once you'd got the travelling bug out of your system. I know you and Nat wanted to go together, but—"

"No." Even to Ash's own ears she'd sounded harsh. "It was never going to happen," she added more softly. Her dream had been shattered, thanks to Nat. Exams failed by Ash's inability to think about anything other than her broken heart. Why would she even have contemplated retaking her final year at school, then following Nat to medical school like some dumb sheep, when Nat had made it abundantly clear she didn't want her any more? No, Ash had decided on that hot August day when her disastrous exam results arrived at her parents' house that she needed to get away. And fast. Start over somewhere. No one would miss her; her parents assumed she was taking a gap year off and were happy for her to have an adventure. Ash's lies had been so convincing and had snowballed to the point her mother and father had actively encouraged her to travel, assuming she'd have it out of her system within a year and would return.

So Ash travelled. She would never have been cut out to be a doctor anyway; that's what she told herself in the months and years following, when she travelled the world seeking answers to her many questions. Perhaps she wasn't as much like Nat and Livvy as she'd thought when she was sixteen, both determined to succeed. All Ash wanted was to be happy and free. Studying for another seven years only to end up in a pressurized career wouldn't make her happy *or* free, would it? If she told herself that enough times, she thought she might start believing it too.

"Livvy told me a while ago you're living in Cornwall now." Judy was speaking. "Is that right?"

Ash blinked at her. "Yes," she said. "I have a house there. Old fisherman's cottage, overlooking the sea."

Or rather, a heap of junk, as Gabe had called it when he first set eyes on it. No more than an empty shell, really. Abandoned, unloved, and infested with mice until Ash saw its potential, bought it on a whim at auction, and slowly transformed it.

Now *that* had been cathartic. Finally choosing to settle back in England after five years of travelling Europe, Holly Cottage had been just what Ash had needed to concentrate her mind on something else rather than herself. Aged twenty-three, with a backpack full of memories, a new best friend in the shape of Gabe, and a vision for the future, Ash had embraced the idea of transforming the cottage into something wonderful. Holly Cottage, it appeared, was the therapy she could have used at eighteen.

"It sounds idyllic," Judy said. "David and I always thought we might like a place by the sea." Her face fell. "Then I lost him, and Livvy needed me more than ever, and…" She cut her glance away. "Now I've lost her too."

"I'm sorry." Ash reached over and captured Judy's hand.

"I have Chloe now to keep me occupied." Judy laughed softly. "I think we'll be good for one another."

"How's she been?" Ash asked.

"Remarkably brave," Judy replied.

"And…her father?"

Ash noticed the flicker of anger cross Judy's face.

"Still in Australia," Judy said, "with his new family and with no intention of coming over, despite everything."

"Classy." Ash raised her eyebrows.

"If there's one thing Stephen isn't," Judy said, "it's classy." She turned her head away from Ash. "She's late." She squeezed Ash's hand, and Ash sensed Judy forcing her attention away from her sadness. "Perhaps not." Judy looked at the clock. "Were you early?"

"I…"

*Chloe was late?*

"More tea?" Judy nodded at Ash's cup.

"I'm good." Ash lifted her cup. "But thanks anyway."

The chime of the doorbell in the hall made Ash turn her head towards the door.

"That'll be her." Judy rose, excused herself to Ash, then left the room.

Ash heard Nat's voice out in the hallway a second after she heard the front door open. Wanting to escape, but knowing she couldn't, Ash drank back her tea. She flicked cake crumbs from her trousers, fussed about with her fringe, tidying it, then cursed herself for caring how she looked. She didn't give a damn about what Nat did or didn't think of her any more. Ash's hand strayed back to her hair. Nat was nothing to her now, and Ash nothing to her.

So why did she feel so nervous?

The closer Nat's voice sounded, the faster Ash's heart decided to beat. Ludicrous. And deeply annoying.

"We're just in here." Judy appeared in the doorway, holding the door open with one hand. "Tea?"

"Perfect." Nat followed Judy. "Thanks."

Nat's eyes settled on Ash the second she entered the room. If seeing Ash sitting in Judy's front room had caused a reaction inside her, Ash thought, she hid it very well in that initial look. There was nothing. No flicker of emotion, no hint of surprise. No warmth. Nothing.

Ash was aware she'd stopped breathing. Adrenaline swept through her, from her scalp to her toes, blurring her vision, heating her cheeks as Nat's eyes rested on hers.

"Ash." Finally Nat smiled.

"How are you?" Ash grimaced at her starched politeness. "I mean—"

"I'm good. You?"

*Fine until a minute ago.*

"Same. Yeah." Ash nodded.

"It's been...how long?" Nat tipped her head to one side like an inquisitive puppy. It was an endearing gesture that was still so familiar to Ash, and one of the many characteristics that had made Ash fall so deeply in love with her, once upon a time.

"Gosh...fifteen years or so?" Ash raised her eyes heavenward, as if thinking hard. *Sixteen years, five months. Not that I've been counting.*

"Has it really been that long?" Nat whistled quietly through her teeth.

"Seems like only yesterday, doesn't it?" Ash replied, probably more tartly than she'd meant to.

"Yes." Nat studied Ash closely, forcing Ash to lower her eyes, uncomfortable at the scrutiny. "In some ways it does."

Ash studied the carpet at her feet with minute precision, desperate to avoid eye contact again with Nat. She was here, right in front of her, speaking to her after so many years. The reality of the situation unsettled Ash almost as much as Nat's emollient disposition—as soothing as her velvet voice—was tangling Ash's senses.

"Well, it's lovely to see you again." It was as though Nat's manners kicked in a nanosecond later, and any hint of Ash's discomfort was lost to her. Nat approached Ash, who sat, dumbly, and stared up at her. "Although I wish it was under happier circumstances," Nat added.

"Indeed." Ash rose, remembering her manners too. She was being childish, she knew, and all the hurt and pain which she'd expected to burst from her at seeing Nat simply hadn't materialized. Ash was surprised. She'd expected something—anything. Bitterness, hate. Melancholy, even. There was nothing. In front of her was the girl she'd loved all those years ago, holding out her hand for Ash to shake, but now, unlike at the wake, Ash felt absolutely nothing. Ash shook Nat's hand, but before she knew what was happening, Nat had pulled her into a quick hug. Ash kept some distance between their bodies without even thinking. An automatic reflex. She sat back down, painfully aware of the fire that she could feel creeping across her cheeks. Had the embrace been for Judy's benefit? Or hers? Inside, Ash squirmed, both at Nat's unwanted tactility and for her own blushing response to it.

"I heard you got it." Judy passed Nat her tea. "Livvy told me. Before...you know." She smiled. "Congratulations. Does this mean you'll be leaving St. Bart's?"

"Thank you." Nat sat down. "It was a lot of hard work, but I got there in the end." She smiled at Judy. "And yes, it means leaving St. Bart's after all this time. But I think I'm ready for the change."

"It's certainly no mean feat at your age," Judy said.

"I was overwhelmed to be offered it." Nat caught Ash's eye.

Ash listened to the conversation, wondering at what point one of them might enlighten her. Suddenly Judy's front room seemed very small and her urge to leave overwhelmed her again; she'd seen Judy, expressed her condolences again, done her duty. Now she was wedged in between her ex-girlfriend and the mother of her dead best friend, and she wanted to leave. Now.

"Consultancy." Finally Judy addressed her.

"I'm sorry?"

"Nat has gained her consultancy at the hospital," Judy said. "At just thirty-five. Livvy always said you'd go far." She addressed a still-smiling Nat.

Ash stared at Nat. "Congratulations," she said, the words sticking in her throat.

"Thank you."

Nat's smile, it appeared to Ash, wavered slightly under Ash's scrutiny.

"Sounds as though you've dedicated your life to your career," Ash continued. If it sounded bitter, Ash was pleased. It was meant to.

"I focused on what I wanted," Nat replied tartly. "And now I have it."

"You sound just like your parents." Ash held her gaze, memories burning inside her. The arguments, Nat's pathological fear of disappointing her parents. Her inability to stand up to them.

"It was all down to my hard work," Nat said, "not my parents."

"Yes, you were always clever," Ash said. "Far too clever for me."

They stared at one another, neither wanting to break the stare. Finally, Nat looked away.

"It's been a lifetime's work," Nat said. She picked up her cup, Ash noting with satisfaction the slight tremble in her hands. "And I had to make…sacrifices along the way. But that makes getting it all the more satisfying, knowing I did the right thing."

That, finally, elicited something in Ash, and she glared at her, infuriated. After years of silence, Nat was actually sitting there in Livvy's old front room, trying to justify her past actions with a pile of bullshit cryptic sentences and knowing looks. Was she serious?

Ash had heard enough. She didn't even want to be in London any more, let alone be sitting opposite her ex-girlfriend while she spouted on about sacrifices and lifetime ambitions, knowing what she'd done to Ash. Ash had her life in Cornwall to get back to, rather than sitting in Judy Fancourt's front room tying herself up in knots because the mere presence of Nat was sending her mind into turmoil. Ash had people who loved her and who needed her. She had her dog waiting for her in the cottage, Gabe and all the guys down at the boatyard. The thought of it wrapped itself around Ash like a warm blanket. Her dog, her adopted family, and her perfect life. Ash glanced up at the clock. Four p.m. If she hurried, she could get the direct service down from Paddington and be back in her cottage by midnight.

"Mrs. F., I'm afraid I'll have to love you and leave you." Ash clambered up from the sofa. "The cake was awesome. Just as I remembered it." She stood, awkwardly, in front of Judy, aware of Nat's eyes still on her.

"You have to go?" Judy looked up at her from her chair. "Of course. I'm sorry, I've kept you." She rose. "I had something to give you from Livvy, as well. And things to talk to you about, but as usual I've gone on far too long."

"Something from Livvy?" Ash asked, glancing again to the clock.

"Listen to me, fussing." Judy held Ash at arm's length. "Of course you must go." Her face was crestfallen, pricking at Ash's conscience. "It can wait, I'm sure."

"I suppose I could…"

"She was desperate for you to have it." Judy squeezed her hands.

Ash glanced at the clock one more time, her heart sinking.

Guess she wasn't getting that train home tonight after all.

❖

"Livvy wrote them," Judy said, "in the hospice. While she still could." She handed a large envelope each to Ash and Nat. "And gave me strict instructions to give them to you when I saw you after she…" She looked away, clearing her throat. "So. There you have it."

Ash's throat tightened. She glanced over to Nat and saw that she too had blanched a little.

"We understand." Nat spoke before Ash could.

Ash turned her envelope over, Livvy's spidery handwriting on the front, still the same from her school days, looking back at her:

*Flash.*

Ash smiled. Her nickname from school. Livvy had circled her name in gold pen and drawn little sparks around the circle. Just like the old days.

She sensed Nat watching her and lifted her envelope for her to see. Nat mirrored the action, a pained smile on her face.

*Crackles.*

Nat's name was surrounded by a cloud, a large sunshine drawn in the top right-hand corner of the envelope.

"I think your nickname always made more sense," Nat said. "Never did get how she came up with mine."

"Do you want to open them now?" Ash asked Nat. She turned to Judy. "Is that okay?"

"Take your time." Judy gathered up the tea tray. "I have things I can get on with in the kitchen."

Discreet. Ash watched as Judy left the room, then focused back on her envelope. No point in putting it off. She sat back down and tore it open, hearing Nat do the same.

A tumble of smaller envelopes fell from inside, each with a number on the front. Ash spread them out on the floor by her feet, counting them. Eight letters. She opened the large envelope further and thumbed out a white piece of A4 paper, folded in half. Frowning, she unfolded it and read:

Dearest Flash,
It's been too long! Last time we spoke (okay, emailed), Widgeon had torn a tendon chasing rabbits in the fields at the back of your cottage. How is the poor fellow? Better, I hope, and not left you with a whopping great vet's bill.
How's the boat stuff doing? Making you shitloads of money, I trust. How's Gabe? Still surfing more than working?

Ash had never read a letter with so much sorrow. Written in Livvy's distinctive handwriting, her voice clear and loud, it was as though she'd just written it there and then and pressed it into Ash's hand.

So, to the serious stuff (yeah, boring, I know). I'm writing this in St. Tom's Hospice. Yes, I know you're probably furious I never told you I was sick, but the truth is, Flash, I never for one moment thought it'd get the better of me. I thought, what's the point in worrying everyone when I'll get better? But I didn't get better. Damn. Them's the breaks, as Mr. Pritchard always used to say in geography class.
Truth is, Flash, I'm worried about Chloe and I wondered if you and Crackles could help take some of that worry away.

Ash looked away at the mention of Chloe's name, blinked, then returned to the letter.

Do you remember the wish list we wrote? You, me, and Nat? That was the night you pulled a muscle in your arm dancing to Metallica in my bedroom and you thought you were having a heart attack so you wrote down all the things you wanted to do before you died because you were convinced you were going to die? Then me and Crackles did the same and it turned out our lists had pretty much all the same things on them? Freaky.

Then when your arm got better and you realized you weren't going to die after all, we all said we'd do our wish list while we were at uni instead.

It never happened. (I'd draw a sad face here, but you know even the mention of emoticons brings me out in hives.) You changed your mind about uni, buggered off around Europe getting up to God only knows what, and the rest is history.

Of course, I always thought that one day we'd all find the time to get back together and then perhaps we could have a right old laugh doing our wish list. Three old ladies running amok. Probably wearing gold lamé, because that's what old ladies wear, isn't it? Gold lamé. And lots of purple.

But, hey, guess what? I'll never get old. I'll never wear purple. I'll never get to complete my wish list.

Poop.

So that's where you come in! I told Chloe about the wish list years ago and we thought we might do some of them together, but now that's never going to happen either.

Double poop.

So I wanted to ask you and Crackles to complete it for me and take her to the places I'll never get to see. It'll be healing for her, I think. Take her mind off stuff, you know? So will you do it for me? Fulfil my wish? Do say you will (pretty please).

Livvy had underlined this last line, adding a note in the margin which said: *with a cherry on top,* making Ash smile.

You've noticed the eight letters inside the envelope, I'm sure. They're numbered one to eight (I'm clever like that). Eight wishes. Yes, I know we wrote at least a hundred and three wishes, but did you really think I'd expect you and Crackles to travel to New York first class? Or invite Brad Pitt out for dinner? (Whose idea was that one? Oh yeah, mine.)

So with the idea of wishes and unfinished business in mind, I've taken the liberty of choosing eight things which I always wanted to do but never got round to doing, and which I think are absolutely doable with a fourteen-year-old in tow. And this is the really clever bit: I've done four wishes for the London area, and four wishes for the sunny old Cornwall area, so you and Nat won't have to be too indisposed. Crafty, hey? If I've got my sums right, you could *totally* do four wishes one week in Nat's neck of the woods, the other four wishes another week in yours. I've given Mum some money for hotels and trains and stuff like that so neither of you will be out of pocket. See? I've thought of everything. Chloe will tell you when she has holidays coming up, so all three of you can do the list in one fell swoop and make me a very happy mother indeedy.

So will you do it? All eight for me? Or at least have a fair old crack at it?

Hmm, I'm going to have to stop there, Flash. I have to write this all over again for Crackles and I'm getting tired, and I'll probably end up writing her an incomprehensible letter and she'll think I've gone quite mad.

Thank you, Flash.

Until another time and another place,

Livvy xxx

Ash gazed at Livvy's name, then traced a finger across the three kisses. It was as though she was in the room with them now, watching over them as they read her letter. It was pure Livvy, her writing sounding just as she'd always done, funny and lovely. Ash stole a look to Nat, reading her own letter. The expression on Nat's face when she finally looked back up told Ash that she felt just as moved as Ash did.

"The wish list," Nat said. Ash watched her as she folded up her letter and placed it back into its envelope. "I'd forgotten about it." She looked at Ash. "Were we…? I mean, were you and I…?"

"Together then?" Ash finished her question. "Yes." Her answer was clipped. How could Nat not remember? "I remember thinking how awesome it was all going to be, but of course I had no idea you weren't thinking the same thing."

"Don't." Nat turned her head away, pricking an irritation in Ash. "This isn't the time or place."

The underlying resentment, dormant since she'd seen Nat at the funeral but never far away, threatened to break cover. Ash was already disappointed with herself for allowing just one flippant comment from Nat earlier about her wonderful life and even more wonderful career to affect her so badly. She'd been determined not to let the death of Livvy rake up old memories, knowing that she'd only managed to bury them just under the surface for the last sixteen years. But there was something about the way Nat had asked if they were together when they'd talked about the wish list that brought all Ash's resentments to the fore.

"Don't what?" Ash took a deep breath, inhaling down the words she was sure were just another look or word from Nat away. How dare she rock up at Judy's acting like they were old friends, and then tell her not to speak her mind? "Don't talk about the past? Or about what you did?"

"This is about Livvy and Chloe"—Nat held up her letter—"not us."

Ash saw her eyes dart to the door, then back to hers.

"Worried Judy will hear the truth about you?" Ash lowered her voice and cast a look to the lounge door as well, imagining Judy just behind it, wondering at their reactions to her daughter's letters. She stemmed her anger. Now wasn't the time to start a fight with Nat, tempting though it was.

With an icy glare to Nat, Ash leaned over, scooping her eight letters from the floor. The amicable conversation she'd hoped for had turned sour. She placed her letters back into her larger envelope, along with Livvy's letter, and stood. "As you say," Ash said, "this is neither the time or place." She made to go.

"Are you leaving?" Nat asked.

"Sure looks like it."

"But…Livvy's letter? Her wishes?"

"Do you really think," Ash said, speaking slowly and clearly, "that I seriously want to spend another second in your company?" She walked to the door. "I'm surprised I managed even this long with you today. You think I want to spend time with you, pretending like we're best buddies?"

"But—"

"It's not happening, Nat." Ash placed her hand on the door handle. "I couldn't bear the pretence in front of Chloe." She held Nat's gaze. "Could you?"

"If it meant honouring Livvy's wishes."

"So sanctimonious." Ash slowly shook her head. "Always *so* sanctimonious."

"But you can't just ignore these letters." Nat waved a hand towards them.

"Who said I'd ignore them?" Ash opened the door and called to Judy. "I'll fulfil Livvy's wishes on my own," she said, lowering her voice as Judy came out from the kitchen. "I'll take Chloe to all the places in these envelopes, and I'll do it just like I've had to do everything else in my life. On my own."

## CHAPTER THREE

The Tube back into London was a total nightmare. Nat sat in her grubby carriage, staring vacantly at the faces around her and fiddling with the now well-worn leather bracelet she wore on her left wrist, wondering why it was no one on the Tube ever made eye contact with their fellow travellers. Ever. She'd often thought, on her daily commute up and down through London, that life in the capital would be so much more pleasant if people would just, on occasion, smile at one another.

Nat glanced across at a young man sitting opposite her, his fluorescent jacket with its blue company logo on it caked in mud, and wondered what he'd been doing all day to get so muddy. Builder? Railway worker? As she was staring, he looked up and caught her eye. She smiled, getting a sullen glare in return. She looked away again.

Feeling embarrassed at being caught staring like a nosy child, and wanting to draw attention away from herself, Nat fished in her bag, pulling out Livvy's letter. Her letter from the grave. Nat shivered, pushing that particular thought away. She gazed down at Livvy's writing, remembering how things used to be between them all. How good it had all been. How much fun they'd all had together before she'd messed it all up because she, Nat bloody Braithwaite, had sucked up all her parents' words like a sponge and had decided being with Ash was more trouble than it was worth.

And why? Because her parents had made her believe that her friends—Nat raised her gaze to the ceiling of the train—would stop her from realizing her dreams. And Ash, Nat had decided, would be the one *friend* who would most definitely hold her back from achieving the only thing she'd ever wanted to do since she'd been a small child.

Nat blinked, clearing the tears that were prickling the backs of her eyes.

Her career back then was more important than anything else. Or anyone else. According to her parents' doctrine, anyway. Nat had been drawn in by their insistence that in order to succeed, certain ties had to be severed, starting with Ash and Livvy. Nat should focus, they said, on her studies, and not be swayed by her giddy friends. Ash certainly had been giddy. Talking about how much fun university was going to be. How wasted they'd be, how they could all finally let their hair down once they'd escaped their boring suburban lives.

Nat didn't want to be giddy, or to get wasted. She wanted more than that. Nat wanted to be someone. Her parents had drummed that into her from an early age: Nat was special. Nat was going places, so that meant when it came to the crunch, there would be no more mucking about, like they'd done at school. If Nat was to become the successful surgeon that her parents, no, that *she'd* aspired to be all her life, then she'd have to knuckle down and sacrifices would have to be made. It had all sounded so plausible back then.

But it had been painful. Far more painful than Nat had ever imagined, and she'd thought over the years, her timing could have been better. But she'd genuinely believed Ash would understand her reasons for finishing with her; Ash knew what Nat's parents were like and would see past the hurt and the pain and realize they could both flourish independently if they didn't each have the responsibility of being in a relationship. And a secret relationship at that. But Nat had been selfish like that back then. Madly in love with Ash but not prepared to tell anyone or to fight for her. She'd just done what she'd always done and listened to her parents as they reinforced in her the determination and drive she'd always had, but had forgotten all the time she'd been free of their demands at school. But she knew medical school would be a whole different ball game and the long hours and focus that would be required of her to achieve her goals made dedicating herself to one person near impossible. Nat convinced herself that being single would be better for both her and Ash—fewer responsibilities, fewer arguments, less guilt.

That was Nat's reasoning, anyway. And, perhaps, at the back of her mind she thought she and Ash could pick up where they left off, further down the line. When the hard work had been done and they were both successful doctors. When they were both free of the responsibilities of their studies, and Nat had finally thrown off the shackles of her parents.

But then Ash had failed her final school exams and had fled to Europe. That hadn't been the plan, but that had been when the reality of what Nat had done had sunk in; she'd ruined everything, thanks to her selfishness and her inability to stand up to parents who'd had her life mapped out for her before she could even walk. She'd ruined both Ash's dreams and their friendship. And there was no turning back.

And now, all these years later, Nat had what she wanted. Her relationship with her parents was strained to the point of minimal contact, thanks to their persistent meddling in her life, an interference Nat had hoped would have stopped when she'd graduated. It hadn't. Instead, their continued intrusion into her life throughout her twenties had widened the gap between them, leaving them with a civility but not the closeness they'd shared when she was a child. Now, at thirty-five, Nat had no one and nothing in her life except for the impending senior consultant's job she'd coveted since medical school, and she'd never been so scared in all her life at what her future now held.

Nat pulled on her bracelet and stared at the blackness beyond the Tube's windows. Stared into her own blackness. Ash's past and current hatred served her right. What did Nat expect? She'd sat in Judy Fancourt's front room and spouted piety about her sacrifices when the only girl she'd ever loved and who Nat had hurt for her own ends was sitting right in front of her. And all for a job which, right now, Nat wasn't sure she even wanted.

Ash would never forgive her, not for anything. She'd well and truly broken Ash's heart all those years ago, not answering her calls, refusing to see her in the days following their breakup.

Then, one day, Ash had stopped calling. Stopped trying to win Nat round.

She'd won. Nat had won, and she'd never felt so miserable in all her life.

❖

Nat panted for air as she struggled to keep pace with Maddie, wondering, for the umpteenth time, why she continued to submit herself to the agony of her weekly spin cycling class with her best friend when jogging was much more her thing.

The sweat that trickled down her chest and plastered her hair to her forehead reminded Nat that the agony ought to be worth it, though. *No pain, no gain,* was Maddie's mantra. Lots of pain, very little gain, more like. Nat cast Maddie a look as her legs pounded in circles, edging her ever nearer to the point where she could finally stop.

"I'm done." Nat raised her hands and slowed her legs. She sat upright on her seat and tilted her head back, sucking air into her burning lungs, her hands clamped against her tight legs. "Over and out."

"Shirker." Maddie grinned over to her. "You could have done at least another ten minutes."

"Not a chance." Nat shook her head. She eased herself from her bike and grabbed her towel, burying her face into it. She breathed in and out slowly, letting her pulse slow with every breath. When she pulled her face from the towel, Maddie was standing next to her.

"So, want to tell me what's eating you?" she asked.

Nat looked at her. "Apart from feeling like I'm going to die, you mean?" she replied.

"You say that every week." Maddie wiped her face. "And every week I tell you the same thing."

"No pain, no blah, blah, blah." Nat lifted her hair from her neck and draped her towel round her shoulders, enjoying the feel of the cool material against her skin. "I know."

"Something's bugging you." Maddie placed her hand on Nat's arm. "I haven't been your friend for these last eight years not to notice when you're not happy."

Nat walked to a bench and sat. How much should she tell Maddie? She watched her friend as she finished towelling her face and arms, then came to join her.

"I'm just…having a hard time again at the moment," Nat said as Maddie sat next to her.

"Hard time, how?"

"There's a lot going on and I'm not sure I'm handling it all so well," Nat said. Wasn't that the truth? The sleepless nights since Livvy's death, having to cope with the grief of that and the thought that soon enough hers and Ash's paths were sure to cross, were testament to that. "I'm just a bit wound up."

"Work?" Maddie asked. "Life? Love?"

"Not love." Nat rolled her eyes. "Definitely not love."

"So, work?"

"I've got to the point where I hate work." It felt good to say it out loud.

"Just as well you're leaving then," Maddie said. "Soon you'll have an even better job, better apartment. More money than you could ever imagine."

"Mm."

There had to be more to life than that. Nat rested her head against the cool of the wall. "What if I still hate work when I move to Ireland, though?" she asked.

"That'll be new job jitters talking." Maddie patted her leg. "Everyone gets them. In the weeks running up to my first day in paediatrics, I was a bundle of nerves. Questioning everything. Was I doing the right thing? Would I cope?" She looked at Nat. "It's perfectly normal to be feeling like this."

"There's something else too," Nat said.

"Go on."

"I saw Ash yesterday."

"Your Ash?"

*My Ash.*

Nat felt a hotness cover her cheeks. She'd always loved the way Ash's name sounded and hearing it now sent a flood of memories cascading around her. Images teased at the edge of her mind, of her and Ash as carefree teenagers. Back to a time when just a look between them would send them into one another's arms, to a time of stolen kisses, of heat and passion and declarations of love. Nat balled her hands into fists, chasing the images away.

"Not *my* Ash for sixteen years," Nat finally said. She swallowed, her mouth suddenly dry. "But seeing her and talking to her again felt like it was just yesterday we were together."

"First loves are like that," Maddie said.

"*Only* loves are like that," Nat corrected. "Loves that you let get away."

"And now seeing her has brought a whole shedload of memories with it?"

"Memories that I think were never far away," Nat said. She sighed. "Now Livvy—the friend I just lost to cancer?—well, she's written to us both. Wants us to hang out together for the next few weeks. Fulfil some wishes she never got to do."

"And I'm guessing that's what's freaking you out."

"Wouldn't it you?"

"But that's the good thing about reconnecting with an ex, isn't it?" Maddie said. "Having the chance to reminisce?"

Nat shook her head. "Ash hates me," she said. "She's flatly refusing to have anything to do with it if I'm involved."

"Mature."

"I can't blame her." Nat would never blame Ash for any of her actions. After all, hadn't Nat been the one who had put all the hate into Ash in the first place? "I wouldn't want anything to do with me either if I was in her shoes."

"You know what you should do?" Maddie said.

"Hit me."

"Call her. Ash. Shame her into doing it by telling her you're not doing it without her."

"I already thought I ought to do that."

God knew, Nat had spent far too much time over the last forty-eight hours staring out of her window in her office wanting to contact Ash. She knew Ash had left Judy her phone number; it would be so easy, wouldn't it, to call Judy and ask her for it. But each time, something had stopped her.

"Then do it," Maddie urged.

"But I'm scared all this will just dredge up the past again." Nat shook her hand, making her bracelet fall down her wrist, then stared at it. "I've already had to make an extra appointment with Callum." She sensed her cheeks flushing again. "Felt I needed it, you know?"

"You need to see your therapist again so soon?" Maddie asked. "Because of Ash?"

Nat was touched by the look of concern on Maddie's face but knew she'd done the right thing, wanting to see Callum.

"Because of everything," Nat replied. "Ash, work. Me." She cut her glance away. Nat's CBT sessions had been a godsend since the day she'd woken up and decided she was unable to cope with life quite as well as she once had. Neither she nor Callum had been able to explain what had triggered that. There had been talk of brick walls and modern life, and even a suggestion of age, which had both amused and annoyed her, but the upshot of it all was the pressures in Nat's life were making her ill. Seeing Ash again had just worsened things.

*You've reached your apex,* Callum had said a long time ago. *People keep ignoring the fact life's getting harder for them. They keep ploughing on until one day they hit that brick wall we talked about. I think you've hit it.*

The brick wall had hurt. It had brought with it panic attacks too, a surreal and completely unwanted side effect that seemed to strike Nat at the most inopportune moments: on the Tube, in meetings at the hospital, in the dead of night. The dead of night ones were always the worst.

"Well, maybe Callum can give you the answers you're seeking," Maddie said. She looked at Nat's wrist. "Or at least help quell your anxieties."

Nat stopped fiddling with her bracelet. "It would be a start," she said. She stood. "The rest, I hope, will follow." She waited while Maddie stood too.

"Another five minutes?" Maddie asked. "Take your mind off stuff?"

Nat followed her gaze to the bikes.

Even another five minutes of agony on the bikes was better than getting sucked into another round of endless thoughts.

"You're on."

Her apartment was chilly when Nat got back from the gym. It was early October. It shouldn't have been particularly cold, but there was a distinct chill in the air when Nat stepped back in through her front door. She immediately flicked the switch on for the heating, allowing herself a wry smile at the thought that once upon a very long time ago Richard would have snapped it back off just to spite her. She dropped her gym bag at her feet, then ran her hands briskly up and down her arms, rousing her blood supply into action, and wandered into the kitchen.

"I'm home!" She called back into the lounge. "Crazy busy shift at the hospital." Nat pulled her refrigerator door open and peered inside, figuring that one pot of yoghurt and half a mouldy carrot did not equal a balanced evening meal. Or indeed a meal at all. "Then my weekly endurance test with Maddie at the gym."

She turned at the sound of soft feet padding towards her across the linoleum.

"Carrot? It's a bit manky but you can pick the worst of it off." Nat bent down and scooped her rabbit up into her arms. "And, yes, I know I'm bonkers for talking to a rabbit. You don't have to tell me." The rabbit stared at her, whiskers twitching. "It's when you start answering me, I have to worry." She kissed his nose and placed him back on the floor, watching as he loped off back into the lounge.

Livvy's letter teased her from inside her work bag still strung around her shoulders and begged to be let out and read again. After pouring herself a glass of claret, Nat eased her shoes off and wandered into her lounge, then sank into her sofa and took a long, slow drink. The claret warmed her as it slipped down, so Nat took another mouthful. Even better.

Setting her drink to one side, she pulled Livvy's envelope out from her bag and emptied the contents on the sofa next to her. She picked up the small envelope with the number one on it. Livvy's first wish. Nat turned it over in her hands, thinking. Was it something she could do alone, considering Ash wanted nothing to do with it, or her? Or would the whole thing be pointless, bearing in mind Livvy had made it clear she wanted her and Ash to do everything together?

"What do you think?" Nat called to the rabbit, busy washing his ears behind her TV. "Should I open it?" She sighed. Asking a rabbit's opinion. Slippery slope.

Nat picked up her glass, drank back the rest of her claret, then, wedging the empty glass between her knees, ripped open the small envelope.

*Crackles,* it began. Nat smiled.

I bet you opened this before Ash opened hers, didn't you? Ha! I'm right. Anyway, seeing (as usual!) you couldn't exercise a little patience, here's the first wish. Do you remember when we were all deciding which university to go to, and you said you wanted to go to Oxford, and I said if we went to Oxford we'd all have to learn to punt because just about *everyone* messes about on the river at Oxford, don't they? You jumped at the idea! Said you'd never been on a boat and so you immediately wanted to add it to your wish list. Now you can! Chloe will love it because she can see the city where her incredibly clever mother got her sparkly law degree, Ash will love it because she loves boats, and you will love it because, well, just because you will. I know you too well.

So, you and Ash choose a day, choose a time, and get punting.

Love you, Crackles.

Livvy xxx

Nat rested her head on the back of the sofa and stared up at the ceiling. Oxford. She hadn't even been able to keep that promise, either. Oh, she could have gone if she'd wanted. Her exams results would have allowed her to be first through their doors. So were Livvy's. But everything changed over that summer. Plans that were made were blown to dust. Three friends had parted. Had Livvy been disappointed? Sure, she and Livvy had had words over Ash, but if Livvy had been upset at the whole Oxford thing, she'd never let on in any of her emails in the years that followed. Livvy had headed to Oxford as she'd planned, but without her two best friends, had aced her exams, become a barrister, and said she'd never been happier. Nat, however, had headed to Edinburgh, aced her own exams, but never said if she'd ever been happier. Probably because she'd been anything *but* happy.

Nat frowned. She'd broken one promise—no, more than one promise—to Livvy and she wasn't about to break this promise. Livvy wanted her to take Chloe punting in Oxford? Maddie was right; she could *so* do that. But she wasn't about to do it alone, so even if it took every ounce of her trying, she'd get Ash to agree to it. For Livvy's sake.

Nat reached into her bag for her phone. Scrolling down until she found the number she was looking for, she dialled.

"Mrs. Fancourt?" Nat said when Judy finally answered. "I need a phone number. I don't know if you can help me? I need Ashley Wells's number."

## Chapter Four

Ash hadn't wanted to do it. She hadn't wanted to search for Nat online, but she had. Even as she'd stared, unthinking, at her laptop screen, she still didn't know what had made her do it. She'd left Judy's house the day before and had returned to Cornwall, still stunned by Livvy's letter, still stunned at the level of vitriol she'd aimed at Nat. Uncomfortable at the reaction that was stimulated inside her just from being in the same room as her. Now, with Nat's photograph right in front of her, her discomfort intensified.

Dr. Natalie Grace Braithwaite.

She looked good. Even Ash had to admit that. There was that smile, the one that used to bewitch her so long ago and make her incapable of rational thinking. There were the beautiful dark eyes that Ash was once so hopelessly lost in, gazing back at her. Ash forced herself to look away. How many times had she looked into those eyes as a teenager? Too many.

She shook her head and typed some keywords into Google. She knew not all of it would be fresh news to her; Livvy had, of course, told her plenty of things about Nat over the years. Had told her of her many successes, and all her promotions, none of which Ash had wanted to hear.

*Remember Nat?* Livvy used to say. *She got the post she wanted at St. Bartholomew's last week. How amazing is that?*

It was always an amusement to Ash that Livvy always, without fail, started any conversation about Nat with *Remember Nat?*

As if Ash could ever forget her.

"So," Ash now murmured, sliding her finger across her touchpad, "what have you got to tell me about her?"

She wanted to know.

She didn't want to know.

Ash looked away while Google found everything it possibly could about Dr. Natalie Grace Braithwaite. Ash knew she was crazy, dredging up a whole heap of information about her ex. But she couldn't stop herself.

Ash looked back. "A whole smorgasbord, it seems," she muttered. Her brow furrowed as hit after hit appeared on the screen. Articles, YouTube clips, interviews, medical journals. All about Nat.

*At today's afternoon session, Dr. Natalie Braithwaite will be delivering a lecture on aortic-valve stenosis. The prominent cardiologist, 35, is currently the lead researcher...* Ash's lips moved as she silently read the words in front of her, the numerous medical terms and Latin phrases washing over her head as she did so.

She sat back in her chair, her mind spinning. Nat was outstanding. A genius. Words and letters swam in front of Ash's eyes as she continued to pull up page after page of articles about Nat, each one lauding her more prolifically than the last.

Ash squeezed her eyes shut. Judy was right: Nat had done it. She'd achieved everything she'd ever wanted to, and it seemed as though Nat's actions had been for a reason all along. Her decision all those years before *had* been for the best—for Nat, at least. Nausea tightened Ash's throat. All those years of bitterness on Ash's part, and Nat had just been carrying on doing what she'd wanted. All those years Ash had pined away for her, wishing things could turn back to how they'd been, missing her more and more each day, month, and year, and what had Nat been doing? Ash's eyes sprang open. Not missing Ash, that was for sure. No, instead, Nat had been carving out a nice little career for herself, congratulating herself on making the best decision she'd ever made.

"Oh, your Nat's clever." Gabe's voice suddenly beside Ash made her heart thump. "She's got letters after her name, look." His finger appeared by Ash's ear as he waggled it at the screen. "Jeez, she's *really* clever."

"Gabe!" Ash puffed out her cheeks. "Do you have to creep up on me all the time like that?"

"You shouldn't leave your door open," Gabe said, sitting down on the sofa beside her. "And if you had a dog that barked instead of letting people step over his sleeping body, you'd be alerted to the fact you had visitors."

Ash felt her face flame. Busted. Another photo of Nat gradually crept down Ash's screen as it slowly loaded, and Gabe's glee at catching her in the act was palpable.

"Not interested, huh?" he asked. "All in the past, huh?" He bumped her arm.

"I got thinking," Ash said, "that I was being childish by refusing to see Nat."

"So you thought you'd check her out online?"

"I was looking for a contact number for her so I could arrange things." Ash rolled her hand towards the screen.

"So you're going to respect Livvy's wishes?"

"Mm."

"Right decision, kiddo." Gabe squeezed her forearm. "You'd only regret it if you don't do it."

Regrets. Boy, didn't she have enough of those? Ash raised her eyes to the ceiling. It was going to be horrendous, she knew, seeing Nat again and hearing how well her life had panned out.

"And it's more for Chloe than me. Right?" Ash said, pulling herself away from that train of thought.

"It absolutely is," Gabe agreed. "I should think Chloe could really use you pair right now."

Ash stared down at the keyboard on her lap, deep in thought. It was true. Ash had watched Chloe grow up, through Livvy's photos and video calls over the years, from a cute-as-a-button kid into an awesome, clever, thoughtful teenager. She adored her as a surrogate niece, just as much as she knew Chloe adored her back as the auntie she'd never had. Ash had guessed, of course, that Nat had also featured in Chloe's life. Apart from Judy, Ash and Nat were about as close a family as Chloe had right now, and Ash immediately felt a smudge of guilt at just how petulant she'd been towards Nat the day before. She'd had no right to dictate whether Chloe should or shouldn't have the chance to fulfil her mother's wishes, just because she hadn't been able to cope with the thought of having to spend time with Nat again.

"And it's your friend's dying wish after all," Gabe said, as if reading Ash's mind. "That's got to mean something, hasn't it?"

"It does," Ash said. "Which is why I'm going to contact Nat right now and tell her we should sort something out for next week." She scanned the screen, looking for a contact number for Nat. "Chloe starts her autumn holidays in a few days, so now could be perfect."

"So Nat's a cardiologist." Gabe looked at Ash's laptop. "That's hearts, right?"

"I'm trying to pretend the irony is lost on me," Ash murmured, tapping at her keyboard.

"That someone who broke your heart has ended up trying to mend others?" Gabe read her mind.

"There's an email address"—Ash nodded at the screen, ignoring Gabe's comment—"for her department." She reached past Gabe and snagged a piece of paper from the table in front of him. "And a phone number."

"So you're going to do it?" Gabe handed Ash a pen.

"For Chloe." Ash scribbled Nat's email address down. Her mind was made up. "And I figure the sooner I get through all this and get Nat back out of my life, the better."

"Well the boat tours will be winding down soon," Gabe said. "So I say, just go for it. The sooner the better."

*The boat.*

Ash snapped the lid of her laptop down. Suddenly she felt exhausted, both physically and emotionally. London had been a whirlwind, but now, half an hour before dusk, and knowing her boat needed her attention if she was to be back down at the harbour ready for the next morning's tourists before all the other boat owners, her day wasn't nearly over yet.

Her boat was her pride and joy. And it was *hers.* She'd worked hard to turn her tour into the only one visitors to St. Kerryan wanted to go on, whether they were interested in wildlife or not. That was another reason she'd been so reluctant to gad about England and God knew where else.

Ash sighed. That was unfair. Of course she wanted to fulfil Livvy's wishes, both for Livvy's sake as well as Chloe's. Using the business as an excuse had been spineless of her. She knew the real reason she didn't want to do it. Nat. Who else?

"What did she say about it?" Gabe asked. "Nat?"

"Oh, she seemed keen enough." Ash shrugged. "Until I told her where she could stick it."

"Well that was very grown up of you."

"Whatever."

"It'll be fine," Gabe said. "How hard can it be? Spending the odd day with her?"

"You don't know how much I dislike her—"

"I'm beginning to."

"—or how much what she did affected me." Ash blinked back angry tears. "How long it took me to get over her." Damn her. Still? She *still* had the ability to do this to her? She'd tried so many times over the years to put herself in Nat's shoes and imagine what she'd been thinking when she'd spoken the words that had ended their relationship. Tried to understand the pressures Nat had been under with her parents. Tried to get inside Nat's head.

"So maybe doing these things with her will give you the chance to tell her just that," Gabe said. "Make her understand how much she hurt you."

"The awful thing is, right now I hate Livvy too," Ash said. "For putting me through this after all this time. This is the way my brain's working right now. Hating my dead best friend because she had the audacity to write—on her *deathbed*, no less—this list that, quite frankly, I'd completely forgotten about." She turned and faced Gabe. "Just how fucked-up a person am I if that's the way I'm thinking?"

"You're not fucked-up." Gabe circled his arm around her shoulder and drew him to her. "Livvy dying has just opened up old wounds, that's all. Brought old memories and old girlfriends back into your life. Made you think about stuff way too much. So just do it. Maybe then you'll stop thinking so much."

Ash rested her head against his shoulder.

"You're the best, you know that?" she said. "My voice of reason."

"That's me."

Ash pulled her head back and looked at him. "You know, if I was straight, I'd have married you years ago."

Gabe kissed her forehead. "And if I was straight as well, kiddo, I'd have accepted years ago."

Nat walked up the now-familiar steps, stopping at the top to adjust the lapels on her jacket, check her keys were in her bag, and then tuck her breeze-blown hair back behind her ears. It was a well-worn routine she'd done for the last few months—a way of delaying the inevitable, even if only for a few seconds.

She entered the building, took the stairs to the second floor, then pushed open the door to the main reception. Today the receptionist with the short blond hair was at the desk. Nat preferred the older one. There was something about the way the blonde didn't ever make proper eye contact with Nat; it was almost as if she pitied her, but that could have been Nat's imagination.

"I'm here for my four o'clock appointment." Nat cleared her throat. "Braithwaite."

"Take a seat, Ms. Braithwaite." The receptionist offered a hand to a waiting chair. "He'll be with you shortly."

Nat snagged a magazine from a pile on a table on her way to her seat and sat down.

*Beekeepers' Monthly.*

Nat resisted the urge to roll her eyes but opened the magazine regardless, trying to summon up some interest at the many pictures of bees inside. When the words started to blur, she glanced up at the clock on the wall: 4.05 p.m. He was late. She hated it when Callum was late. All she ever wanted when she had to endure these visits to her therapist was to be in and out and back at her apartment with the minimum of time and fuss. Nat returned to her magazine.

*The queen bee is the heart and soul of the honey bee colony...*

Defeated, Nat flopped the magazine back down and looked around her. Quite without warning, an image of Ash appeared at the edges of her consciousness, taking her by surprise. Her eyes rose to the clock again. Now 4.07. What did Ash do at 4.07 on a Wednesday afternoon in October? Nat knew Ash ran her own boat business, thanks to Livvy and her updates over the years, not to mention her constant suggestions that they should go and visit her. Nat would never have gone though, not even if Livvy had begged her. Which she hadn't, of course. But the suggestions were always there.

The email from Ash the previous afternoon had taken Nat by surprise. She remembered the feeling now, the unexpected butterflies at seeing Ash's name sitting in her inbox, and shifted slightly in her chair, certain that Blond Receptionist could sense her unease.

*I've been thinking,* Ash's message had said, *that to disappoint Chloe would be churlish when it's her mother's wish that we do just this one thing for her.*

A phone number had appeared at the end of the message.
*Call me.*

Nat had. The prospect of ringing Ash had sent her—what was it Callum called them?—*apprehension issues* rocketing to the point where it was all she could think about. It niggled at her, on an hourly—no, half-hourly—basis until she finally bit the bullet and did it.

Their conversation had been brief. Nat had been glad, because the minute the call was over, her heart could go back to its normal pattern, her hands could stop sweating, and she could finally channel her mind onto something other than The Phone Call to Ash That I Had to Make.

"Natalie. I'm so sorry for the delay."

Nat looked up at Callum's voice. How long had he been there? She stood and shook his hand, then followed him out of the waiting room.

"Take a seat."

Nat took the seat that was offered to her and placed her bag at her feet. She waited while Callum opened a window, saying something about the October weather which she didn't quite catch, then smiled at him as he sat in the chair opposite her.

"How've you been?"

She looked at him, unsure how to answer truthfully.

"How've I been?" Nat took a deep breath. "Hmm. That's a tricky one to answer."

"Take your time."

"I've been using the bracelet more"—Nat lifted her hand—"because I've felt like I've needed it more."

"Like we've always talked about?" Callum said.

"Just like we've talked about."

"And it's helped?"

"Mm. A bit." Nat considered her answer. "But I've been feeling a whole new set of anxieties just lately."

"Because?" Callum asked.

"Stuff." Nat sighed. "Just…stuff." She looked at him. "Work and…stuff." What else could she call it? And did Ash slot into that vague category too?

"I see."

She noted the frown on Callum's brow. One step forward, two back.

"It's important to remember the breathing exercises too," Callum said, "as well as the distraction methods." He looked at her. "I know you find your bracelet works to take your mind off things, but remember listening to music, concentrating on your breathing, things like that can all work well too."

Nat nodded, feeling like a little girl lost. This shouldn't be her, this uneasy, nervous person sitting in front of her therapist talking about how a piece of material round her wrist could help stave off panic attacks. She was successful, confident. The person her team at St. Bart's looked to for inspiration and advice. She should be stronger—she should have *always* been stronger. Callum often reminded her that it was the strong ones who ignored their anxieties, and tried to carry on regardless, but that never seemed to make much sense to Nat.

"I think I have a lot of things going on in my life right now," Nat said, "that I can't seem to manage inside here." She tapped her temple. "It feels like a computer trying to access too many files at once." Her mind, as she was talking, sought out Ash. She'd find this amusing, Nat thought. An ironic justice. Nat had never been the strong one in their relationship, her strength of character only emerging when pushed into making a decision which was out of her control.

"You spoke last time about a new job." Callum leaned forward, resting his elbows on his legs.

"Mm." Nat looked at him. When he didn't continue, she took that as her cue to talk. But where to start? "Just thinking about it scares me." She laughed quietly, more out of embarrassment than anything else. "But everyone I know is telling me I fully deserved it."

*Even Ash. Even if her congratulations were dripping in sarcasm.*

"Do you think you deserve it?" Callum asked.

Nat frowned, sensing her father breathing down her neck, his admonishments as clear in her mind as they'd always been.

*Some people in this life are destined to just get by, Natalie,* he'd say. *Others to excel in everything they do. You are one of the latter.*

"Yes," she eventually said, "I think I do."

"Then you must take that knowledge with you to your new job," Callum said. "Take that strength and use it."

Nat nodded. Strength? Right now she felt anything but strong. She felt weak and defeated, bowed down under the pressure of a new job she wasn't sure she was up to, and the prospect of having to spend time with Ash, knowing that Ash loathed her and resented everything about her.

The next few weeks, Nat knew with a quick glance to her wrist, would either make her or break her.

Somehow she thought it might be the latter.

## Chapter Five

Oxford was bathed in a mellow glow of midmorning sunshine when Ash finally arrived there, two weeks after her afternoon tea with Judy. Sun-soaked ancient spires watched over the city, sitting curiously amongst the bright-red tour buses and tourists, almost as if the eyes of a thousand former Oxonians—from Betjeman to Tolkien—were quietly assessing them.

Time had passed slowly since Livvy's funeral. According to Judy, Chloe had been handled with cotton-soft care, grief had had time to mellow—even if it hadn't nearly disappeared altogether—and Ash had gradually grown used to the idea that the next two weeks would be the first step on the road to having Nat temporarily back in her life again.

Not that the idea sat any easier with her. Over the previous fortnight, and much to her dismay, her melancholy at what Nat had done to her all those years before had taken a leap forward again, after lying dormant for so many years. They'd exchanged phone numbers. That had been weird, and even though Ash had flatly refused to speak to Nat again after their initial phone conversation, she knew they'd have to communicate somehow if their forthcoming two weeks together were to run smoothly. Texts, Ash figured, would do, but each new text from Nat, asking for confirmation of dates and times to meet, was met with a renewed sense of dread at what Ash was about to do. She hated it all. Hated the way she felt each time she saw Nat's name illuminate her phone. Hated the anxiety that choked her throat when she thought about seeing her again.

Now, as Ash strode towards their agreed meeting place, her mind—hitherto desperately trying to dismiss her nervousness—took itself on a journey where it sought out Nat, because Ash's brain needed to quickly process how it was going to feel at seeing her again, and needed to be fully prepared. For her own sanity, she had to anticipate exactly where Nat would be, what she'd be wearing, and how she'd look. How would their initial meeting fare? Who would see whom first? Who would smile first? Would Nat try to hug her again, like she had at Judy's house? Ash frowned at the thought, dug her hands deeper into her pockets, and walked on. Faces and colours coalesced as Ash sidestepped and weaved her way through the crowds milling around shopfronts, with no one apparently in any hurry to get out of her way.

Nat was already there, waiting for her. Ash cursed under her breath that she hadn't been the first to arrive but couldn't quite fathom why that would unsettle her so much. She'd wanted more time to gather her thoughts before Nat arrived, that much she already knew. But had she also wanted Nat to have the gut-wrenching anxiety *she* was now experiencing, knowing that she would have to seek her out and then approach her through the crowds, just as Ash was now?

Ash's feet slowed. She didn't want Nat to see just how nervous she was. Didn't want to give her the satisfaction of knowing that Ash was dreading having to spend the day with her. Finally, Ash stopped walking and stood, hidden by the crowds, and watched Nat through the sea of heads in front of her, feeling a coldness spread about her chest as she did so, as though the ghosts of her past were shimmering right through her heart.

If Nat *was* as uneasy as Ash was, she was hiding it well. Instead, she was pointing something out to Chloe, standing beside her, bending her head slightly to hear Chloe's reply. Laughing lightly and easily. Nat looked beautiful. Composed. Ready. Ash blinked slowly, hardly able to tear her eyes away. Nat was confident and poised.

More importantly, though, Nat was quite unlike the shivering mess who was watching her, with increasing dread, through the crowds.

❖

Nat knew she was watching her. It would have been so easy just to turn her head a fraction, catch her eye, and beckon her over. But she couldn't. Why? Nat fixed her gaze dead ahead of her, not daring to allow her line of sight to wander over towards Ash, still standing watching her. Because if she did beckon her over, then that would mean this was all real.

It was anything but real.

"See that building there?" Nat dragged her attention from Ash and pointed to a rounded building just to her left. "That was where your mum had her graduation ceremony." Ash's presence still bored into her. "Where she finally received her law degree."

"It's fancy." Chloe looked in the direction Nat was pointing.

"Sheldonian Theatre," Nat replied. "Been standing since Charles II's time."

"That's a long time, right?" Chloe smiled at Nat.

"You could say that." Nat laughed lightly, aware that her laughter sounded hitched tight. Nervous anticipation, she figured, did that to a person.

Why was Ash not moving? She knew they were there, waiting, but still she hung back. How much longer did she want to draw this out?

Nat allowed herself a half glimpse in Ash's direction. Finally, she was striding towards them. Walking confidently and with purpose. Ash looked ready to take on anything. Ready to take her on.

Mostly though, Nat thought with a sinking feeling, Ash looked quite unlike the shivering mess who was watching her, with increasing dread, as she pushed her way through the crowds towards her.

❖

"Clo." Ash warmly embraced Chloe and held her close. With a quick, final squeeze, she released her. "I'm so glad you came. Did your grandma put you on the train?" She picked a small ball of fluff from Chloe's shoulder. "Which station did you travel from? Did you sit at an aisle seat like I said?" Ash was gabbling. She knew she was gabbling, but her mouth wouldn't stop.

"She travelled with me." Nat spoke before Chloe could answer. "I didn't want her travelling alone."

"Neither did I." Ash met Nat's gaze.

They stood, a sliver of ice lying between them.

"Even though I travel across London every day." Chloe smiled. "And Grandma was totally okay with me coming to Oxford alone."

"Nat stepped in anyway?" Ash raised an eyebrow. "Well there's a surprise."

"You'd have a fourteen-year-old travel alone?"

"She's fourteen, not four." Ash gave her best bored look. "And if Judy was okay with it…" She shrugged.

"I'm here. It's cool." Chloe gave Ash another hug. "You two are stressing way too much."

Ash caught Nat's eye. Stressing. Understatement of the century.

"So." Nat dropped her eyes. "What first?"

"Your mum," Ash said, pulling Livvy's letter from her bag and ignoring Nat, "wanted you to see a river called the Cherwell today." She opened her letter out. "It runs through Oxford or something." Ash rolled a hand vacantly in the air, then stuffed Livvy's letter back into her bag.

"It's where she spent a lot of her summers," Nat added. Her gaze met Ash's again. She looked tired and drawn, Ash thought. As though, just like Ash, this was the last place she wanted to be, and the last thing she wanted to be doing.

"Messing about on the river like something out of *Wind in the Willows*?" Chloe smiled. "She used to tell me about it."

"I used to come with her." Nat lifted her eyes to the sky, and Ash sensed her remembering. "When I visited for weekends, you know?"

"You guys used to come here together?" Chloe looked from Nat to Ash and back again.

Nat shook her head. "I don't know whether Ash ever came."

Ash stole a glance to Nat. Memories of time spent with Livvy on her own tumbled about her. Both before she left for Europe and after. Weekends spent desperately hoping Livvy wouldn't mention Nat's name, and desperately hoping she wouldn't bump into her. She should have been more of an adult, Ash thought now. She should have dealt with it. Relationships happened, and break-ups happened. But she'd never been able to, just like she'd always assumed Nat had never been able to either.

Sadness enveloped her once more. Grief at her losses. Ash circled an arm around Chloe's shoulder and steered her along, hoping to send her grief scuttling away again. "Trust me, Clo," she said, "there'll be more than just a bit of messing around this afternoon." She glanced back over her shoulder to Nat and felt her heart grow heavy again.

It was going to be a long week.

Nat rested her head back and stretched her legs out in front of her. The soft sound of water lapping against the side of the boat, coupled with the heat, both from the sun and the warmed wood, all conspired to make her dozy. Her eyes, leaden with tiredness, refused to stay open. Ash's and Chloe's murmured voices entered and left her ears, while the occasional sound of child's laughter from the riverbank, or an accompanying boat, let her know she was still partially awake.

Their boat was meandering its way down the river, having left Oxford far behind. Once various landmarks had been pointed out to Chloe, and memories had been shared, a silence had settled over the boat. That was when Nat's eyes had grown heavy, and she had been happy to lie back and let Ash carry on punting the boat.

A jolt instigated a stretch from Nat. She locked her arms above her head and slowly eased one eye open, slitting it against the sun, and peered down the boat. Ash and Chloe were sitting next to one another, still talking in lowered tones, apparently oblivious to Nat's stretching. Ash had one hand gripped tight around the boat's punting pole but had stopped propelling it, happy for now just to aid its steering and allow the boat to continue its way down the river without any other help.

Nat settled back down. Her gaze, though, remained on Ash, following the line of her hand, gripping the pole, up her arm, to her face. Nat blinked. Ash always did have an expressive face and now, as she talked animatedly to Chloe, her expressiveness shone through. Ash's voice was different too. Her London accent had faded to warmth, thanks to its new southwest twang. Living in Cornwall had obviously helped shape her new, more grounded accent, and Nat liked it.

The cool teenager she'd known had grown into a striking woman, with the same confidence and strong personality she'd always had, and as Nat studied her, fresh regret gripped her. Ash had barely said two words to her the whole afternoon, let alone made any proper eye contact. Instead, it had been Chloe who had been the lucky recipient of Ash's kindness, humour, and company since the moment Ash had met them, and Nat was jealous. That was it. Nat had felt an uneasiness all afternoon, one which she hadn't been able to put her finger on, but now, watching Ash giving Chloe her total attention, the reality hit her. She was jealous. She squeezed her eyes tight shut, embarrassed at her own feelings.

The jealousy refused to budge.

Ash was still a closed book to her, and Nat hated it. More than that, on the few occasions Ash had actually looked at her, she had looked at her with such wounded, lifeless eyes it was as though they had never once known one another intimately. Had never kissed, never lain naked together, had never lived and breathed one another, or had never been so lost in one another's gaze that the outside world hadn't existed to either of them.

Now, fast-forward sixteen years and Nat knew hardly anything about Ash—only the few snippets Livvy had told her—and while she knew she shouldn't be interested, the truth was, she was curious about her. Ash had asked her nothing of her life, either. That hurt. Wasn't Ash just as curious to find out what had happened to her and how her life had eventually panned out in the intervening years? Nat peered down towards them again. Was she really going to have to grill Chloe on the train back to Judy's house about Ash? Had it really come to that?

"You're awake!" Chloe called down to her. "I thought we were going to have to dunk you in the river to wake you up."

Nat stretched again, as if to show she really *had* just woken up. Such an act. It was all such an act.

"Sorry." She sat up, then rubbed her face. "Blame the sunshine." She yawned, clamping her hand over her mouth when she saw Ash watching her.

"We were talking about tomorrow." Ash addressed her.

Nat sat up straighter. "Yeah?"

"And that we should open letter number two," Ash said. She paused. "When you'd finished your beauty sleep, that is."

Nat stared at her. Had she noticed the hint of a smile from Ash? If she had, that would have been a first all day. She stood, holding her arms out to her side as the punt wobbled slightly, then gingerly made her way closer to them.

"Letter number two," Nat said, raising herself an inch off her seat to retrieve Livvy's letter from her back pocket, "to be opened after wish number one has been completed." She smoothed the envelope out onto her knee and watched as Ash leaned backwards slightly to pull her own letter from her jeans pocket.

"Do we all agree wish number one has been completed?" Ash asked.

"Punting in Oxford," Chloe said. "Check." Nat watched, gratified, as Chloe gazed about her. "And it's been awesome," she added.

"We aim to please." Nat caught Ash's eye for an instant, then looked away.

"Letter number two," Ash said. Nat watched as she slid her index finger under the envelope's flap, pulled out the letter, and unfolded it. *"Dear Flash,"* Ash read, *"how was Oxford? Just as I remembered, I hope. Did you show Chloe Magdalen on your way down the river? What did she think of it?"* She lifted her eyes to Chloe.

"Awesome." Chloe smiled, the sadness in her smile resonating with Nat. "The fact that Mum went there and was all kinds of wonderful and clever and brilliant is mind-blowing." Nat sensed Chloe's shoulders slumping. "And it makes me miss her more than ever."

"We all do." Nat smiled at her. "So it makes it all the more important that we have the best time over the next two weeks and fulfil her last wishes." She looked at Ash. "Right?"

"Right." Ash nodded. She lowered her eyes again. *"If you're all willing,"* she read, *"it would be brilliant if you'd head back to London after you're done messing about on the river and take in a show in the West End. Nothing too fancy, mind you. I never could abide all that la-di-da theatrical stuff. Remember how once Nat wanted to go see some Chekhov play at the National and we both said we'd rather swim down the Thames naked?"*

Nat's smile matched Ash's at that last comment. The Chekhov play had remained unwatched, she recalled. As had all the other plays they'd pledged to go and see. Time had marched on, and friends had parted, never to fulfil their wishes.

"We never did go, did we?" Nat spoke her thoughts aloud. "You wanted to see *Phantom*. I said I couldn't cope with all the cloaks and singing." She laughed. "Do you remember?"

"Seems there was a lot we couldn't agree on back then, wasn't there?" Ash replied. The sharpness in her tone stung Nat, leaving her laugh hanging awkwardly in the air. "Where was I?" Ash returned to Livvy's letter, Nat's attempted pleasantries to her apparently unimportant.

Nat concentrated on her breathing, hurt and unnerved by Ash's instant return to coldness. She stole a look to Chloe, apparently unaware of the resentment that was now radiating from Ash's direction as she continued to read Livvy's letter. Nat sighed. Her trip to Oxford had, until that moment, turned out better than she could have ever hoped, offering her hope that the next few days might actually not be as bad as she'd feared. Now, as she continued to watch Ash, her nerves that had dissipated as the punt had bobbed its way along the river returned with a vengeance.

How was she ever going to get through the rest of the day, let alone the next week?

## CHAPTER SIX

It was a small hotel. Some might even say poky. The view from Ash's window down to the grubby courtyard below, where the hotel's chefs gathered to smoke their break-time cigarettes, wasn't much better, either. Of course Nat had suggested another hotel that she knew, closer to Kensington, but Ash's stubbornness and reluctance to allow Nat to have any say over where Ash should or shouldn't be overruled her. Now, staring around her claustrophobic room and knowing this was to be her temporary home for the next four days, Ash regretted her pig-headedness.

How had she even managed to get herself into all of this anyway? Oxford had happened, and, yes, the punt down the Cherwell had been far more enjoyable than she could ever have anticipated, but now she was booked into a hotel in North London, pacing the floor with an ever-increasing sense of dread because she knew that in two hours' time she'd be sitting in a theatre. With Nat.

It was all madness. Chloe was excited though, both at the thought of going into the West End and at spending more time with her and Nat, and it was only the thought of her exuberance that would get Ash through the rest of the evening.

Ash's gaze fell to the minibar. She couldn't, could she? Weren't the two beers she'd just drunk with her dinner downstairs enough? She pulled her hands through her hair. It would take more than just a couple of beers to see her through the evening. Ash walked over to it, opened it, and crouched in front of it, her face illuminated by its internal light. Just the one. To settle her nerves. She pulled a bottle from inside, opening it in an instant, and chugged back a mouthful. Wiping her mouth with the back of her hand, she stood, closed the minibar's door with her foot, and sat on the edge of her bed.

Since when had Nat turned into the sophisticated woman she'd just spent the day with? Ash stared down at her feet, brooding. True, she'd always had class, but age had just made her classier than ever. And so beautiful. Ash studied the label on her bottle. *So* beautiful. She shook her head, smiling at herself. Even after all this time, there was no one to match Nat. Never had been. People like Nat only came along once in a blue moon, and that was what had made their parting so painful. Ash had known at the time she was lucky to have Nat as a girlfriend. As far as Ash was concerned, Nat could have had anyone she'd wanted in school. But she'd chosen Ash. She'd *chosen* her. Then she'd chosen to finish with her, just like that. Ash's frown deepened and she drank back some more beer, as if to swallow down the resentment that was threatening to rise up inside her again.

Her phone rang inside her pocket, making her jump. When she saw Gabe's name illuminated, her relief was palpable.

"You saved me," she said, once she'd answered.

"From what?" Gabe's voice was like a steadying hand on her arm.

"From myself." Ash laughed. "And my thoughts."

"Beware the demon thoughts," Gabe said. "How was Oxford? Full of clever people?"

"Oxford was…actually okay," Ash replied.

"You didn't tip Nat out of the boat?"

"Not once."

"Good girl."

"Didn't even try."

"Have a Gabe gold star." Gabe laughed.

"We're going to the theatre tonight," Ash said. "Some drama at the Barbican." And, boy, hadn't they taken forever to choose just the right play to see.

"You've been London-ized." Ash imagined Gabe, ever the drama queen, clutching at his chest. "This is another Livvy wish, yes?"

"Mm," Ash replied. "Another thing we always said we'd do but never got round to doing."

"Did you pack a posh outfit?"

"What do you think?" Ash stared down at her legs. "Chinos are okay for the theatre, right?"

Despite the tiredness of the day muddying her brain, Ash had, to her surprise, managed to leave a small pocket of it free to devote itself to think about her evening's clothes. Even if they did only stretch to navy chinos and a patterned top that matched it perfectly.

"Guess you'll find out when you get there," Gabe replied, not altogether helpfully, Ash thought.

Nat, Ash was sure, wouldn't be wearing chinos tonight. She glanced at her legs again, then to the clock on the wall of her room. Too late to bomb into town and buy something smarter? Ash sighed. Way too late.

"She'll have to take me as she finds me," Ash said, unthinking.

"Who?"

"Nat."

"You care?"

"Nope." Ash rubbed her temple. Yes, she cared. "I don't want to look a total scruff-pot, that's all."

"You'll look beautiful," Gabe said soothingly. "You always do." He paused. "Do that thing with your eyes that makes me go all hetero. You know, when you make them up all dark and lovely."

"Maybe."

"Chicken, with your hair and skin tone, trust me—no one will notice whether you're wearing chinos or not." Gabe laughed. "You'll knock Nat sideways."

"Who says I want to impress Nat?"

"Your tone implies it," Gabe replied, his mischievous note not going unnoticed by Ash.

"If anything," Ash said, rising from her bed, "I want Nat to know I can still look good, even if I *do* spend my days mucking about on stinky boats." She glanced down at her weathered, tanned hands and stubbed fingernails. "So if that means slapping on a bit of eyeliner, then I guess I'll do it."

"And if it impresses her, all the better?" Gabe offered.

"Far from it." Ash walked to the mirror and looked at her reflection. "I went there once before and got burned." She stared into her own eyes. "When it comes to Nat, there's most definitely no going back."

❖

Nat fussed with the hem of her jacket, wishing, for the umpteenth time since she'd left her apartment and headed across London, that she didn't feel quite so trussed up. She'd bought it on a whim, on her way back to her apartment that afternoon, and now it struck her as ludicrously formal. Why she'd chosen to buy something so starchy was anyone's guess. After all, did anyone even bother dressing for the theatre these days? She looked over to Chloe, dressed as you'd expect any normal teenager to dress for a night out watching a play. Chloe looked cool and comfortable, the polar opposite to how Nat was feeling.

"She's late." Nat lifted her head and squinted over the sea of heads milling about the theatre's foyer.

"No, she's not," Chloe replied. "We're early."

"Are we?" Nat looked at her watch. It seemed as though they'd been waiting for Ash for hours. Or did anticipation just make it feel like hours? "Which station's she coming from again?"

"I told her Moorgate," Chloe replied. "Depends if she's coming straight from her hotel or whether she's already in town." She laughed. "You know Ash. She'll have been in a bar somewhere ever since we left her earlier."

*You know Ash.*

Nat stared, unthinking, ahead of her. So hanging out in a bar was typical of Ash, was it? When was the last time Nat had gone to a bar alone? Actually, scrap that. When was the last time she'd even set foot in one? That had never been Richard's thing. Had *anything* ever been Richard's thing? She lifted her eyes to the sky. That was always what she'd loved about Ash: her confidence and her sociability. At school, everyone had loved her, and while Nat had been just as popular, there had always been something about Ash that had made her stand out more. Ash could walk into anyplace she liked and brighten it up instantly. When they were together, it had always been Ash who could stride into a place oozing confidence, while Nat had always been the one walking just a few paces behind, letting Ash do all the talking. Ash had never once had any inhibitions about anything, but Nat had never been like that, and certainly never later in life when she'd been with Richard.

But then, everything with Richard had been an act.

"Hey, guys."

Thoughts of Richard melted into the crowd around her as Nat turned her head and saw Ash, standing next to her. Her stomach balled tight at the sight of her.

"Ash." Nat shook her head. "I was miles away. Sorry." She smiled.

"Been here long?" Ash, Nat noted, addressed Chloe more than her.

"Five minutes or so," Chloe replied.

Nat glanced at Ash, taking in the chinos, biker boots, and battered jacket, and felt her own jacket sitting even more formally about her shoulders. She felt like an old maid in comparison to Ash and resolved there and then to pull her wardrobe apart when she got home and throw out anything that made her look as awful as she was sure she looked tonight.

While Ash spoke with Chloe, Nat watched her. Ash's hair was different tonight: sleeker and straighter than it had been earlier. She'd darkened her eyes too, Nat noted. Just how she'd always loved them. Her dark eyes, combined with her different hairstyle, gave Ash a casual look. A typical Ash-doesn't-give-a-damn air.

And Nat loved it.

While Ash and Chloe talked, Nat found she couldn't pull her eyes from Ash. She was standing, hands in her pockets, smooth hair falling about her eyes, her flawless honey-coloured skin making her look the picture of health. Nat thought in that moment she'd never looked so good, but she also knew, from experience, that Ash had no idea just how good she looked. That had always been her style, right from an early age. Scruffy but cool. Casual but put-together. Turning heads without even knowing it.

"Isn't it?" Chloe was talking. How long had she been addressing her?

"Isn't it what?" Nat was sure her face had reddened.

"Supposed to be, like, *the* play to see right now?" Chloe asked.

"The one we're about to see?"

"Well, *durr,*" Chloe replied playfully. "Yes, the one we're about to see."

"Yes. Of course." Nat pulled herself straighter. She was being stupid, she knew. Just because Ash had rocked up looking like she'd just stepped off the cover of a magazine didn't mean Nat had to lose all rational thought. "Shall we go in?" She moved away.

"She's tired." Nat heard Chloe talking to Ash. "That's why she's away with the fairies."

Nat walked on in through the foyer, her mind in turmoil.

If only it was as simple as plain tiredness.

The darkness of the auditorium wrapped itself around Ash like a blanket. As she sank down into her seat, her long legs just touching the seat in front of her, a contentment settled over her. Much to her surprise, the day hadn't been as gut-wrenching as she'd thought it might have been. Oxford was okay. London was bearable, as was Nat. While Chloe talked ten to the dozen next to her, Ash shifted slightly in her chair and stole a look to Nat from the safety of the other side of Chloe, watching her with a mixture of curiosity and intrigue as Nat absorbed herself in the theatre programme. Ash only had half an ear on Chloe, chattering about a boy at school who was blowing hot and cold on her and who was also in the audience and whom she desperately wanted to avoid. Ash knew she should be listening more. Her mind, however, was focused on Nat.

There had been no bitterness at seeing Nat again, no regret, no sadness, and only a handful of memories to nudge Ash and remind her just what Nat had meant to her, once upon a time. The day had been cathartic. Ash knew that now. If she'd thought that morning, when she'd been choked with nerves at the prospect of being with Nat again, dreading what reaction seeing her would fire in her, that twelve hours later she'd be sitting in a theatre feeling as relaxed as she did now, she'd have never believed it.

Neither would Gabe, she thought with a wry smile.

Ash rested back into her seat and stared ahead of her to the stage, still cloaked with its velvet curtains. But they hadn't talked all day, her and Nat. Well, not *talked* talked. Perhaps they should. Wasn't that what old friends did? Ash's smile deepened in the dark.

*Old friends.*

She wondered how much Livvy had told Nat about her. Did she want Nat to know anything about her life? Was it even important, bearing in mind she and Nat would be strangers to one another again in less than two weeks?

Ash's thought process had arrived too late. As the curtain rose and the first sharp footsteps rapped across the stage, any thoughts of Nat slowly spiralled like a thin wisp of smoke up to the auditorium's ceiling.

❖

"He was great."

"Which one?" Ash placed a hand on Chloe's back and guided her through the crowds in the theatre foyer.

"The bloke from the telly."

"The detective?"

"Yeah." Chloe allowed Ash to steer her towards the exit. "How did he remember all his lines?"

"Who knows?" Ash laughed. "I have trouble remembering my shopping list sometimes."

She threw a look back over her shoulder to Nat, picking her way carefully through the crowds towards them.

"Okay?" she called.

Nat nodded, a hint of surprise, Ash thought, flickering across her face.

Once safely back out on the street, Ash pulled her jacket closer around her against the chill night air. She glanced at her watch: 10.30 p.m. The street where the theatre sat heaved with people. Rowdy pub drinkers intermingled with the more sedate theatregoers. Lights twinkled against a clear inky-black autumn sky, and loud voices and laughter bubbled out from the bars and restaurants that lined the street, whilst a seemingly never-ending procession of night buses ebbed and flowed up and down the road.

Saturday night in London. Ash looked about her, missing the peace and quiet of Cornwall with each excitable person that brushed past her. This wasn't her any more. Her life was now so far removed from any of this, it was astonishing to think she'd ever lived in London.

"Do you want to go to a bar somewhere?" Chloe asked.

Ash leaned in to her to hear her above the noise.

"You're fourteen," she replied, more sternly than she'd intended. "So, no."

"And you berated me earlier today for wanting to travel with her on the train." Nat raised an eyebrow. "Now who's the fussy auntie?" A hint of a smile passed her lips.

Ash looked at her steadily. "There's a world of difference."

"Is there?"

"Yes." Ash held her stare, but unlike earlier that day, there was a smile behind her look.

Nat returned her smile. "I'm joking with you," she said. "I wouldn't want to take her to a bar either." She paused. "Anyway, haven't you seen enough bars today?"

Ash looked at her, confused.

"Earlier," Chloe said, "when we were waiting for you. I said you'd be hanging out somewhere."

"Wouldn't be seen dead in one." Ash looked across the sea of heads and shuddered. "Not my scene any more."

"Ah, I forgot you're all about the clean living now." Chloe linked her arm through Ash's. "You're all boats and sea and fresh air these days."

"Well, as the three beers I had in my hotel earlier will testify," Ash said, "not as clean as you think."

She caught Nat's eye and winked, then dropped her eyes as she saw Nat hastily look away, colour spreading across her cheeks.

"We should go," Nat said, moving away. "It's been a long day."

"Of course." Ash watched Nat's retreating back. Ash noticed her entire body was tense and she wondered if she found her annoying, or if she was as unhappy at being placed in this situation as she was.

Ash unlinked her arm from Chloe's and followed after Nat, feeling foolish. Why had she winked? Nat had looked so embarrassed. Too friendly? Perhaps. After all, they were essentially strangers to one another again.

And strangers they'd stay.

## CHAPTER SEVEN

Sunday morning broke, sunny and dry. Nat's socked feet scuffed a muffled rhythm against her carpet as she mooched about her apartment, cradling her second coffee of the morning. She thought of Chloe, a long stone's throw away over at Judy's house in Wimbledon, regaling her with tales of punting and plays, and smiled to herself.

Chloe was great. More than that, she'd proved herself to be a steadying influence the previous day, once again showing a maturity that was far beyond her years. Nat had been grateful for her company too. For constantly taking her mind off her nerves at seeing Ash again, and for intervening whenever the conversation dried up over the course of the day. She'd been just the distraction Nat had needed, the third person required to keep everything flowing. Of course, without Chloe, there would have been no visit to Oxford or the West End, but Nat was grateful nevertheless. And she'd enjoyed herself too. Far more than her nausea the previous morning that had prevented her from even contemplating breakfast would have had her believe.

Today was a new day, with a new request from Livvy. Nat sought out her letter, placed in readiness on her coffee table the night before. It would be another day in London; after all, that was Livvy's wish for this week. But where? Nat placed her now-empty coffee cup on her mantelpiece and reached for the letter. She sat down. *Dearest Crackles*, it began.

How was the theatre? I hope you didn't all have drinks at the interval. West End theatre prices are *so* overinflated, and I'm afraid I only supplied enough ££s for the play itself. Was it enough? I do hope so.

So, another day dawns, and with that comes another wish from yours truly. I was thinking, as I was lying in bed today (not much else to do) that in all the years we lived in London, we never visited the Tate, yet it was one of the things that was at the top of my wish list when I was sixteen. Why did we never go? The coolest art gallery in all of London and we never went. Last year I promised to take Chloe and show her some of Dali's stuff there because she studied Dali at school in year nine last year and I thought she'd enjoy it.

We never made it there.

Will you fulfil that promise to her? She'll love it, and you and Flash can explain all the complicated paintings to her because you're both hideously clever.

It's free to get in, but Mum has money for you for eats, so you can get that off her when you go to collect Chloe. Give Mum a hug from me when you see her?

Until letter number four,

Livvy xxx


Nat placed the letter on her knees, then linked her hands behind her head and rested against the back of her sofa. She closed her eyes. The Tate Modern. Hideous, and absolutely not her cup of tea. Nat opened her eyes and stared up at the ceiling. She doubted it would be Ash's either, if her taste in art had remained the same over the years. True, Livvy had pestered them to visit the Tate when they'd been at school, but she and Ash had always made an excuse not to go. But now? Now they were adults and had to step up to the plate for Livvy and Chloe. A huge smile escaped Nat's lips as she imagined the look on Ash's face when she too read her letter.

Automatically, Nat reached for her phone and scrolled down until she found Ash's number. Her blood pulsed warm under her skin as she heard the ringtone, her heart drumming a quicker beat the longer the phone rang out. Finally, Ash answered.

"It's me." Nat grimaced. Of course it was her.

"Hi."

"Did you read the...yeah, hi." Nat cleared her throat. "You good?"

"Well, I just woke up." Ash sounded groggy. "But yeah, good. You?"

"Shit, sorry. Did I wake you?" Nat sat up straighter. "What time is it? Is it early?" She pinched the bridge of her nose, wishing she could start the whole conversation over again. "Sorry."

"Don't apologize." Ash chuckled. "It's cool."

"Did you read the next letter?" Nat asked, wishing her voice didn't sound so thin. "It's why I'm ringing."

"I read it last night when I got back," Ash said. "The Tate? Ugh."

Nat heard the groan of despair coming down the phone and couldn't help smiling again. "I thought you might say that."

An awkward silence settled. Nat could faintly hear Ash breathing and wished one of them would speak. No words came to her, though.

"So," Nat said when the silence became too much, "where shall we meet later?"

"Inside?" Ash asked.

"How about lunch? First. Before we go in, I mean. I know a nice place. Nearby. Near it." Nat groaned at her ineptitude. Why did she sound so stilted?

"No, we'll go straight in," Ash replied. "Get it over with sooner."

*So you can get away from me quicker?*

Nat's brow creased at the thought. "Sure," she finally managed to say.

"One thirty?" Ash asked.

"Sure," Nat repeated, her flood of anticipation at offering Ash lunch trickling into a dried up stream of disappointment at Ash's disinterest.

"See you later, then."

Their call ended abruptly. Nat sat back, tapping the edge of her phone against her lip. Despite her upset at Ash's indifference, the thought of seeing her later warmed Nat as much as the thought of the Tate chilled her. But feeling happy at the thought of seeing Ash again was a good thing, right? It meant she finally felt comfortable in her company, rather than being knotted up by the anxieties that had hampered her the day before.

But, to Nat's dismay, it also meant that a thousand new questions were beginning to worm their way into her brain.

The walk along the Thames down towards the Tate had always been one of Ash's favourites when she'd lived in London. No one had told October that it should be wet and windy; instead the sun shone down radiantly through trees that looked only slightly more spindly than they had in September, and the crunch of fallen dusty leaves underfoot reminded Ash that it hadn't rained in weeks.

Ash had come off the Tube so that she could walk across the Thames at London Bridge and walk down Bankside, always keeping St. Paul's Cathedral in her line of vision. She didn't know if it was a superstition, or just a personal quirk, but she had, even from an early age, gained comfort from seeing St. Paul's. She was also never sure if that was because it was a symbol of strength—after all, neither the Great Fire nor Hitler's Luftwaffe had been able to defeat it—but Ash knew with absolute certainty that the day St. Paul's disappeared would be the day the world ended.

To Ash, it was as simple as that.

Nat had laughed at her about that when they'd been teenagers. But her ribbings had never been anything more than just that. Quite the reverse; Nat had told Ash in the years they were together that her opinion about St. Paul's had just been another of her many quirks.

*Another beautiful layer to your personality,* she'd said. *You have so many beautiful layers.* They'd spent many moments walking hand in hand after dark along the river, looking up at the cathedral together. Whenever they were in its vicinity, Ash would always want to go and see it, even if it meant taking a long diversion. Nat always, without exception, complied with her wish.

Ash's feet slowed as it appeared to her now, remembering. She stopped and lifted her eyes skyward. How many times had they stood, side by side, and stared up at its dome just like she was doing now? They'd only ever stop and look for a second before moving on, but it had become a habit in their relationship that made them both laugh at the sheer peculiarity of it. A pang of regret for past times swirled about Ash, swiftly followed by a wry internal smile at her stupidity.

She glanced at her watch and knew she should move on. Nat and Chloe would be waiting inside the Tate, as arranged. Her feet, however, remained rooted to the spot.

There had been no one quite like Nat since they'd parted. Sure, there had been acquaintances, but Ash had never been able to give her heart to another woman since Nat. She was her first love and no one else had ever understood her like she had. No other woman had ever felt quite right, and Ash knew that was because of her, not them. As much as she hated to admit it, her heart had stayed Nat's property for years after they'd parted. Nat was the one who had broken it, and she was the one who had kept it all that time. How else could she explain the regret of a lost love that had followed her right round Europe, back to England, and down deep into Cornwall? It had never left her. *She* had never left her.

Ash's gaze roamed over the familiar dome. The sadness at her and Nat's parting should have left her years ago. She knew that. Gabe was right: people come and go in each other's lives; people get together and break up. They were teenagers, for goodness' sake. Teenagers break up all the time.

So why had it felt so different when she and Nat had done it? Why had she been unable to shake it off? Sure, she hadn't thought of Nat for a while now, and seeing her again was bound to stir up old feelings and old wounds, but seeing Nat again had done so much more than just that. Seeing her had brought it home in stark clarity to Ash just how much their parting had affected her. Now she yearned for her past again, for her lost teenage years, after managing to so successfully lodge them in the back of her mind for so long.

Enough. She couldn't change the past. Ash shook her head and quickened her step, leaving St. Paul's behind her, hastening towards Bankside before her thoughts could overwhelm her. She forced her mind ahead to make it think of something else—anything else—so that her nostalgia wouldn't get the chance to catch up with her. By the time she arrived at the Tate she'd be her usual self again, and neither Nat nor Chloe would be able to guess that she'd just spent the last half an hour wallowing in self-pity. More than that, though, she wouldn't let Nat know she'd been thinking—again—of *them.* She hadn't thought of her and Nat for so many years, and she wasn't about to change that.

If only her mind would comply.

From inside the Tate's café, Nat's phone buzzed on the table in front of her. She glanced over to see Ash's name lit up and shot a look to Chloe, hoping she hadn't noticed the shift in her that seeing Ash's name had triggered.

"She's on her way." Nat picked up her phone and read Ash's message, placing it back on the table at Chloe's nod of acknowledgement.

"You know, I'm very grateful," Chloe said. "To both of you."

"For what?" Nat asked, surprised.

"For doing all this with me," Chloe replied. She paused. "I think it's a bit of a chore for you both."

Nat lowered her head and caught Chloe's eye.

"Clo, it's not a chore," she said. "Far from it."

"But it feels strange for you both," Chloe offered. Nat watched as she picked up a paper napkin and turned it over in her hands. "Spending time together again after all this time."

"It's odd, but nice." Nat smiled. "Stops me thinking about my new job all the time." The now-accustomed knot of nerves hit Nat's throat at her own words. New job, new life. It was what she wanted—a new start away from London—but the panic she felt at having to start over in Ireland on her own welled up inside her each and every time she thought about it.

The job she could cope with. Nat was confident in her own abilities as a surgeon—after all, the consultancy post she'd been offered had been everything she'd worked her whole life for. No, the uncertainties lay in the thought of packing up her soulless apartment in London and transferring its belongings to another soulless apartment in Belfast, where she would continue her life alone. Just as she'd done all her life—before, during, and after Richard.

"Does Ash know you're moving to Ireland?" Chloe asked.

"Why would she?" Nat knew she sounded harsher than she'd meant to. "She knows I have a new job, but she doesn't know it's in Ireland."

"Guess you two haven't really talked much, have you." Chloe looked at Nat. "This weekend, I mean."

"No. Guess not."

"Perhaps you should," Chloe said. "Clear some old air."

Nat looked away as Chloe pulled her phone from her bag, read something, then placed it back in her bag. Her mind ticked over. "Perhaps," she murmured, sliding a look to Chloe. The kid was smarter than she realized.

"Mum always said you two were great together," Chloe said slowly. "It seems a shame."

"Your mum told you about us?" Nat asked.

"That you were all close friends?" Chloe smiled. "The Untouchables? Of course."

Nat nodded. If only it had been that simple.

"I used to ask her why you two never came to visit us at the same time," Chloe continued. "When I was smaller, Mum used to say it was because Ash was in France and you were in Scotland, and blah, blah."

"Then?"

Chloe shrugged. "When I was older and able to understand better, she told me you two fell out when you were eighteen and didn't speak any more."

"Sounds so uncomplicated when you put it like that." Nat looked away.

"Why should it be complicated? Oh, she's here." Before Nat had to think up an answer, Chloe patted Nat's arm, then rose and went towards Ash the second she appeared in the doorway. Nat watched, grateful for the intervention, but resenting the nip of envy that instantly returned at the sight of Chloe's ease around Ash, when all Ash did was make Nat tense up. Ash certainly didn't look tense, and Sunday museum dressing, it seemed, meant nothing to her. Instead, she'd chosen faded jeans, slightly frayed at the bottoms, and a top low enough even for Nat to appreciate the smoothness of her neck and chest from where she was sitting. The combination looked good on her, Nat thought. Effortless but with just enough about it to turn heads in admiration.

Nat saw Chloe say something to Ash, point, then heard Ash laugh uproariously. The insecure woman inside her wondered, just for a fleeting moment, whether Chloe had said something to Ash about her, but she knew she was being oversensitive.

"I just told Ash about the painting we saw in the foyer over there." Chloe flopped down in her chair next to Nat again. "Told her I'd give her some crayons and she could replicate it later."

"It looks like a five-year-old drew it," Ash said, snagging the seat opposite them, "so it shouldn't be too hard." She eased back in her chair, crossing one long leg over the other. Despite her eyes begging her to look lower, Nat kept her focus on Ash's face.

"I wondered what had made you laugh," Nat said.

"Have you seen it?" Ash flicked her thumb over her shoulder. "If that's the standard of paintings here"—Nat smiled as Ash lowered her voice—"then it's going to be a long afternoon." Their eyes met across the table, and in that moment, Nat sensed a slight shift happen between them, the first tangible feeling of positivity and change she'd felt so far. Ash had seemingly brought with her an energy that had up until now been missing, a shared knowledge, mixed in with something Nat could only comprehend as fun. Nat didn't think she'd ever felt so grateful.

"So are we good to go?" Chloe stood. "The Dali exhibition's the one I'd like to see first."

Ash unfurled her legs and stood, the look of mischief in her eyes telling Nat everything she needed to know about what she thought about the prospect of viewing some Dali paintings.

Nat followed suit, watching Ash and Chloe make their way across the foyer, her eyes on Ash's back.

It was going to be a long afternoon, sure. But, still thinking about that shift, suddenly Nat didn't care.

The exhibition, to Ash's surprise, wasn't the complete drag she'd expected it to be. In fact, the whole museum had turned out to be a pleasant surprise and she knew she had Chloe to thank for that. Her keenness for modern art, exacerbated by good old-fashioned teenage enthusiasm, taught Ash far more than she'd ever expected. She knew she wasn't about to go out into London immediately afterwards and bag herself a reproduction Picasso for her bathroom at home, but Chloe had cleverly shown her that the best way to appreciate the works she was seeing was to not think too much about what she was looking at. That suited Ash just fine. Her mind, annoyingly, was on anything but modern art. Instead, it was on Nat. She looked great, and although a shadow of anxiety remained, she looked far more relaxed than she'd looked the day before. Happier too. A relaxed and happy Nat, Ash now thought as she slipped a look towards her as they left the museum, suited her well.

"Dinner," Ash said, looping an arm around Chloe as they stepped back outside, "is on me. There'll be a McDonald's round here somewhere I'm sure."

"You mind if I take a rain check on dinner?" Chloe pulled her phone from her pocket and waved it in front of Ash's face.

"Better offer?" Ash cocked her head to one side and smiled. "Better than a McDonald's?" She clutched at her heart. "I'm hurt."

"Something like that." Chloe batted Ash's hand away and laughed. "Couple of friends from school want to hang out," she said, adding "and we'll all travel back down to Wimbledon together, so don't worry," when Ash's concern had been noted.

"Have you heard this?" Ash turned her head to Nat. "Blown out for some friends."

"Don't be a drama queen." Nat walked past her, smiling back over her shoulder. "Just because you had to endure Dali doesn't mean poor Clo has to endure McDonald's with us pair."

"Funny." Ash hurried to catch her up. "Now what am I supposed to do?"

"Put up with me on your own," Nat said, still walking. "I hope you're hungry. I'm bloody starving."

## CHAPTER EIGHT

From the outside, the restaurant was no different to the dozens of others in London. The glorious aromas wafting towards Ash as she and Nat approached it, however, were enough for them both to stop seeking something slightly more expensive and plump for it. It looked as though it would be a good choice, and certainly better than her planned McDonald's, Ash thought with a smile. Entering the dimly lit belly of the restaurant, the plush ruby seats, tasteful decorations, and ambient lighting gave it the air of a place that was perhaps only one step down from something more at home in Mayfair. Ash looked down at her jeans, frayed at the ends, and wished—not for the first time—that she'd thought to pack better evening wear, annoyed with herself that she hadn't known better.

"Too posh or okay?" Nat's hair tickled her cheek as she leaned closer to be heard above the hubbub in the restaurant.

"It's okay," Ash replied. "I'm too hungry to worry."

They were shown to a table close to the bar, tucked away in a darkened corner, their waiter giving them his undivided attention. Tips, Ash guessed looking at the upmarket clientele that surrounded her, had to be earned in this particular place. She waited for Nat to be seated first, glancing around as the waiter fussed around her, then waved him politely away as he attempted to seat her too.

"I'm good," she said, sitting down. "Could we just get some drinks, please?" She hated his formality. Drinks would ease her own unease. "Beer would be good for me, thanks."

"Oh." Nat, Ash thought, looked a little taken aback. "Whatever house red you've got will be great." Nat smiled at him. "Thanks." She looked at Ash. "No perusing the drinks menu, then?"

"Beer for me," Ash replied, shrugging, "wine for you. Who needs a drinks menu?"

"You're uncomfortable, aren't you?" Nat asked.

"It's just a bit stuffy for me, that's all." Ash wrinkled her nose. "Starched napkins, starched waiter. Makes me feel nervous."

"I remember the look."

"What look?"

"You always used to get that look on your face when you felt uncomfortable," Nat said. "A sort of grumpy, panicked look."

"Thanks." Ash rested back in her seat as her glass of beer arrived. She waited while Nat received her wine, then leaned forward again. "Grumpy *and* panicked?" She picked up her glass and smiled over the top of it. "Cheers." She lifted her glass higher, watching as Nat did the same, then drank her beer.

"Whenever we went somewhere where you felt out of place," Nat said, "you'd always get prickly. Like you held it personally responsible for making you feel uncomfortable."

"I don't recall us going to many places like that," Ash replied. "Only that one time when you tried to drag me off to the ballet."

"You wore your shorts." Nat nodded.

"It was the middle of summer."

"No one wears shorts to the ballet."

"I did." Ash took another sip. She remembered it well. They'd laughed so much at how out of place Ash had looked, in amongst the suits and dresses, that they'd narrowly avoided being asked to leave by the stuffed shirt on the door. "They were nice shorts," she said. "I didn't think there was a problem."

"You never did worry about what people thought." Nat grinned. "You were too cool to care."

"Life's too short." Ash's glass paused midair. "Pardon the pun." She drank some more beer back.

"That's one of the things I loved about you when we were together," Nat said. "Not much bothered you, did it?"

"Only some things." Ash picked up a menu as a distraction to Nat's words. Talking over the past wasn't going to be on her agenda tonight; she'd promised herself that, the second she'd realized she'd be dining with Nat alone. Her evening with Nat would be spent discussing Livvy's letters, or Chloe, or London. Anything but their past.

"You having a starter?" Nat picked up her own menu. Had she sensed Ash's unease? Ash stole a look over the top of her menu; if Nat had sensed it, she was hiding it well.

"I'm going to plunge straight into the main course, I think." Ash frowned, trying to concentrate on the words in front of her. The letters coalesced.

*That's one of the things I loved about you when we were together.*

Nat had loved her once, but now it all seemed like such a long time ago that Ash had forgotten what it felt like to be loved. That feeling had never been bettered but also had never returned after Nat had left her. Looking across the table to Nat now, Ash tried to remember back to a time when they'd told one another they loved each other. When the words just rolled so easily from their mouths. When they both really meant it.

"The duck here is supposed to be the best this side of the river." Nat's words pulled Ash back.

"Sounds good to me."

"And some sides to go with it?" Nat, Ash noted, was deep in concentration, studying the menu.

"Why not." Ash took another drink, wishing she could shake the feeling Nat's earlier words had provoked.

She watched as Nat turned her head and sought out a waiter. With one effortless rise of her chin and a smile that could charm the birds from the trees, the waiter was instantly at her side. She ordered, not waiting for confirmation from Ash, and it struck Ash that Nat was as comfortable in such a formal dining setting as she was ill at ease.

"What?" Nat's smile alerted Ash to the fact she'd been staring at her.

"Nothing. I—" Ash dropped her gaze. "I was just thinking how at home you look here." She shook her head and frowned. "I mean, when I feel so tetchy at the primness of it all."

"I've been here before," Nat began slowly, "so I guess I'm used to it." That was a question, Ash assumed, more than a declaration. "I don't know." Definitely a question.

"You've been back in London long?" Ash asked. "Livvy said you left Edinburgh when you, you know, finished at medical school. But…" Her words petered out. Did she want to know more about Nat? Her head said no. Her heart, though…

"It'll be, let me see"—Nat stared at a spot just past Ash's shoulder—"nearly ten years now." She sat back and whistled through her teeth. "Never realized it was that long."

"Time flies, huh?"

"Something like that." Nat smiled. "And you? How long have you been in Cornwall?"

"About the same," Ash replied. "Mm. Maybe a bit longer. Maybe twelve years." She nodded.

"You like it there?" Nat sat back.

"Love it." Ash looked squarely at Nat. "It's just…me. It's everything I am," she said. "There's something strangely comforting about being tucked away in the furthest corner of England, in a cottage where my garden practically falls into the sea." Ash smiled, almost hearing the rush of the sea as she spoke. "Does that make sense?"

"Perfect sense."

"Like I'm sure London is everything you are or want to be," Ash offered. "After all, you fit very well into a place like this. Whereas me"—she waved her hands up and down in front of her—"I'm more at home in a burger shack on the beach." She laughed.

"I think—" Nat paused as the waiter arrived at their table with cutlery.

An awkward silence settled across the table as the waiter busied himself setting down knives and forks. Ash drained her drink and asked for another, putting the offer to Nat, who declined. Her wine, Ash noted, had hardly been touched.

"You think...?" Ash prompted once the waiter had left again.

"I can't remember." Nat laughed through her nose. "How silly." Her face, Ash thought, looked pained.

"Senior moment?" Ash smiled.

"I think perhaps London once was my sort of place," Nat said quickly, almost as though she needed to get the words out before she changed her mind, "but not any more." She looked at Ash. "Maybe Belfast will be."

"Belfast?"

"The consultant's post that Judy was talking about at her house," Nat said, "is at the Royal Victoria Hospital over there. I just have to accept the post and then I'm off. Could be there this time next month."

A strange sensation flickered inside Ash. Barely distinguishable, but there all the same.

"Isn't that funny?" Ash thought her voice sounded odd. "But for some reason I assumed it would be in London."

"Well I *was* offered a post at St. Bart's," Nat said. "Where I am now, you know?"

"Mm-hmm."

"But"—Nat wrinkled her nose—"I fancied a clean break." She hesitated. "You know I was married once?"

"Livvy told me." Ash caught Nat's eye. Richard Thornton, senior cardiologist. Two divorces, five kids, nine years Nat's senior. Numbers, numbers. But all important. The marriage, according to Livvy, had lasted barely a year. Another important number. "Richard, wasn't it?" His name was out before Ash realized.

"You know his name?"

Nat looked distressed, Ash thought.

"Livvy mentioned it once." Ash broke eye contact. Livvy had mentioned his name more than once when Nat had been with him.

"He helped me...get my head around stuff," Nat said. "After you."

"After me?" Ash replied drolly. "Livvy said you met him in your twenties."

"I did."

"I was long gone by then." Ash looked up as her beer arrived. She immediately picked it up and drank some back, the liquid choking down some more words she knew were desperate to be spoken.

"Physically maybe," Nat said, once the waiter had left. "Emotionally for me? Not so."

"You're expecting me to believe that you married Richard as a way to get over me?" Ash stared at Nat. "After you dumped me? You're really serious?"

"I cared about you more than you realized," Nat said. "When I knew you, I…"

Her words hit a nerve.

"When you *knew* me?" Ash sensed the colour flash across her face. "You think it's okay to catalogue what I felt for you as just being an *association*?" She sat back. "You're priceless."

"I didn't mean it like that." Nat shook her head. "You misunderstood me. I genuinely cared for you."

Her words were like a slap across Ash's face. "You cared for me so much you were prepared to do that to me?" She leaned forward again and lowered her voice. "The one thing I do understand is the only person you ever cared about was yourself," Ash said bluntly. "All your life, Nat Braithwaite was your number one priority. So don't give me that."

Ash stared at her, forcing Nat's gaze away from hers. Ash watched as she fiddled with her hair, picking at some stray strands, and then cleared her throat.

"I don't want to argue," Nat finally said, "I was just trying to make conversation." Her voice was light and flippant, and Ash knew her point had struck home. Ash's sense of satisfaction was profound.

"By telling me that you stumbled into the arms of some man as a way to get over me?" Ash felt her own tension hitch up again at the thought. "The only reason you hooked up with this Richard guy was for your own ends."

"Meaning?" Nat's face hardened.

"Meaning it would be good for your career," Ash countered. "Because everything you've ever done has been for your own benefit."

"That's rubbish and you know it." Nat, infuriatingly for Ash, sipped at her wine and looked away, indicating that as far as she was concerned, the matter was over.

It was far from over for Ash.

"Like leaving me," Ash said.

"Why rake that up now?" Nat asked.

"Because I'm trying to make a point here." Ash fought back her annoyance. "You're sitting there, all holier than thou, pretending you were heartbroken over me and that it took you years to get over everything, when we both know the truth."

"The truth," Nat said, looking evenly at Ash, "is that we were both young, and it would never have lasted through university anyway."

"Your parents' words or yours?" Ash said.

"Mine."

"So, despite knowing I loved you and would have done anything for you, you made the decision to end it," Ash said. "Just like that."

"We wanted different things." Ash watched Nat stare down into her glass. "We had different mentalities back then." She looked back up at her. "We were just kids, Ash."

They were just lame excuses, Ash knew. Nat was happy to reel out the same old excuses about them needing space, needing time apart. About their relationship being too much too soon. Nat, Ash realized with increasing frustration, was as determined to fight her corner as Ash was to point out her faults. The combination didn't make the atmosphere across the table particularly comfortable.

"Did you regret it?" Ash asked. "Us?"

She watched as Nat circled a finger around the rim of her wine glass, apparently deep in thought. Finally she looked up at Ash.

"I wish I *could* tell you I regret us ever being together," Nat eventually replied. "Like you told me the night we parted."

Ash remembered that night, remembered her words and her vitriol. There had been so much anger and hate; Ash's heart hadn't meant the things she'd said to Nat, even if her mouth, at the time, had.

"But I can't tell you that," Nat went on, "because I don't regret any of it, and that's the truth."

"I loved you." Ash held Nat's gaze. "But it wasn't enough for you, was it?"

"What did we know about love, Ash?" Nat looked away.

"I knew you were everything to me," Ash said, "and that I would have done anything for you."

Ash shifted back in her chair as their waiter arrived with their plates. Her words hung uneasily between them, and Ash wished she could take them back. Seconds felt like hours as the waiter served them and asked, again, about drinks. Finally, at the shake of their heads, he left.

"Maybe," Nat eventually replied. "But—"

"But it wasn't going to get in the way of what you—or your parents—wanted?" Ash replied. She picked up her fork and prodded at the small pile of vegetables on her plate, then looked back to Nat, an unwanted sense of guilt sweeping over her at the wounded expression on Nat's face.

Ash opened her mouth to speak again, another confrontation forming on her lips, but stopped herself. Instead, she drew in a long, slow breath. Maybe Nat was right, and this really wasn't the time to rake over the past. "So tell me about Richard," she said, almost forcing the words out.

"Richard was a mistake." Nat looked away.

"No shit." Ash raised an eyebrow. "You're gay, remember?"

"Yes, I know."

Ash bent her head and caught Nat's eye. "No one can kiss another girl like you did and call themselves straight." She held her gaze long enough to make Nat look away first.

"Richard was just…there," Nat said. "Conveniently put there by my father at a time when I was lost and unhappy."

"Your father?" Ash was confused.

"Richard was a colleague," Nat explained. "Same department as my father."

"And your father orchestrated something?"

"Didn't he always?"

Ash's mind fell back almost twenty years. Yes, her father had always had a say in Nat's life. Had preached the importance of success to her until she got to the point where she would comply with his wishes just to get him off her case. But that was then. Somehow, though, Ash thought that by her twenties and living away from home Nat would have had enough of his meddling. Apparently not.

"Were you happy?" Ash hadn't meant to ask the question, but the minute it was out she knew it had been inside her, desperate to be asked, for years. "You and Richard?" Images tapped at her as she said his name out loud. Nat with Richard. Richard with Nat. She cut her glance away, annoyed at herself for the jealousy she was feeling.

"No." Nat's face, Ash saw when she turned back to her, was shrouded with misery. "He just made me even unhappier."

"So why…?"

"He wanted a wife," Nat said. "I wanted a shoulder to cry on at a time when I was vulnerable." She looked at Ash. "And don't look at me like that. I already told you why."

Ash stared at her, hearing the pain in her voice.

"You mean you really did regret finishing with me?" she asked.

"Every day," Nat said. She picked up her knife and fork and Ash sensed a change of direction for the conversation. "What about you?"

"Me?"

"Is there…someone?"

Ash picked up her glass of beer and swirled it around, watching the liquid eddy inside.

"No," she eventually said, "there's no one." Ash slowly looked up, sensing, as she always used to, Nat's gaze on her. "There's not really been anyone since…"

"Us?" Nat finished the sentence.

"Yes. Since us." Ash held Nat's gaze. "No one ever really compared."

"I really fucked up, didn't I?"

Ash slowly drank back her beer, figuring her silence was all the answer Nat needed.

"And now I only have myself to blame, don't I?"

"It's been a lot of years, Nat." Ash shrugged. "We're past all that, surely?" She looked at her, surprised at the pain she saw in Nat's eyes.

This was Nat's way of vindicating her past actions and Ash knew that right now this was merely scratching at the surface of what had happened. What good would arguing even more do? Nat had had years to justify to herself why she'd ended things, and to convince herself that what she'd done was right for both of them. Arguing with her now would just bring all that pain and bitterness to the surface again and leave them strangers to one another once more. Ash was tired of fighting. Tired of hating.

Now all Ash felt was...*what*? It was hard for her to separate all the different emotions she was feeling at that moment as Nat sat opposite her. Was it anger? No, she would have expected anger; that would have been fully justified. Instead, there was something stronger dancing around the edges of her consciousness. Relief, perhaps. Or an understanding.

And none of it made any sense to Ash at all.

## CHAPTER NINE

Dearest Flash,

How's the weather? Isn't that how you're always supposed to start a letter?

Ash turned her head away and stared at the raindrops pooling, like brimming tears, at the bottom of her window. She blinked slowly, unsure why reading Livvy's fourth letter made her feel so sad. Maybe dinner with Nat the previous evening had stirred up too many emotions for her to cope with in less than twelve hours. Who knew? All Ash did know was she'd coped with Livvy's other letters, but for some reason, the start of her next one pinched a sadness in her chest.

Ash wiped her eyes with her sleeve and read on.

Anyway, I hope you're enjoying your time in London and making your way merrily through my list. How's Chloe? I'm sure she's having a ball with you pair. Give her a hug from me and tell her I miss her?

I was lying in bed this morning, thinking back—as you do—to when we were seventeen and your dad gave you £200 for passing your driving test. Do you remember? You got terribly grumpy about it all because you knew he couldn't afford it, but he wouldn't take it back because he said you'd worked so hard to pass your test.

Ash smiled. Of course she remembered. She'd run home, light-headed with relief that she'd passed her test, and her father had pressed two hundred pounds into her hand the second she told him. *I got it from the bank before you'd even gone to take your test,* he'd said. *I was that confident.*

She'd refused the money. Her father, out of work for the previous two years, could ill afford to give her ten pounds back then, let alone anything more. Ash's attention returned to the rain, still slamming against her window. That had been one of the reasons her parents had both upped sticks and headed to New Zealand when she was twenty and already halfway round Europe with no intention of ever returning home herself.

He wouldn't take the two hundred pounds back, of course. Pride. He still had buckets of pride. He told her to treat herself—and her friends—and do something she'd never ordinarily be able to do. They'd come close to it too: a spa day, tea at Claridge's, a personal shopper at Harrods. Ash's smile deepened. That last idea had been Livvy's. But they did none of those things. Instead, Ash bought her parents a bench for their garden, as a thank you to them for everything they'd ever done for her. She'd never have tolerated a personal shopper waggling dresses in her face, anyway.

Ash shifted in her chair and returned her attention to Livvy's letter.

> We never did get to have tea at a posh place, did we? Or that massage at Champney's? You were your usual lovely, gorgeous, generous self and that's why we all loved you, even though Nat said at the time she didn't because she'd always wanted to go to Champney's. She was joking, btw.

Ash raised an eyebrow.

> So now you can make it up to her! I've sent buckets of money to Claridge's—you know, the terribly posh place in Mayfair?—so you can all go and have afternoon tea there. Just pre-book a time, give them my name, and

hey presto! Oh, and Flash? Don't wear your jeans (I bet you wore them to the theatre, didn't you?) because you'll get booted out. And for goodness' sake make sure Chloe looks smart too. You're as bad as each other. Ask Nat what to wear if you're worried—you always used to ask her opinion when you were together, and come on! She was usually right, wasn't she? Admit it.

Okay, time for my afternoon nap. I do hope you'll all enjoy your posh tea. Remember not to slurp, and think of me when you're there, will you? I'd like that.

Until the next missive,
Livvy xxx

Although this particular letter made her sad, it was, Ash thought, easier to deal with than the others. She couldn't put her finger on why though. Perhaps it was because she found comfort in it, almost as though Livvy was reading it aloud to her, and that she could clearly hear Livvy scolding her for wearing jeans or glugging down her tea. Ash rested her head back. It had been too long since she'd heard Livvy's voice.

Her head still resting against her sofa, Ash's hand fumbled for her phone next to her. Lifting it up high to see its screen, she found Nat's number. New message. Ash tapped her finger on the screen.

*Hiya.*

Delete.

*Hello Nat.*

Delete.

Ash's brow furrowed. *Just write the damn message.*

*Hey, how're you?*

Ash nestled down further into her chair and formulated her message.

*Have you read Livvy's next letter yet? What time shall we meet? 3 p.m. or thereabouts? Livvy says I have to ask you what to wear. Ha! Bloody cheek (she knows me too well). Ash xxx*

Ash stared at her kisses, then hastily deleted them before sending her message to Nat. She sent kisses to everyone in her texts—usually at least four to Gabe—but for some reason, it felt weird sending them to Nat. Ash placed her phone on her chest, closed her eyes, and wondered what to wear. She was surprised to feel her phone buzz straight away. The feeling inside when she read Nat's name was even more of a surprise.

*Hey,* it said. *I read Livvy's letter over breakfast. 3 p.m. sounds perfect. I'll call Chloe and arrange to meet her at the station.*

Ash wrote her reply: *See you then.*

Inside, she wanted to say more but couldn't quite figure out what. Why should she want to keep the texts going? Her hand strayed to her stomach. Because of the sensation of anticipation receiving a text from Nat gave her, that's why.

Her phone vibrated.

*Do you need me to take you round Selfridges before we go, though? Buy you something smart? I hear ladies wear dresses these days... ;)*

Ash couldn't stop the smile that spread across her face.

Her finger automatically hit reply.

*Haha! Make it pink and taffeta and we have a deal ;)*

She tapped send, hoping Nat would reply immediately. She did.

*And some pretty shoes? With sparkles?*

Ash grinned. She started to reply, her typing interrupted by another text from Nat: *I enjoyed dinner last night, btw.*

Okay. Unexpected.

So Nat had enjoyed herself, despite Ash having a go at her over Richard. Ash put her phone down, then picked it up again.

*Me too.*

Send.

Should she have said more? Should she have made a joke about the waiter's trousers, or the noisy lady sitting at the next table to them as well? Should she have told her that she'd enjoyed herself too? Far more than her brain was allowing her to tell her?

*We should do it again.*

Ash's stomach fluttered at Nat's reply. She puffed out her cheeks in exasperation at her own knee-jerk emotion. It was just an offer of another dinner, that was all. Not a date. Definitely *not* a date.

They could take Chloe with them this time, if they decided to go out again. Her fluttering eased. That was it. They'd all go out together. Lunch today. Ash nodded to herself, decision made.

*How about lunch today?* She wrote. *Then on to Claridge's afterwards?*

Nat's reply was immediate: *Sounds perfect. After lunch we can both go and collect Chloe from Bond St. Station and head straight for Claridge's.*

Awkward.

Should they just go alone? Ash stared blankly at a mark on the carpet by her feet. No, Chloe had to come too. Where Nat was concerned, it was best to keep things simple. They'd forged something of a superficial friendship over the last three days; if either of them delved any deeper they ran the risk of old feelings rematerializing. And what would that actually achieve? Ash leaned her head to one side. The mark on the carpet looked like a butterfly, she thought. Nat was going to Belfast, sooner rather than later, it seemed. Ash was happy in Cornwall. The emotional attachment they once had might pull them together again, and Ash knew beyond any doubt that she wouldn't—couldn't—chance falling for Nat all over again.

She zapped out a message to Nat: *I thought it'd be nice for Clo to come along too. Tell her I'll see her at the station at midday.*

It had been painful enough at eighteen when it had ended. For it to all end again at thirty-five? Unthinkable.

Send.

Silence filled the room. Just the sound of Ash's steady breathing, and the imaginary whirr of her brain turning everything over. She'd always have feelings for Nat. She'd known that all her life, but fear of rejection would focus her mind, give her clarity, and always stop her from acting on those feelings.

Ash looked at her phone. Once, twice. Three times, as though suddenly she'd lost the ability to hear it vibrate. Nat hadn't replied.

A buzz. Finally.

*Okay. See you later.*

Ash stood. She felt flat. Confused. Angry, even, but she didn't know why. She grabbed her coat from the back of the door, jiggled the pockets to hear her keys inside, and left the safety of her hotel room.

❖

Why did having lunch have to turn into such a big deal? Not that *having* lunch was a big deal, per se. But the whole process of lunch, and everything it could have meant, had now somehow turned into something way bigger than Nat felt comfortable with. And she knew it was all her own fault.

Nat walked to her window. Soft autumn rain fell like champagne bubbles outside, soaking into the parched grass of the park opposite her apartment. She watched as it drank it back gratefully, sucking it in. A blackbird appeared on her windowsill outside. He fluttered fretfully, and Nat could see his feet were tangled up in the small messy cotoneaster that swirled about her window box, and which acted as the pathetic sum of her garden. Nat watched, heart in mouth, wondering if she should open her window and help him, relieved when he finally freed himself and flew off, chattering angrily at the sheer indignation of it all. Nat watched for as long as she could as he flitted left, then right, before finally disappearing into the rain.

She ran her finger down the condensation on her window, then rubbed the water on her finger away with her thumb. What she wouldn't have given over the years to spread her wings and fly away. Disappear into the rain like the blackbird. Maybe Ireland would be different; perhaps Belfast would give her wings and she would finally find the change in her life she'd been seeking since medical school.

Nat's hand fell to her phone in her pocket. She needed to reply to Ash. Of course Chloe should come to lunch too. Nat felt foolish; why would she even think otherwise? It wasn't even as though she and Ash had rekindled anything remotely like closeness. No, all they'd managed to do over the last few days was snag back a scrap of the friendship they'd once had. Why would either of them want more?

*Because you want more?*

Nat felt unable to silence the voice in her head. She abruptly pulled out her phone, shooing away that train of thought before her brain had a chance to make anything more out of it.

*Okay. See you later.*

That was all that needed to be said.

❖

"Claridge's has a dress code?" Ash stared at Chloe. "You're kidding, right?"

Chloe held up her phone. "Elegant smart casual," she read, "no shorts, vests, sportswear, flip-flops, ripped jeans, or baseball caps."

"To drink *tea*?" Ash asked. "I guess trousers and suede boots are okay though."

"Sure you don't want to go shopping for that dress after all?" Nat raised a brow.

"Did I ever suit a dress?" Ash asked.

"Well now you mention it…" Nat shrugged and grinned.

Ash wiped the corner of her mouth with her napkin. They were in Luigi's, a small Italian café just a five-minute walk from Mayfair. Lunch had been good; Nat had been okay too, dispelling any worries Ash might have had that she'd spoiled her plans by asking Chloe along. Her thought process had been ridiculous—she knew that now. After all, the whole point of the last three days in London had been for Chloe's benefit. Hadn't all of this been for Chloe?

"Ash," Ash now heard Nat saying to Chloe, "was such a tomboy when we were kids."

"No change there, then." Ash shrugged.

"I used to envy her casualness," Nat said. "And the fact she'd look good in whatever she wore."

Ash caught Nat's eye.

"And I used to *love* trawling the clothes shops with her." Nat looked away.

"She did," Ash agreed.

Shopping trips. Oh, so many shopping trips. Ash remembered them well. Nat loved to shop; Ash didn't. But she loved Nat, and when you love someone, you grit your teeth and fit in with what they want to do. Especially when you're first dating and trying to impress them. And for quite a large chunk afterwards too.

Ash dug a finger into the corner of her eye, hiding a wry smile with her hand.

She hated the shopping. But because she loved Nat, she made out she loved it too, because she knew it made Nat happy. But she never felt so uncomfortable as when she was standing next to Nat, trying to make all the right noises at the clothes Nat would hold up for her, when secretly she thought they all looked the same and that, quite frankly, she'd prefer to see Nat *out* of her clothes rather than in them. That used to happen later, of course. Nat knew Ash loathed shopping, so her reward was given to her in her bedroom later, door locked, parents oblivious downstairs.

Now that had been worth all the hours traipsing round the shops.

The smile that Ash had fought to conceal broke out as she remembered, with a sudden, stark clarity, one particularly satisfying recompense. Nat had been very grateful, she recalled.

"What?"

Ash looked over to see Nat studying her quizzically.

"What's so funny?"

"Nothing." Ash shook her head. If Nat could only read her mind...

"I can read you like a book." Nat's stare was intense. Too intense for Ash's liking. "Something's tickled you."

"Just remembering stuff." Ash sat back in her chair. "About you dragging me round the shops with you."

"You were always so patient," Nat said. Ash laughed as she clutched her chest. "Such a hero."

Ash lowered her eyes.

*I would have done anything for you back then.*

She returned her gaze to Nat, putting voice to her thoughts.

"I wanted to do it," she said. "Whatever you wanted, I'd have done it."

"I know." Nat's voice was quiet.

They held one another's gaze, a shared knowledge seeming to leap between them in amongst the clinking of crockery and chatter of the tea room.

"You two are a total cheesefest," Chloe said, breaking Ash's stare first. "Total. Cheese. Fest." Chloe picked up her phone, her words dissolving into a yawn.

While Chloe scrutinized her phone, now oblivious to both Ash and Nat, Ash looked over to Nat and their eyes met.

Neither said a word. They didn't have to.

❖

Claridge's, an art deco masterpiece of a hotel, appeared to rise up magnificently from the pavement as Nat, Ash, and Chloe approached it from Luigi's. A flitter of nerves hit Nat as she recalled the last time she'd been to the hotel, nearly ten years before; dinner, with Richard and his cronies, hadn't been the best experience of her life.

She stared ahead to the ornate foyer as they walked down the street towards it, Ash and Chloe oblivious to her discomfort. Richard, Nat remembered, had insisted she wear shoes that pinched, and a dress that suffocated her. All to impress his friends. Nat's face shadowed. They'd argued; she'd begged him to let her stay home. He'd bullied and belittled, and refused to acknowledge that Nat was crying inside. Because that had been his way. His previous wife—a lawyer in Chelsea—had warned her. Nat hadn't understood at the time why the second Mrs. Thornton would think to seek out her email address and contact her at work, offering her some friendly advice.

"You coming?" Ash called back over her shoulder. Nat had unknowingly slowed, her thoughts dragging her back.

"You go on." Nat waved her on. "I'll catch you up."

"And make me go in here alone?" Ash stopped. Her friendly smile immediately soothed Nat. "This is far more your kind of place."

Nat fell into step with them.

*He'll try to dominate you,* Meredith Thornton had said. *You don't seem to understand what a strong character he has.*

Nat should have listened. It wasn't even as if she loved him, so why she hadn't just run when she had the chance was beyond her. She slipped a look to Ash. She didn't run because Richard wasn't Ash. Ash had been right too, in her withering assertion of Nat and Richard's sham marriage: Richard could also help open doors for her, and if doors were opened then everything she'd done in the past, everything she'd done to Ash, would have been justified.

Marriage was never part of her plans though. Nat's pace slowed as they arrived at Claridge's. The proposal and marriage part of her *interaction* with Richard was akin to being on a roller coaster; she'd got herself onto it, and suddenly she couldn't get off again. It had all happened so fast. Yes, she'd had dinner dates with him, and yes, she'd liked him. But not like that. Never like that.

Then she'd been trapped like the blackbird outside her window.

The concierge outside the hotel tipped his hat as Nat, Ash, and Chloe wandered up the steps towards him. With a sweep of his arm, the door to the hotel was opened, and Nat was inside.

And she'd been trapped ever since.

"I just wanted to say thank you again to you guys."

Nat licked her finger, then dabbed it on her plate, gluing up the last of her cake crumbs. "You don't need to keep thanking us, Clo," she said. She sucked the crumbs from her finger.

"You've been awesome," Chloe said, "and, well, I'm sure Mum's up there looking down thinking the same."

Nat caught Ash's eye.

"I hope so," Ash said.

"And I've had a blast," Chloe continued. "Punting, theatre, posh afternoon tea…"

"More than some people do in a year." Nat grinned. She sat back in her chair, her shoulders, previously taut with stress, now relaxed. She looked around her, then to Ash. A sense of gratitude tumbled about her, because this time she was in Claridge's with Ash, not Richard. Grateful that she'd felt more at home with Ash in the last hour than she had ever done with him. Thankful that Ash had made her return to the hotel less traumatic than she thought it would be, and loving that the cool, unflappable Ash that she'd once loved so much was still very much alive and kicking.

They'd laughed so much over tea too. Over the years, Nat had wondered if she'd lost the ability to laugh. Happiness had become a stranger to her, but being with Ash had made her realize she was still alive after all.

Nat looked at Ash, talking with Chloe. Their first day together, just two days previously, seemed like a lifetime ago. Their stiltedness towards one another had rapidly diminished. They were smiling at one another, joking with each other. And Nat had never been so thankful.

"So we have one more day left in London." Ash was talking to her.

*Then four days apart.*

Nat blinked. The drone of noise in the tearoom continued.

"Nat? One more day." Chloe. "Then off to Cornwall. I can't wait."

"Yes." Nat picked at the corner of her eye. Focus. "One more day."

A teacup spilled to the floor somewhere across the room, shattering. Nat jerked her head round, grateful for the interruption. Her mind was tailspinning, dangerously out of control, then quite without warning—and just like all the other times—her heart started to pound. Thoughts of Richard had eaten away at her. Thoughts of Ash. Of parting with her again. Of being alone again with just her thoughts again.

It was starting, and she needed to get out. Now.

"Give me a sec, will you?" She stood. "Just need to go." She signalled towards the sign for the ladies'.

Nat walked from the table, the palpable sense that the room was closing in on her hard to ignore. One foot in front of the other. She'd be okay.

Once in the safety of the toilet cubicle, she placed the seat down and sat. Cradling her head in her hands, Nat let out a long, juddery breath. She lifted her head from her hands and pulled on her bracelet, tears lurking just under the surface. It had been nearly two weeks since her last panic attack. Two weeks of respite, but it was understandable, she thought as she fought to get her breathing back under control, that things would have sooner or later hit her again.

Nat looked to the closed door of her cubicle, trying not to think too hard about Ash and Chloe, waiting for her at their table. She'd have to move soon, she knew, before one or the other came looking for her.

"Get a grip," Nat muttered under her breath. "Thirty-five and acting like a kid."

She pulled her hands through her hair, her fingers feeling cold against her scalp. Ash was at the heart of all this, she knew it. She still cared for her, that much was obvious now. But those intense feelings from all those years ago, when no one else in the world mattered but Ash, they were long gone now, weren't they?

Nat heard the door to the ladies' open.

"Nat?"

Nat groaned. Ash.

"You okay?"

How long had she been sitting there? Barely minutes, surely?

"Yeah, I'm good," she called out. She pulled in a large breath and peeled off four sheets of toilet paper, blew her nose, then stood, just remembering to flush the toilet before she left her cubicle.

Ash was standing outside.

Everything was the same as it had always been, except now everything was different.

"Chloe says she has to scoot soon," Ash said. She leaned against the sink, arms folded. "DVD night with her besties, apparently."

Nat smiled as Ash rolled her eyes as she said *besties*. She turned on the tap and put her hands under the running hot water, savouring the heat on her clammy skin. "I'm on it," she said. "I'll go with her to the station. We can head down the Jubilee Line together."

"It's been good," Ash said quietly. "This whole day."

"Claridge's didn't bring you out in a Socialist rash?" Nat raised her eyebrow.

Ash pinched her finger and thumb together. "Just a teensy bit," she said.

Nat laughed. Her heart slowed.

"So I'll see you tomorrow?" Ash asked. "Depending on what delights Livvy has for us."

Nat moved as she pushed herself away from the sink.

"I'll open my letter tonight," Nat said, "then text you later."

They both made for the door. A jumble of voices fought to be heard in Nat's head. She held the door open for Ash.

"Although…" Nat went through the door.

"Although?" Ash followed her.

"You could bring your letter over to mine tonight?" Her words were out before she knew it. It was madness, she knew. Spending time with Ash was madness. "We could open them together."

Nat was surprised at her boldness. She was even more surprised at Ash's reply.

"I couldn't think of anything I'd love to do more," Ash said.

## CHAPTER TEN

Ash could barely wait to get back to her hotel so she could talk to Gabe. She needed to hear his voice, to listen to his practicality, and for him to tell her it was perfectly normal that two old lovers could actually hang out with one another and—heaven forbid—be civil to one another.

So why couldn't she stop thinking that going over to Nat's later was one huge mistake?

London, everything about it—Nat, Chloe, and this whole wish-list experience—was lunacy. She was away from home; personalities sometimes changed away from their normal environment, right? People did things they would never dream of.

*Like going round to your ex's late at night.*

*An ex you still have feelings for, even though you won't admit it to yourself.*

Ash threw herself down on her bed and stared up at the ceiling of her room, seeking patterns around the light fitting. She dialled Gabe's number, contentment spreading over her like a warm blanket when she heard him answer.

"How's it going, chicken?"

Ash nestled her head back into her pillow. "It's been crazy," she said. "I can't wait to come home tomorrow night." Wasn't *that* the truth?

"So what have you been up to?" Gabe asked. "Your texts have been…vague." He chuckled.

"Eating, mostly." Ash smiled up to the ceiling. "Lunches, dinners, afternoon teas at swanky hotels."

"Swanky hotels?" Gabe sounded impressed. "I hope you brushed your hair."

"I'm going over to Nat's tonight." Even as she said it, it sounded wrong.

"Ooh, that's an unexpected development."

"We're getting on okay, actually," Ash said, "which I think is a surprise to both of us."

"No awkwardness?"

"Oh, loads to start with." Ash frowned. "Mostly from me. Then I realized I was being a jerk, figured the best way to get through my time with her was to thaw out a little and then…" She hesitated. "We sort of started to get on okay."

"And so it's a cosy dinner chez Braithwaite tonight?"

"No." Ash looked at her empty McDonald's box. "Nothing like that. I'm just going over to open Livvy's next letter with her." She pulled in a long breath, then exhaled slowly. "Gabe?"

"Yuh-huh?"

"It's okay for me to want to go to Nat's, isn't it?" Ash frowned. "It doesn't have to mean anything, right?"

Gabe laughed loudly, forcing a smile from Ash. "Honey, it's totally okay," he said. "I'm guessing she asked you?"

"Yeah."

"So she wants to hang out with you," Gabe said. "You think she's sitting at home right now, fretting like you are about whether she should have asked you or not?"

"Doubt it."

"Well then."

"It feels…I don't know." Ash sighed. "Odd. Reconnecting with her after all this time, you know?"

"Remember I used to go out with a guy called Danny, years ago?" Gabe asked.

"Mm."

"And remember how cut up I was when he ended it?"

"How could I forget?" Gabe, usually the life and soul of the party, had hid himself away for weeks. Retreated to his cottage, refusing to answer her calls, until in desperation Ash had called the police. Gabe was found sitting, wrapped in a blanket, a plethora of empty whisky bottles strewn at his feet, watching *Kramer vs. Kramer* with the lights off.

"I thought I'd never get over him," Gabe said. "Thought I could never walk down the street again in case I bumped into him."

"I wasn't cut up like that over Nat," Ash lied. "It was totally different."

"That's as maybe," Gabe said. "What I'm trying to say—badly—is that pretty much everyone at some point in their lives will have to see, speak to, and interact with an ex. I met Danny again a few years later and I survived it. We had coffee together, and it felt like the most unnatural thing in the world to do, but I did it and I got completely confused over him all over again, because spending time with an ex will always stir up a myriad of emotions and memories and regrets and all those other nasty little things that having an ex stirs up."

"You should be a psychiatrist."

"I'll send you my invoice later."

"So it's okay to go over?"

"I already told you. It's *totally* okay."

"You're the best."

"I know. That's why you love me."

Travelling on the Tube, Ash thought as she studied the map, should be like riding a bicycle. Once mastered, you never forgot how to do it. Seventeen years away from London, though, made her feel like a tourist again. She'd navigated her way successfully around central London over the last few days with just a few wrong stops along the way. Nat's apartment, however, was proving far trickier to get to.

Her route finally understood, Ash sat on the first of the requisite four trains needed to get her to the remote pocket north of the Thames, where Nat would be waiting for her.

Gabe's words followed her. She'd been reassured by what he'd said, so why did the persistent shadow of doubt follow her too? Ash put her hand on her jacket pocket, feeling Livvy's letter inside. This was what it was all about—what everything had been about. It was important to remember that the London trip wasn't about meeting Nat again, or getting confused over her again. It was for Chloe. Besides, getting confused over Nat would get her nowhere. Ash knew the best thing she could possibly do right now was put her feelings to the back of her head, remember how Nat had treated her when she was eighteen, and remind herself that Nat was still the ambitious, successful girl she always was. To keep her at arm's length and not get caught up in her emotions was the only—and best—thing Ash could possibly do.

Her fingers touched her phone, next to Livvy's letter. She pulled it out and texted Nat: *Running late. Took me forever to work out route at Charing Cross! Out of practice ;) see you later.*

It was only polite, she figured. She put her phone back into her pocket, pulling it out again when she felt it vibrate against her palm as she waited on the platform for train number two.

*You've been away from London too long! Don't stress. See you when I see you xxx*

Kisses. Ash stared at them. They were new. She liked how they looked, next to Nat's name. Liked the feeling they gave her.

*Keep her at arm's length.*

Ash stuffed her phone hastily back into her pocket and shook her head. She looked up and scrutinized the underground map in front of her. The adverts to the left and right of it too. Anything to take away the image of those three kisses, because thinking of kisses *really* wasn't a good idea right now.

Ash was late. That was okay, though. It gave Nat more time to get her brain used to the idea that she would be stepping in through her door anytime now. Gave her heart a chance to slow, knowing that Ash would soon be with her, in her personal space. Alone.

"I know, I know." Nat bent down and scooped up her rabbit with one hand. She smoothed his ears flat against his head. "When was the last time anyone outside of work came here? Maddie included?" His ears sprang back up, compelling Nat to smooth them back down again. She walked to his crate in the corner of her lounge and placed him inside it, shutting the door behind him. "And if you catch me talking to you when Ash is here, shoot me."

Nat straightened up at the sound of the intercom. Her blood thrummed warm under her skin as nerves tapped out a steady beat.

*Keep calm.*

"Hey." She spoke into the intercom's handset. "Come on up."

The time it took Ash to come up the four floors to Nat's apartment stretched like elastic. Even though she was ready for her when she eventually knocked on her door, Nat still felt tense.

"You found me eventually, huh?" Nat opened the door. "It's not the easiest route up here. The Metropolitan Line's not the prettiest either, is it?" She stepped to one side. "A change here, a change there." She swallowed. "Nightmare."

Ash came past her and stood, silently, in her lounge. Nat watched as she glanced around her, taking in her surroundings, and smiled.

"It was okay," Ash finally said. "Just took a bit of working out."

"Is it still warm?" Nat's brain floundered. "Outside, I mean."

"It's nice, yes," Ash said, touching her jacket. "Warm enough for just this."

"Drink?"

The look on Ash's face was tangible.

"Beer, if you have it," Ash said.

"You never did like wine, did you?"

"Hmm. No, not really."

The woodenness of their conversation hung between them, filling the room. Nat gestured for Ash to go further into the lounge, then made for the kitchen.

"You have a bunny."

Nat poked her head out from the kitchen to see Ash walking towards the crate.

"I couldn't bear to keep a cat locked up in an apartment all day," Nat said, "dogs need walking, and fish are boring." She joined Ash at the crate, bringing with her a bottle of beer and a glass of wine. "It's not ideal, but Smudge here seemed like the best option."

Ash took her beer, thanked Nat, then took a long drink. "I needed that," she said.

"Tube really that bad?"

"Worse."

Ash crossed to the window, raising a hand to her eyes to shield them from the low sun. "This is a nice room," she said.

"It gets the evening sun." Nat joined her, her own glass of wine in her hand. "Not much of a view though, even though we're four floors up. But you can just about see the tip of The Shard if you peer between those buildings there." She pointed to a spot somewhere towards Ash's right.

They stood close. Ash leaned her face closer to the window, trying to see where Nat was pointing. Nat watched as her eyes darted then finally locked on to it.

"I see it. The sun's glinting off the glass." Ash moved back, almost, Nat thought, as if she was suddenly aware of their proximity. "Very nice."

Nat motioned for Ash to take a seat. "You're out of practice," Nat said. "The Tube?"

"Not too many trains in my corner of Cornwall." Ash sat down. "Thank goodness."

"You like it there?"

"Cornwall?"

"Mm." Nat took a small sip of wine. "And your little corner in particular."

"I love it." Ash sank back onto Nat's sofa. "I love everything about it."

"You said you live alone?"

"Yup. Just me and the dog."

"Called?"

"Widgeon."

"Nice."

WHEN I KNEW YOU

"He seems to like it."

A silence skittered across the room.

*Think of something to say.*

Nat moved in her chair, then drank back some more wine. "Beer okay?"

"Fine. Great." Ash paused. "Thanks."

"Are you hungry?" Nat asked.

"No, I...yeah," Ash said, "starving."

"That's a relief." Nat stood. "I got a few bits and pieces in," she said, throwing a look towards the kitchen to the array of foods bought hastily on her way back from Claridge's, despite telling herself not to make too much of a fuss. "You know. Just in case."

Nat's apartment was spartan, Ash concluded. Beautifully and tastefully decorated, but with the hint of being the sort of place that someone didn't spend much time in. She flicked a gaze about her, skimming the magnolia walls, the mantelpiece with the few things on it perfect and neat. To the plush curtains and expensive dining suite by the window. It was all typical Nat—sophisticated yet unpretentious.

There were no photos or paintings anywhere though, Ash noticed. Nothing to give a visiting stranger—such as herself—any hint as to the character of the person living there. Every house or apartment had *something*, even if it was just a small print hanging above a fireplace, a piece of colour or texture to break up the monotony of the walls. Nat's had nothing.

In her mind's eye, she wandered to her own cottage, so full of colour and chaos. The contrast with Nat's apartment was stark, and Ash knew which she preferred.

"Your apartment's way tidier than mine." Ash voiced her thoughts. "My place is a muddled mixture of dogs and boat parts." She turned and smiled as Nat appeared to her in the doorway, a tray of food in her hands.

"My apartment's always going to be one of those places," Nat said, coming further into the room, "that's never going to be finished."

Ash leaned forward in her seat and cleared a space on the table in front of her as Nat approached. She sat back again, then waited as Nat set the tray down in front of her.

"You still like dim sum, I hope?" Nat asked.

Ash's heart pulled a little. Each plate had been beautifully arranged with little parcels with small sprigs of something green that Ash couldn't immediately identify in between as a garnish. Ash, wishing she'd not bothered with her McDonald's, knew this wasn't simply something Nat had thrown together in a hurry. It was clear she'd taken the time and trouble to make it look appetizing and special.

Ash's heart pulled a little more.

"I love dim sum." She looked up and smiled at Nat. "Especially the prawn ones."

"I remembered." Nat looked pleased as she sat back down. "You'll like these then." She waved a hand towards one of the plates. "Prawn and—"

"Coriander?" Ash widened her eyes.

"Coriander." Nat sank back, laughing, her laugh matched by Ash's. "I know what you like."

"I'm grateful." Ash nodded. "You really shouldn't have gone to so much trouble though."

"It was no trouble." Nat looked at Ash, then drew her gaze away.

"It doesn't look unfinished." Ash finally spoke again. She looked around her. "Your apartment. It looks…nice."

*Nice but characterless.*

"I moved here eight years ago." Nat smiled. "Half my boxes are still in the spare room, still waiting to be unpacked."

"After eight years?" Ash raised her brows. "You don't believe in rushing things, do you?" At Nat's gesture towards the tray of food, she took a plate and placed two small parcels onto it.

"Work," Nat said, mirroring Ash's actions, "got in the way."

"Of course," Ash said quietly, "your work." She sensed a shift in her own demeanour at the mention of Nat's work.

"I'm never here," Nat said.

Ash might have guessed. She bit into a parcel, cupping her hand under her chin to catch some bits as they fell. Nat's work was at the core of everything in her life. No change there, then.

Ash nodded, her mouth too full to answer.

"There's no such thing as a nine-to-five in what I do," Nat added.

*And whose fault is that?*

Ash chased the thought away. Nat had done all this for her. Why argue?

"I'm never here," Nat repeated. "Often it's past midnight when I get back." She frowned. "It's tough sometimes."

"You chose that path, though," Ash said, wishing she'd been able to ignore the argumentative voice in her head. "You chose to dedicate your life to your work." She paused. "At the expense of everything and everyone."

"I did."

Ash was poking at a hornets' nest, she knew. But the devil in her didn't want to stop. "So you can hardly complain now if it's a grind."

"No," Nat replied, "I can't really complain."

Ash chewed thoughtfully on her food, wondering why Nat was refusing to disagree with her, like she had in the restaurant the night before. It was both impressive and frustrating, Ash thought. And way more mature than Ash was acting.

"Although…"

Ash looked up.

"Although…?" She prompted.

"Sometimes I imagine giving it all up to go and live in a tent somewhere," Nat said. Her laugh was light, but Ash noted a certain hollowness behind it.

"Seriously?" Ash asked.

"No." Nat frowned. "I'm joking. Some more?" She gestured to the plates.

Ash took the smallest piece from the plate and placed it onto her own plate, not quite able to force another morsel down. She'd sensed a note of something in the delivery of Nat's *no* which she just couldn't put her finger on. Knowing she shouldn't keep asking, but unable to stop, she asked, "But you enjoy it. Your work." The question came out more as a statement than a question.

To Ash's surprise, Nat didn't answer her immediately.

"I don't know," Nat said. "It's just…"

Ash saw that Nat's gaze was distant, her fingers absently working the cuff of her shirt, her expression blank. Nat opened her mouth to say more, then stopped, and Ash knew whatever it was Nat wanted to say was now gone, withdrawn back inside to the place where unwanted thoughts hid. Why was she reluctant to talk about it? Ash had assumed she'd be bubbling over with enthusiasm at having the opportunity to talk about her love of her work, like Ash would if prompted about her own business.

"Of course I enjoy it." Nat took a sip from her drink, apparently snapped out of her reverie. "Like I'm sure you enjoy yours."

*So she was a mind reader after all.*

"But…"

"But…?" Again, Ash sensed Nat's confidence wobbling, and had the notion that she was holding back some important truth from her. The frustration was infuriating.

"Nothing." Nat smiled. "Have some more food, won't you? I think I bought enough to feed an army."

With the memory of her McDonald's still sitting dumpily in her stomach, and her uneaten morsel of food still staring up at her from her plate, Ash nevertheless leaned forward and took some dim sum. When had Nat bought all this food, anyway? On her way home from Claridge's earlier? Immediately, the thought of Nat making a special effort—unless Nat ate party food all the time, it was blindingly obvious it had been bought for Ash—pricked at Ash's conscience and she felt embarrassed all over again for her attempts to goad Nat into an argument earlier, and for pushing her now into telling her something Nat obviously didn't want to confess. Equally, she was touched that Nat would think to buy beer, rather than trying to foist wine onto her, and her shame in her petulance increased. Nat, she guessed, probably didn't buy beer too much.

"The beer's good." Ash voiced her thoughts. "The food too." She paused. "Thanks for it all. Totally unexpected, so thanks."

"I didn't know what beer to buy." Nat rolled a hand towards Ash's bottle. "I hope it's okay."

Ash's lips twisted into a smile. "I figured you might not buy this stuff much." She lifted her bottle. "It's perfect. Thanks."

"Remember when I wanted to take you to that wine bar in Soho for your eighteenth?" Nat asked.

"Oh God, yes!" Ash widened her eyes back at her. "How could I forget?"

Nat smiled and studied Ash long enough to make Ash feel the need to look away.

"And I said if you loved me..." The words died on Ash's lips. She frowned and stared at the label on her bottle, then cleared her throat. "I said if you loved me you'd not put me through that," she continued.

"So that's why I took you to Planet Hollywood instead," Nat said. "Because I loved you."

"You hated it there." Ash laughed. Still staring at her bottle, she rubbed at her temple as if encouraging the memories to come flowing back. "You were never a Planet Hollywood kind of girl, were you?"

"I loved you."

Ash looked up at Nat's unexpected declaration.

"You told me the other night at dinner that you'd loved me, and I didn't reply," Nat continued. "So I'm telling you now. I loved you."

"I know you did. Once upon a time." Ash looked up, catching Nat's eye, and suddenly once upon a time didn't seem like so long ago.

"Didn't we get ourselves in a terrible jumble, though?" Nat laughed through her nose.

"Jumble?" Nat's analogy had caught Ash off guard and she felt unable to answer properly.

"But I think it all worked out for the best, don't you?" Nat said. "I think if we'd stayed together—"

"I'd have held you back?" Ash offered, sensing a hardening in her tone. "Isn't that what you told me at the time?"

"We'd have been on a collision course," Nat corrected. "It was so…intense."

"Love is intense."

"But at eighteen?" Nat asked. "When we wanted so much from life?"

"When *you* wanted so much, you mean," Ash said. "I was just in love. My ambitions back then were just to love you wholeheartedly." She thought for a moment. "And you really can love someone wholeheartedly at eighteen, you know. Love wasn't and isn't just the privilege of non-teens."

"I know—"

"You make it sound like we were kids experimenting," Ash said, her mouth saying the words even though her brain was telling her not to, "but I know what I feel—felt—for you was real."

"Our lives were always going to take different paths, Ash," Nat said. "My parents. You remember what they were like."

Ash sat back. Of course she remembered Nat's parents, because Nat's parents were everything her own weren't.

"You still in touch with them?" Ash asked. "Livvy said—"

"No." Nat's answer was firm. "It was one thing after the other, until…"

"Enough was enough?"

That made Nat look back at her, and in that split second Ash felt desperately sorry for her. She'd spent her life being scared of her parents, always wanting to impress them. It had never been enough.

"It was when I left Richard," Nat said slowly, "and everything that followed afterwards." She paused. "Well, that seemed to be the final straw. For all of us."

"Because you had the audacity to divorce someone you allegedly never loved?"

"Not allegedly," Nat said. "I didn't even particularly like him." She looked at Ash. "It was when I told them about me and you. That was when we stopped speaking."

"You told them?" Ash moved in her chair. She leaned closer to Nat, her beer bottle still grasped in her hands. "Even though…" Her mind was in turmoil. Nat telling her parents was the last thing she would have ever done.

"You never left me," Nat said. "The loving wholeheartedly thing? It was the same for me too."

"But it still wasn't enough to stop you leaving me."

"Don't you think I've had to live with that all these years?" Nat asked. "Don't you think I haven't wondered how things might have been different if I hadn't been so scared of my parents?"

"I know you dumped me because of them," Ash said. "It just astonishes me and always has done that you would ruin everything we had, ruin my future plans, because of what you thought your parents might say."

"Did I ruin your life, though?" Nat asked. "Really? From where I'm sitting, you've done okay for yourself."

"I could have been a doctor." Ash's voice raised a notch. "I wanted to be a doctor. But my head was so fucked-up—by you—that I could barely hold a pen in my hand, let alone sit my exams."

The argumentative Ash returned as the bitterness that she'd kept under control for the past few days rose in her throat, and she had to slam down the rest of her beer in order to calm her anger again.

She stared at Nat, angry that a few simple words from her could rake the past up so vividly. She was over it all now. Nat surely no longer had the ability to stimulate any kind of emotion in her—not anger, nor bitterness, nor resentment. Nothing.

Nat's gaze met hers, sparking a flint inside Ash that was anger mixed in with…with what? Ash broke eye contact, her confusion terrifying her. She was so over Nat, wasn't she? She just had to be.

## CHAPTER ELEVEN

Tell me some more about your life in Cornwall." Nat wanted to change the subject. Defuse the growing tension that threatened to splinter the atmosphere between her and Ash. She hadn't meant to start raking over the past again, and the look on Ash's face right now told her she should have stopped at her talk of wholehearted love. Why had she even thought to say that anyway? Because Ash had already said it?

"Cornwall's the best."

Nat sensed Ash pull in her breath, almost as if to calm herself. Now, the hint of the smile that touched Ash's face after her previous annoyance was enchanting, Nat thought.

"It's everything I hoped it might be," Ash continued, "and more."

"And your business is doing well?" Nat wanted to know. It was important to her that Ash liked her life.

"Very well." Ash nodded. "Better in the summer, naturally," she said, "but you'd be surprised at the number of people who still want to get out on the sea in the winter too."

"When the weather cooperates?"

"The sun always shines in Cornwall." Ash grinned. "Well, nearly always." She shrugged sheepishly.

"You sound like you're happy there."

"I am," Ash said. "I suppose…"

"You suppose…?" Nat dipped her head to catch Ash's eye.

"Well, I wonder sometimes if I'm not happier doing this than I would have been being a doctor."

"You wanted to be a doctor, remember?" Nat echoed Ash's words from before.

"I did." Ash's answer was firm. "But would I have been as happy?"

Nat sat back, the anxiety that had been clutching at her for the last few minutes easing its grip on her stomach slightly. Would she have been happier if she'd taken a different path in life? Nat shook the thought away. "That's good to hear," she finally said.

"Mm."

Nat watched as Ash finished the last of her beer.

"You can see for yourself next week anyway," Ash said. "I guarantee in the short time that you're there you'll fall in love with the place too."

Ash was happy. The iron grip inside Nat eased some more. Ash's life hadn't been blighted as much as Nat had often feared over the years, and now to hear it from her directly and see it in her eyes made her guilt over everything she'd done to Ash lessen. Albeit only slightly.

"I'm looking forward to it." The conviction in her statement was as much as a surprise to Nat as it seemed to be for Ash. But she meant it. After spending the last four days in Ash's company, going down to Cornwall—to Ash's stomping ground—didn't seem like the daunting task it had seemed last week. "Depending on what Livvy has in store for us," she added quickly.

"We have to get through tomorrow first," Ash said.

Livvy's fourth and final London letter. Nat threw a look to Ash, her anger no longer apparent. Had the mention of returning to Cornwall mellowed her again? Now, annoyed Ash had been replaced with relaxed Ash, her head resting against the back of her chair, empty beer bottle nestled between her knees, her cleared plate in front of her. Over the course of the evening, Nat had completely forgotten about the reason for Ash being with her. She glanced up at her clock, dismayed to see it was past ten o'clock already. She didn't want the evening to end, but she knew they had to open their letters soon, and that once they had, Ash would leave.

Not that Ash looked like she wanted to go anywhere. Nat soaked up the unusual sight of having someone sitting with her in her lounge after dark. Sure, colleagues came and went—usually with their partners while Nat flew solo—but no one Nat genuinely wanted to be there. Colleagues were...colleagues. She had Maddie—wonderful, supportive Maddie—but she had a husband and family of her own who all took up her time, and that was absolutely understandable. Nat's other colleagues, she knew, only came by because sometimes the easiest place to talk about work was far away from the workplace. But they'd talk shop endlessly. Discuss which particular research they were currently working on. Moan about their kids. Then they'd wait a respectable amount of time after coffee had been finished before they'd make their excuses and leave again, thanking Nat for her hospitality and stressing that next time they'd be the ones to invite *her* over so that she could meet David, or Tom, or whichever other poor singleton they'd drag along just to make up the numbers. Nat shuddered. The downside of keeping her private life just that—private—was that others assumed things about her. Marrying Richard had never helped, either.

Nat sighed. Now wasn't the time to start picking over the broken glass of her solitary life. She stood, sensing Ash watching her, and crossed the room to where her bag was slung over the back of a dining chair. Nat pulled out Livvy's letter, returning just in time to see Ash pull hers from the back pocket of her jeans.

"What do you think?" Nat flopped back into her chair. "Opera? Fine dining at the Ivy? Or another trip out to the West End?"

"You could just kill me now."

Nat laughed as Ash shuddered. She flipped open the envelope, thumbed the letter out and shook it open.

"Shall I?" Nat nodded her head to the letter, smoothing it out flatter when she saw Ash give her the thumbs up in response.

"*Dear Crackles,*" she read aloud. "*Well, this is it. Your fourth and final letter for your London jaunts. How's it been? Has Flash grumbled incessantly about having to spend nearly a week in the capital? I do hope so! If she reads this, tell her that was a joke, by the way.*" Nat lifted her eyes to Ash's, relieved to see her smiling.

She returned Ash's smile, pleased by the shared joke between them, then resumed reading. "*Remember when we were thirteen and Ash got that magnificent bike for her birthday? And we were both terribly jealous of her?*" Nat looked up to Ash again. "Bike?" She frowned. "BMX." Ash grinned. "I bugged my parents for months about it. It was yellow, with these fab blue flecks all over it. Livvy was jealous as hell because she wanted one but her parents were worried about her cycling in London."

"I remember." Nat sat back, crossing one leg over the other. "I put a sticker on the crossbar about a week after you got it and you wouldn't speak to me for three days."

"It was my pride and joy, that bike."

"You were obsessed with it."

"Then you slapped some damn pink stickers all over it."

"One sticker!" Nat laughed. "You exaggerate so much."

"One sticker too many," Ash replied. "And…hello? Did I ever look like I liked pink?"

Nat loved the look of feigned indignation on Ash's face. The years peeled back: the banter, the jokes, the looks. All here now. She held Ash's look, her gaze finally dropping away before Ash's.

"In hindsight," Nat said, a smile tugging at her lips, "pink wasn't the best colour for you."

"I rest my case."

Nat returned to Livvy's letter. "*I never got a bike. Cue sad music,*" she read, "*but I did cycle round Oxford an awful lot when I finally got to uni. I know you never had time for the whole two-wheel business, Crackles, but trust me, it's huge fun! So, with that in mind, I wondered if you'd take Clo cycling round Richmond Park. She was always like you—adamant that it was boring—but I did finally persuade her that she and I ought to hire some bikes one day and have a blast round the parks of London, and she was really up for it. Of course, like with most of the other things we'd planned to do, time ran out. For me, anyway. I never got to go cycling with her. So will you two? Will you convince her that it's a darn sight better than sitting on a grubby Tube, or being slumped in front of her iPad twenty-four seven?*"

"Sounds right up my street, that," Ash said, her voice pulling Nat's attention away from the letter.

"Still the adventurer?" Nat asked.

"Every bit of it."

Nat watched as Ash stretched her legs out straight in front of her and stifled a yawn. Nat checked the clock. Ten fifteen.

"Guess that's tomorrow sorted then." Ash stretched again. She lifted herself slightly from her chair, stuffed her still-unopened letter back into her pocket, and flopped back down.

Nat watched her, wondering if she ought to ask her when she was going. Or would that make it sound as though she wanted her to leave? Her brain waged a war, but before it had a chance to outwit her, she blurted out, "Fancy another beer?" then felt relieved, happy, and grateful in equal measures when Ash nodded.

She walked to her kitchen, tossing another look over her shoulder to Ash as she went. If she could squeeze another half an hour of Ash's company, then she'd be happy. Make it an hour and she'd be happier still. Nat lurked in the doorway of her kitchen and studied the back of Ash's head, the thought of being alone again once Ash finally went deadening her heart.

Finally she pushed away from the door frame. The thought of being alone at all just deadened her heart further.

## CHAPTER TWELVE

I am *not* riding that." Ash pointed to a line of bikes on a rack. "All it needs is a basket on the front. I'll look like bloody Miss Marple pootling around on that thing."

"When Mum said cycling round the park," Chloe said, "I think maybe she meant mountain biking."

"Now you're talking." Ash looped an arm round Chloe's shoulders. "I always said you were smart."

"Ash, I'm thirty-five," Nat said.

Ash raised an eyebrow at Nat's concerned face. "Thirty-five, not eighty-five," Ash replied.

"Even so, I'm not dressed for mountain biking," Nat argued.

"You're wearing Lycra." Ash flitted a hand in Nat's direction. "Of course you're dressed for mountain biking."

Ash heard an audible sigh. She struggled to stop the smile that was threatening to escape. Why was an indignant Nat so funny? Her pique was hilarious but curiously cute at the same time. And her Lycra? Ash bit back another smile. Nat in Lycra took cuteness to a whole different level. She worked out, that much was obvious. Nat's figure, hitherto partially hidden beneath a range of loose-fitting jackets, tops, and trousers, was perfection now it was clad in her tight-fitting cycle clothes.

"Okay, but if I fall off I'm suing your arse."

Nat's voice pulled Ash's attention away from her body and back to her face. Ash wondered if she'd been staring. If she had, nothing in Nat's expression suggested that she'd minded one little bit.

"Deal." Ash grinned. "Although I'll make sure you don't fall off."

"I'll hold you to that."

"By all means."

"So when you two are finished winding each other up," Chloe said, "can we go get us some bikes to ride?"

Ash moved her arm as Chloe stepped away from her.

"Were you two always like that, by the way?" Chloe asked, waggling a finger in Nat's direction. "Like some kind of comedy act?"

"That, Clo," Ash said, ruffling her hair as she passed her, "was nothing. Just wait until we get onto the bikes. That's all I'm saying."

The breeze was warm against her face as Nat freewheeled down the hill. The wisps of hair that had escaped from under her helmet in the wind batted against her cheeks, tickling her skin so that she was constantly lifting a hand from her handlebars to scratch at it. Ash and Chloe were ahead of her, cycling smoothly now they were back on the flat, and Nat could see they were deep in conversation. Ash had been right. Taking the slightly longer off-road route around the edge of the park had been just the right decision as it offered more of an endurance test than the rest of the park. They were in Richmond Park, heading towards Wimbledon Common, having looped the park's trail once already, and Nat knew the long climb up the bridleway would give them all an even stiffer test of their fitness.

The park was beautiful at any time of the year, but in autumn, it seemed to put on an extra-special effort to spiral the senses. The bloody hues of the trees—a clattering of russets, reds, and oranges—took Nat's breath away, and she wondered, as she reached the bottom of the hill and started pedalling again, just how many words for the colour red she could think of before she caught up with Ash and Chloe.

"You were miles away."

Ash had stopped just round a bend, Chloe a little ahead of her. Nat hastily squeezed on her brakes and came to a standstill next to Ash.

"Physically or mentally?" she asked, slightly out of breath.

"Both. Slowcoach." Ash grinned. "But I meant mentally. You were away with the fairies."

"Then the fairies were helping me count the number of words for red." Nat undid the chin strap of her helmet and pulled it off, then ran her hands through her hair. "They came up with five."

"As you do." Ash mirrored Nat's action of removing her helmet and tousling her hair.

"Don't you think it's lovely here?" Nat slid forward off her saddle and rested her arms on the bike's handlebars, her helmet dangling loosely from one hand. "It's the centre of London but it could be the middle of the countryside."

"If you think this is impressive, you'll love Dartmoor," Ash said. "I'll take you. Next week, without Chloe perhaps. You could come a day early." Then, as if realizing what she'd said, she added, "I mean…if you want to."

"I'd like that." Nat meant it.

"Assuming we have time." Ash frowned, then stared out at a point beyond Nat's shoulder. "It's a long drive from mine, and, well, you know."

"No, I'd like to," Nat repeated, noting the slight flush on Ash's cheeks. "Really. If we have time."

"Sure." Ash flicked a look Nat's way, then away again. "Shall we get on?"

Nat watched as Ash fumbled with her helmet, her fingers apparently too thick for the straps, then crammed it back onto her head, tightening up her chin straps afterwards. Ash was flustered. Anyone could sense that. Nat studied Ash's back now she'd turned from her. But Ash didn't do flustered, did she? Nat smiled as she too replaced her helmet and watched Ash slowly cycle away.

No, Ash never did flustered.

❖

Dartmoor seemed like a million miles away from where Ash was now. As her tyres crunched along the path leading towards Wimbledon Common, the voices inside her head all cried out to be heard. She had no idea what had made her offer to take Nat to Dartmoor, when to do so meant deviating from the very reason they would be in Cornwall. And deviating meant one thing: Ash wanted to spend more time alone with Nat. But that wasn't the plan. That had never been the plan. The plan had been to get the two weeks over with as quickly as possible, then part again.

But then Nat had asked Ash to dinner, and to her apartment, so she had deviated there too. More than that, she'd enjoyed being alone in Nat's company far more than her brain was allowing her to think she did. Nat had also just apparently jumped at the chance to go to Dartmoor with her, so did that mean Nat was just as keen to spend more time with her as well? Away from the restrictions of the list and Chloe? Ash shook the thought from her head, choosing to stare down and concentrate on the whirring of her front wheel, rather than trying to work out the whys and wherefores of the past four days, and the impending four further days.

"So I'm not invited to Dartmoor but Nat is?"

Ash looked up, swerving slightly to avoid Chloe, who had slowed down to speak with her.

"You heard?" Ash sat up straighter. "Don't take what I said to Nat as a—"

"I'm kidding you." Chloe held up her hand. "I totally get you'd want to hang out with Nat on your own for a bit without me getting in the way."

They cycled on, side by side.

"It's not like that."

"I told you before," Chloe continued. "I'm stoked you pair are even doing this for me." She looked over to Ash. "It's been a blast so far, and I've still got another four days in Cornwall with you guys, so it's all good."

"You're a good kid."

"Don't call me a kid."

"Okay, you're a good"—Ash lifted her eyes skyward—"dude. Better?"

"Ish. Dude is a bit cheesy though."

"I don't even know why I suggested Dartmoor to Nat," Ash said truthfully. She felt the need to explain. Felt the need to speak her thoughts out loud. "I think it was one of those spur of the moment things."

"You should do it, though," Chloe said. "Impress her with your knowledge of wildlife and all things cosy and Cornish."

"Who said anything about impressing her?" Ash asked, frowning. "I just thought it would be nice. I don't think she's ever been."

"Yeah, right."

"Seriously." Ash lifted herself from her seat slightly as they approached a small incline.

"You two seem to be getting on okay." Chloe glanced over to Ash. "Why did you fall out with each other again?"

"Oh, long story." Ash laughed. She cast a look back over her shoulder to Nat, some way behind them on the path again. "And that's all I'm saying."

"Whatever the reason," Chloe said, "it's a shame."

"Perhaps." Ash sat back down as they levelled off again.

"I mean it," Chloe said. "You're like Beth and Emily at school. They're mates, then they're not mates, then they are again. I'm always being, like, just *get* on with it, will you? It's so boring."

"Sorry if I'm boring you." Ash laughed again, her laugh masking her discomfort at being analysed by Chloe. "Nat and I are *not* like Beth and Emma."

"Emily."

"Emily. Yes, Nat and I were friends a long time ago, but now?" Ash shook her head. "We're just acquaintances."

"Inviting her to Dartmoor would suggest you want to be her… friend."

"I told you," Ash said, drawing her words out to indicate her exasperation, "that was a spur of the moment thing."

"So you keep saying."

"Anyway, who made you the expert?" Ash asked. "You're fourteen."

She ignored the withering look that Chloe flashed her.

"So why did you fall out with her?" Chloe pressed.

"You're like a dog with a bone." Ash twisted her gear stick, shifting up a gear. "We were young," she said. "We wanted different things from life." Ash looked away. Well, Nat did, anyway.

"Mum said you and Nat were always so close."

"We were," Ash said, "but it was all a long time ago now."

"It's a shame," Chloe said. "A real shame."

"Do you ever stop?" Ash reached over and poked Chloe's arm, grinning when she squealed.

"Never." Chloe started to pull away. "Oh, and by the way, just so you know? Mum let me in on a secret," she called out as she raced off, "and I have a feeling that secret might just happen soon."

"Since when was October supposed to be so hot?" Nat flopped down on the grass next to Ash and Chloe. She pulled at the neckline of her top, then flapped it back and forth, enjoying the cool air it produced. "October is all about burnished leaves and Halloween. Not sweat."

They had come to an agreed stop part way round Wimbledon Common, the long climb up to the Common, combined with the unusually warm weather, having temporarily defeated them. Now, lounging on the grass, their bikes scattered about them, Nat, Ash, and Chloe lazily watched a steady stream of cyclists, joggers, and dog walkers file past.

"That last stretch finish you off, did it?" Ash asked.

"All I can say is that spin cycling with my friend Maddie in a gym must be different from cycling up evil hills." Nat lay back and shielded her eyes from the sun. She rolled her head and looked at Ash. "How come you were barely out of breath at the top?"

"I'm as fit as a flea." Ash closed her eyes. "Working on a boat every day helps."

"Will you take us out on it next week?" Chloe asked. Ash opened an eye and peeked at her. "Sure, if you want." "Nat will love it," Chloe said. "Right, Nat?"

*Ash's boat.*

Nat smiled inwardly. She couldn't think of anything lovelier than a day out at sea. With Ash. She cupped her hands over her eyes against the sun again and voiced those thoughts aloud. "I couldn't imagine anything nicer." She turned her head, catching Ash looking at her. Their gazes held for a moment, before Ash turned away again. Ruffled by Ash's stare, Nat pulled herself upright and sat, her knees hugged tight to her chest, afraid that Ash would notice her discomfort.

"I'll take you both out on the route we do with photographers," Ash said, still lying down, "to see the seals. Interested?"

"Only if I can steer," Chloe said, laughing.

Nat followed Chloe's gaze as she waved to a boy walking across the Common.

"Back in a mo." In a heartbeat, Chloe had scrambled to her feet and run across the grass to speak to him.

"Nice to see one of us can be tempted across a park by a boy," Ash said, the drollness in her delivery provoking a spontaneous and uproarious laugh from Nat.

"Sure never happened when we were fourteen," Nat said when she'd stopped laughing. She looked back down to Ash. "Sure as hell isn't going to happen now."

"Amen to that," Ash murmured, her eyes closed again.

"At fourteen we were all about the netball," Nat said. "Remember?"

"Ah, netball." Ash smiled, her eyes still closed. "Lovely, lovely netball."

Nat rolled onto her side, propping herself up on one elbow. "So, tell me some more about Cornwall," she said. "So that I'll know what to expect when I get there next week."

"You never got round to going, then?" Ash asked.

"You knew my parents." Nat chuckled. "When all the other kids went to Cornwall for their summer holidays, mine preferred France."

"I used to hate it." Finally Ash opened an eye. "Your three weeks each summer in France. I used to count the hours until you got back."

"I know." Nat gazed down at her. "So did I."

"Do you remember the necklace you brought me back the first time you went after we got together?" Ash asked. "Different colour blue beads on brown leather?"

"From Biarritz." Nat smiled. "I found it quite by chance in this amazing little shop on the seafront. Bought it on the spur of the moment."

"I've still got it."

"No way."

"Mm."

"After all this time?" Nat was genuinely shocked. The necklace had been bought because she'd been missing Ash like crazy, and buying her something had made her feel closer to her. She remembered sitting in the bedroom of the gîte her parents had rented, turning the necklace over in her hands, imagining how and when she'd give it to Ash when she got home. Missing her more and more with each feel of the necklace, her sadness escalating, knowing it would be weeks until they'd be together again.

They'd been so in love back then. Unable to spend barely a day apart, let alone three weeks. The four summers they were together became an annual roller coaster of agonizing emotions, their tears at Nat's departure only matched in intensity by their happiness and rush of renewed love for one another when they were finally reunited.

"It's a nice necklace."

Ash's voice blew Nat's memories up into the sky and away from her.

"It should be," Nat said quietly. "It cost me a fortune."

A sense of disappointment stabbed at her when Ash gave no sign of having heard her. Instead, Ash closed her eyes again, threaded her hands behind her head, and turned her head away from her.

Safe in the knowledge that Ash couldn't see her, Nat allowed herself the luxury of staring at her. Her thoughts fluttered back down to her, stronger this time, tinged with regret. Nat knew she'd never experience the kind of love that she and Ash had shared as teenagers ever again, and she knew she'd never miss anyone like she'd missed her back then. The necklace hadn't been a spur of the moment present, despite what Nat had said. She'd spent days searching for the perfect present for Ash, fending off questions from her parents as to why she'd prefer to trawl the markets and shops rather than sunbathe. It had all been for Ash, and as Nat now sat watching her gently breathing, she absorbed the implications of her thoughts and knew with a sinking heart that she would never match the strength and passion of their relationship ever again.

Nat looked away, tears needling the backs of her eyes, and stared blankly out across the grass, across to Chloe, still standing under a far-off tree with her mystery boy. How had Nat ever let Ash go? She had been the best thing to ever happen to her and Nat had treated her like she didn't matter.

"All I need right now is the sound of the sea and I could be back home."

Ash's murmured voice sounded next to Nat. Nat stole a look to her, Ash's head still turned away.

"You still haven't told me about Cornwall." Nat lay down.

"What do you want to know?"

"Describe it to me," Nat said, "in your own words."

"Hmm," Ash said. "Well it's nice."

"No." Nat flapped an arm at her. "Tell me exactly what it's like."

She heard Ash breathe slowly in, then out again.

"Let me see," Ash said. "Cornwall is vibrant. It's…a clash of countryside, sea, moors."

"More. I need to see how *you* see it."

"Well," Ash began, "the sky is pale in winter. Like you can't see where the sea ends and the sky starts. But then in summer? In summer, the sky turns this amazing deep blue colour, and the sun sparkles off the sea, almost as if it's dropping handfuls of diamonds onto it."

Nat smiled.

"Night skies so clear you can see stars like millions of beads."

"Like beads?" Nat repeated. "I like the sound of that."

"And sometimes," Ash said, finally turning her head to look at her, "I like to just sit and listen to the breaking of the sea on the beach. Gabe always says you can't be stressed when you're listening to the sea."

"Sounds perfect."

"It is."

Nat sensed contentment radiating from Ash.

"And the boat?" Nat asked.

"Oh, the boat's my life," Ash replied. "Out on the boat, you can almost taste the sea." She hesitated, then propped herself up on one elbow. "Close your eyes," she said.

Nat peered at her.

"Just close them," Ash said.

Feeling slightly self-conscious, Nat did as Ash wanted.

"You want to see Cornwall as I see it?" Ash asked.

Nat nodded.

"Imagine golden fields of corn in summer," Ash said, "all buttered by the sun and gently bowing their heads in a breeze so soft it feels like it's caressing you."

"I feel silly." Nat's smile hid her self-consciousness.

"Then forget I'm here," Ash said, "and just transport yourself there."

"Okay."

"So, can you see it?" Ash asked. "The corn?"

"I see it."

"Now see the contrasting skyline, as intense a blue as you'll ever see," Ash continued, "and then look behind to see emerald hills, sheep dotted across them. You see them?"

"Mm-hmm."

"Now start walking," Ash said, "and feel the corn tickling your fingers as you walk."

"It's nice."

"What do you see ahead?"

"The sea." Nat's eyes grew heavy, her muscles loose. Ash's voice, low and soft, swirled about her, muddying her senses. "I see the sea."

"Now, listen."

Ash's voice was closer, Nat was sure. She wanted to take a look, but the comfort of the images that now blessed her closed eyes was too lovely to break.

"Seagulls." Nat smiled. "And waves crashing, the sea breeze whispering." She laughed. "Listen to me, all poetic."

"It's nice, isn't it?" Ash asked. "The contrast of sea and land and all the clash of colours and sounds that brings with it."

"It's perfect."

"So do you see it now?" Ash asked. "Cornwall? Just as I see it?"

Nat's smile increased. "I see it," she said. "Thank you. I see it."

"Good, because I think I'm all poemed out."

That was, Nat thought with a pleasant twinge inside, typical Ash. She'd always been very good at dizzying Nat's senses, then saying something daft to cover up her embarrassment. It had always been like that when they'd been together, Nat remembered. Declarations of love from Ash had always been swiftly followed by a dry comment.

Nat heard Ash move and sensed she'd lain back down again. Nat lay, her eyes still closed, her senses pulsing—both from Ash's soft voice and her own memories—and listened to both of their quiet breathing. She rolled over onto her side and looked across at Ash, lying facing her with her head nestled in the crook of her arm. Their bodies were barely inches apart, their faces close. Ash's eyes fluttered open and locked onto hers with an intensity Nat hadn't seen from her all week. Without thinking, Nat reached out and brushed a strand of hair from Ash's eyes, her heart pounding faster when Ash didn't attempt to stop her. Knowing she shouldn't, but unable to stop, Nat drew her hand from Ash's hair and traced it down her arm, finally finding her hand and capturing it in hers. Their fingers entangled, Nat continued to gaze at Ash, wanting to say so many things but at a loss as to where to start.

Hearing Chloe's familiar laugh in the distance, Nat pulled her eyes from Ash's and saw Chloe hugging her friend, their conversation apparently over. Untangling her fingers from Ash's, she hastily pulled herself upright, clambered to her feet, and walked away from her. Behind her, she sensed Ash's eyes still on her and felt her chest fill with a mixture of longing and regret. Had Ash felt it too? The aching tension and desire that had just passed between them?

"Hey." Nat lifted a hand to Chloe and walked over to her, grateful to put some distance between her and Ash.

She needed to forget what she'd just done, forget that she still wanted Ash. What had just happened had been a moment of weakness, a reminder of a love lost, and now Nat needed to be strong all over again. Ash was heading back out of London on the first train in the morning, doubtless without even so much as a single thought about Nat. She had her own life now, a life that didn't include Nat, and for Nat to confuse things for her now, when she was obviously so happy, would be unthinkable.

She and Ash had an understanding, a reconnection after so many years pretending the other didn't exist, and Nat knew, as she strode towards Chloe and ever further from Ash, she should never do anything to confuse or compromise that.

# CHAPTER THIRTEEN

"Come home to me!"

Ash couldn't help but laugh at the mock anguish in Gabe's voice.

"Seriously, it's been what? Four or five days?" She sat on the edge of her bed. "I've hardly been away ages."

"Five days ago you were ringing me telling me you'd barely made it through a day in Oxford without throwing Nat out of your boat," Gabe said.

*Five days ago, Nat was still a stranger to me.*

"A lot can happen in a week." Ash shuffled herself back on the bed, then propped herself up against the wall behind it. "Things can change."

And things had certainly shifted off kilter that afternoon, Ash thought with a frown.

"And feelings?" Gabe asked. "Have they changed too?"

"Spending time with someone can change your perception of things," Ash said. "And that's all I'm prepared to say on the matter."

"So you've had a good time?"

"The best." Ash leaned back against the wall. "And I never thought I'd say that."

Nat's image returned to her, leaning over her, her dark eyes on hers. Then her hand, drawing slowly down Ash's arm, stimulating a shiver of pleasure from Ash even now as she remembered it.

"Any idea what Livvy's got planned for you next week?" Gabe asked.

Ash, grateful for his intervention to her thoughts, looked down to her rucksack, packed and ready for the morning. Inside, Livvy's final four letters for Cornwall awaited.

"I figured I'd wait to open the next one until Nat and Chloe get down on Sunday evening," Ash said. "Did you book the B and B like I asked in my text the other day, by the way?"

"I booked the posh one in Trevelyan, just like you wanted," Gabe said. "A double room each, Nat's with sea views. Again, like you asked."

"You're a gem."

"I know." Gabe paused. "It'll be nice for Nat to see your home county at its best."

"And Chloe." Even Ash knew she didn't sound convincing. Gabe was absolutely right; choosing the perfect B & B had been deliberate. Even before their closeness that afternoon, she'd known she didn't want Nat shacked up in any old place; it had to be classy—just like Nat. The one Gabe had booked, just a ten-minute drive from Ash's own, much smaller village, was perfect.

"Of course," Gabe replied.

Ash detected a note of amusement and scepticism in his voice. That was understandable. Even Ash found the idea of wanting to impress Nat absurd, but that was exactly what she wanted to do. Sure, she told herself it was because she wanted Nat to envy her, to realize that she was doing okay, and that she'd become a success despite everything, but the truth also was that she wanted Nat to admire the life Ash had made for herself without her, because it was important to her that she saw Ash wasn't the flighty girl Nat had known and loved. Maybe because Nat was so successful, Ash was quietly embarrassed at her physical job—she was never quite sure. She had always been so proud of her business—and still was—but there still sometimes niggled the deep-seated feeling that running a boat business in Cornwall was never what she'd set out to do, despite how happy she was.

If Nat could see her little corner of the world and understand how much it meant to Ash, then perhaps that deep-seated sense of failure might, after many years, finally go.

"So, what time is your train tomorrow?"

Gabe's voice rumbled in Ash's ear, pulling her back.

"First thing." Ash scratched at her hair. "I'm not sure. Nine-ish."

"Text me," Gabe said. "I'll meet you at the station."

"I will. Thanks."

"I'm sensing you'll have a lot to tell me," Gabe continued. Ash heard his pause. "About how you and Nat got on."

"I already told you," Ash said. "We got on great."

"I can't wait to meet her," Gabe said, the mischievous intonation in his voice clearly audible to Ash.

"Because?" Ash asked, trying to deflate his playfulness.

"Because I've heard so much about her," Gabe replied.

His answer was far more sensible than Ash had anticipated.

"Well as long as you don't put her off—or Chloe—and send them both fleeing back to London." Ash smoothed the linen down on the bed next to her leg and stared down at it. "I *do* want to have at least one day where I can take them out on Doris."

"I'll be on my best behaviour, I promise," Gabe said.

"You better be."

"So I'll see you tomorrow afternoon, then," Gabe continued. "And the grilling can commence."

"About?"

"You know what I mean."

"I do," Ash replied, "and there'll be no grilling, thank you very much. There's nothing to tell, anyway."

She frowned, letting her own words sink in as a snapshot of that afternoon wheedled its way into her brain. She'd wanted more that afternoon, she was sure of it, and the arrival of Chloe at the park had been opportune. If she'd not come back when she had? Ash wasn't sure what would have happened, but she knew she'd have done nothing to stop it. Despite her protestations to Gabe, Ash knew that Nat was slowly drawing her back, just like she'd always done. The sensation of her hand on hers again, after so many years, Nat's eyes locked onto hers, her very presence all making Ash feel as though she were the most important person in the world.

Ash could keep telling herself, Gabe, and anyone else who would listen that it wasn't true, but the reality was she was slowly, tenderly, deliciously falling for Nat all over again.

And the thought absolutely terrified her.

Paddington Station was exactly like it always was the next morning: hot, crowded, noisy. Ash stood on the concourse, staring vacantly up at the endless screens above her head, her concentration constantly interrupted by either intercom announcements or people bumping into her. Her eyes darted from left to right, trying to find which platform her train departed from. There was too much information on the screens for her confused brain to take in. She squeezed her eyes tight shut against the bright lights that were threatening a headache, hitched her rucksack a little higher, and tried again.

Truro. Platform twelve. At last.

Ash looked at her watch, grateful she'd thought to allow herself enough time for a coffee before she left. Throwing a look over her shoulder, she spotted a coffee stall not far from where she was standing, and made for it.

"What can I get you?" An Australian accent floated out from behind the counter.

"Latte would be good." Ash shrugged her rucksack from her shoulders and shook it down, then placed it at her feet. "Thanks." She dug in her trouser pocket, pulling out a handful of coins which she then placed on the top of the counter.

Taking her drink, Ash picked up her rucksack again and settled herself at a table which allowed her a clear view of the announcements board. She glanced around her, the feeling of despondency that had followed her around since the previous afternoon still shrouding her, and sipped at her coffee. Inside her jacket pocket, her phone vibrated. Her latte instantly forgotten, she immediately pulled it out, sensing her cloak of discontent tighten around her further as she read the text on her screen. *Dude! Train time? I can't pick you up if I don't know what train you're coming in on later xxx*

Gabe. Not Nat.

Ash crammed her phone back in her pocket, her longing for the text to have been from Nat nearly suffocated her. Why hadn't she texted? Why hadn't they even spoken once since they'd parted at Bond Street Tube the night before, when Nat knew full well Ash was getting the first train out of London the next day? Especially after what had happened at Wimbledon Common. What *had* happened anyway? There had been something there, and afterwards Ash had made her way back to her hotel, buzzing from the day, happiness consuming her, and fully expecting at least a text or call from Nat to wish her a safe journey the next day or, heaven forbid, tell her that she'd enjoyed the day just as much as Ash had.

Ash picked up her latte and sipped at it again, frowning at its heat.

She should have known better than to let herself get drawn into Nat's web again. The frowning increased. She might have guessed that she'd get swept up in seeing her again, confusing herself, because that's what Nat had done to her all her life. Confused her. Over the years, all it had taken was a comment from Livvy about Nat to send Ash's mind hurtling over to her, wondering where she was, how she was, or whether she still thought of her.

Ash blew across her coffee, watching the liquid ripple. It had happened all her life. Nat *was* her life. The coffee tasted awful, Ash decided. She pushed it away, fighting the nausea that seemed to hang around far too much for her liking just lately, and looked around her again. Why wasn't Nat here? Because Ash wasn't Nat's life, that's why, and Ash was stupid to even begin to think she could be.

The notion that a distance could have opened up between them, just when Ash thought they might be getting close again, frustrated her even though she had no right to be frustrated. Much of her annoyance stemmed from not knowing what could have caused it in the first place, or what could be done to close the gap. The one thing she was sure of, however, was she desperately wanted to feel some of the closeness they'd begun to share over the past few days again.

Ash stood, scraping back her chair, and scooped up her rucksack from the floor. Her coffee lying dully in her stomach, she strode across the concourse to resume her position underneath the announcements board.

Ten minutes. In ten minutes her train would pull out of the station and take her back to her normal life, away from fretting about whether Nat had or hadn't texted her, and why she wasn't here to see her off. Away from the magnet that persisted in pulling her to Nat, when she knew that it was all so pointless.

Ash looked over to her platform, longing for her train to arrive so she could climb on board and get away from London. Go home and re-establish some semblance of order back into her life and mind. Yet despite her urging the train to hurry up, another louder voice wouldn't stop suggesting to her that she could quite easily walk straight out of the station right now and seek out Nat.

She ambled closer to her platform, her hands deep in her pockets, then stopped. Seven minutes to go. Ash looked up at the board, relieved and pained in equal measure that her train was still on time.

Nat's voice sounding next to her sent Ash's heart pounding in her chest. She cast Nat a look and tried to ignore the accompanying flipping inside her stomach.

"Oh. Hey." Ash tried to look surprised. "What're you doing here?" The convincing edge to her voice pleased her.

"I…came to see you off." Nat smiled at her. "I was at a loose end. Passing by. You know."

*Passing by Paddington Station?* Ash didn't care whether it was true or not. She was here, and at that moment, that was all that mattered to her.

"You didn't have to," Ash said, as blithely as she could muster.

"I wanted to."

Ash saw Nat narrow her eyes and peer up at the board.

"Well I'm glad you did," Ash said. She followed Nat's gaze up to the board, making sure she didn't look at her. "Very glad."

"Well I needed to make sure you got on the right train." Nat bumped her arm. "I know what you're like."

*You do. You know me better than anyone else.*

Ash felt Nat's level gaze but didn't answer. She wished she could, but no words would come. Instead, she hooked her thumbs into the straps of her rucksack and jiggled it higher onto her shoulders. In the corner of her eye she could see people starting to gather at the gate to her platform and knew it would soon be time for her to go.

"I should…" She lifted her head in the direction of the platform.

"Are you off?" Nat followed Ash's look. "Is it time?"

Ash started to walk away, knowing with every step that while she was happy to go home, she just didn't want to leave Nat. As she walked, and Nat followed, Ash desperately wanted to talk to her about what had happened at the Common, or at the very least tell her how much she'd enjoyed the last few days. But she couldn't. Instead, a deafening silence followed them, cranking open the awkwardness between them, it seemed to Ash, even further.

"This is me, then." Ash died inside at her politeness. She saw Nat look past her shoulder, to the train waiting for Ash, then back to her.

"I…" This time Nat looked skyward.

"I should go." Ash's heart thrummed a steady beat. There was so much she wanted to say. The more she thought about that, the faster her heart thumped. "So…I'll see you Sunday?"

"Yes, Sunday."

The awkwardness intensified. Wimbledon Common was confined to the past.

Ash nodded, then turned to go. Before she knew it, Nat had pulled her back to her and gathered her in her arms, Ash returning the hug. When Ash went to pull away after a couple of seconds Nat squeezed even harder and spoke softly in her ear.

"Not yet. Not quite yet."

Nat's whispered words sent Ash's senses spiralling high up into the station's domed ceiling. She drew Nat closer still, melting into the hug, her body coming alive at the feel of Nat's body against hers, forgetting everything else that was around them. But she knew it had to stop. Reluctantly, Ash pulled herself away, her confusion saddening her.

Wasn't this what she'd been wanting all morning? For Nat to appear at the station to say goodbye to her?

"I can't…" Ash shook her head. "I can't do this."

"Can't do what?" Nat's face was a mixture of confusion and longing.

"All this." Ash hitched her rucksack higher and tried to ignore the nausea that was making her throat close. "*Us*."

"But"—Nat shook her head—"I thought you felt the same as I did."

"I don't know what I feel any more, Nat." Wasn't that the truth? Ash stared up at the glass ceiling of the station, her heart feeling too big for her chest. "I think I'm past feeling anything other than confusion right now."

"You don't have to feel like that," Nat said, taking Ash's hands. "There's nothing to be confused about."

"There's plenty to be confused about." Ash laughed quietly.

"But you must have felt the connection between us again, surely?" Nat asked. "Because I have."

"No." Ash let her hands fall from Nat's. "I can't."

"It never went away, Ash," Nat said. "I never stopped loving you."

Ash turned her head away. "I've heard this all before. Believed it all before. You telling me you loved me."

"But we were kids then." The pain in Nat's voice was evident. "Just kids. We're both so different now."

"I was old enough back then to know that you nearly killed me." Ash looked back at her. "I'm damned if I'll let you do that to me again."

"Do you know how many times I nearly came back from medical school to tell you I was sorry?" Nat asked. "To tell you I'd been an idiot and to beg you to take me back?"

Ash stared over towards her train, unable to formulate an answer. Voices ebbed and flowed around her; people bustled and bumped past her. But the only thing she was aware of was her and Nat, and the beating of her own heart.

"I have to go," she eventually said. "My train…"

"Not until I've told you all the things I've been wanting to tell you for years," Nat said. "About how I've felt about you all this time. About how I came this close to giving it all up." Nat pinched her finger and thumb together. "I tried, Ash. I tried so hard."

"Yeah. Felt like it." Ash rued her petulant tone.

"All I knew was that you'd buggered off to Europe," Nat said. She threw out her hands. "Where did I start? Where did I even start looking for you in Europe? France? Germany? How on earth could I know where you were?"

"You didn't need to come looking." Ash turned away and looked over to her train, its doors still closed. "I went to Europe to get away from you. I didn't want you finding me." She didn't need to look back to see the look on Nat's face.

"But that was all a very long time ago," Nat said. "We're sixteen years down the line from there."

"Some things are hard to forget." Ash slipped her thumbs through the strap of her rucksack again. "What you did is hard to forget."

"And if I had my time again I would never have done it," Nat implored. "I've gone over and over it in my head and I wish I could change what I did, but I can't." She came closer to Ash. "I can't change the past, can I? All I can do is tell you how I feel about you and tell you I'll never do anything to hurt you again."

Ash sensed frustration from Nat. Well, tough. Nat couldn't swan back in her life, and then think they could pick up where they'd left off all those years ago.

"I'm a different person to what I was then." Nat pulled Ash's hand from the strap of her rucksack and held it again. "I don't have my father breathing down my neck, telling me what I can or can't do. I'm free. For the first time in my life, I'm free."

"Can you hear yourself?" Ash wrenched her hand away. "You managed okay all those years ago, didn't you? Managed without me then."

"Who says I managed?"

"And whose fault it that?" Ash asked. "Answer me that. We had everything we could have ever wished for but you were too cowed by your parents to stand up for this beautiful, amazing relationship you had."

"But I'm not afraid any more," Nat said. "Finally I know what I really want."

Ash's mind tailspinned. They could make this work. They could. Nat could stay in England and forget about Belfast and...

"How can I ever believe anything you say to me?" Ash asked quietly, staring down at her feet as if they held the answer to all her questions. "How can you even ask me to try?"

"You've felt the tension between us, surely?" Nat asked slowly. "Every time we're together. Each time our eyes meet. There's still a chemistry there, Ash. You know it, I know it."

"Do you know how long it took me to get over you?" Ash snapped her head back up. "Years. I spent years trying to convince myself that I was okay. That you finishing with me hadn't screwed me up." She glared at her. "I stumbled around Europe, too afraid to come back to London because that was where all the bad memories were," she said. "Then when I finally found the courage to return, all I wanted to do was hide myself in a small corner of England where I knew no one knew me." Ash felt her face flaming. "That was all down to you. So while you were swanning around London, climbing the greasy pole with the help of some bloke you didn't even really like, I was hiding away finally trying to make something of my life."

The hurt on Nat's face was deeply satisfying.

"So when you tell me you still have feelings for me," Ash said, "you can kind of understand why I'd be sceptical. Wouldn't you?" She stepped back, suddenly weary.

"So why did you want to kiss me when we were on Wimbledon Common?" Nat asked quietly. "I know you wanted to, just as much as I wanted to kiss you."

Ash's insides flipped over. "Don't." Ash's voice was quiet. "Don't do this."

It was all so impossible. How could they ever have a future when Ash knew that the past still haunted them? They could try but Ash knew deep down all the old bitterness and regret that had corroded and stultified and eventually ended their friendship would eventually return.

"I love you."

"I said, *don't*."

"It's true, Ash," Nat said, capturing Ash's hands again. "I can't keep kidding myself. I love you and I know you feel the same way about me."

Pain burned in Ash's chest.

"You'll hurt me again," Ash said, hating the words that came out of her mouth. "I can't risk that."

Ash held Nat's gaze. She was everything Ash had ever wanted in someone: adorable, funny, generous, beautiful. She loved her. She'd never stopped loving her. The only thing hiding herself away in Europe had done was numb the pain of losing her. Now that Nat was standing in front of her, telling her she still had feelings for her, was Ash prepared to lose her all over again? All she had to do was tell Nat she loved her too, and maybe they could work something out.

Ash remained calm and rational. "I can't, Nat," she finally heard herself say. "I just can't risk falling in love with you again."

Finally, Nat released Ash's hands. Knowing there was nothing more her racing heart would allow her to say, Ash turned and hastened to her train without so much as a backward glance.

## CHAPTER FOURTEEN

N at stared down at the small granite tablet with the ornate white engraved writing and sighed. Anyone could tell it was new, placed there just that morning. After so many people had attended Livvy's funeral, Livvy's mother had been adamant she just wanted a quiet family interment. Livvy's friends had granted her that wish.

Nat wasn't sure what it was that had compelled her to visit Livvy's ashes so soon. When she'd heard the tablet was in place, she'd determined to leave it awhile before visiting it, but she'd woken the day after Ash's departure from London feeling so low, she knew the only person she could talk to was Livvy.

The flowers Nat had brought her were perfect, she thought. Well, it was more of a pot plant than flowers, but then Livvy had always liked cyclamen, so Nat had thought it fitting. As Nat crouched and nestled the pot next to the small posy of flowers laid down by Judy and Chloe, her thoughts drifted to the day before. She glanced around the small church graveyard, making sure she was alone, then, feeling slightly self-conscious, spoke quietly.

"So what do I do?" Nat settled herself down on the grass. She pulled her knees up closer and hugged them. "About this whole situation?"

She looked about her again, convinced someone would hear. The graveyard was empty.

Nat stared down at the tablet, choosing her words. "I only saw her yesterday, you know. Ash. But I miss her already. There. I said it, Liv. I miss her already." The inevitability of it sat in her stomach like a rock. "Want to hear a secret?" She looked about her again, then spoke. "I feel like I need to be near her again, sort of, *all* the time, you know? Just like before." Nat frowned. "We can spend hours together but the second she's gone, I miss her." And missed her like crazy. "Which is all a bit silly really, considering I thought I'd buried my feelings for her away so deep I'd have to get a JCB digger to find them again."

*Perhaps not.*

"You know what this all means, of course. It means I still love her." Nat stared down at the stone. "Yes, I know, I know," she said. "I know what you're going to say." She lifted her head and looked out across the churchyard. "Why did we never tell you we were together all those years ago?" Nat sighed. "Maybe we should have done. But I suppose we both just got to a point when it seemed too late to tell anyone." She picked a blade of grass and rubbed it between her finger and thumb. "Then all that stuff happened"—Nat flicked her hand—"and Ash left, and…"

And what? Nat wasn't sure. All she knew was, at the time, she'd had no desire to confess to Livvy that she was responsible for it all. Nor in the years later, either, when the secret dragged on.

"I guess this is my punishment, hey?" Nat said. "Wanting her, and knowing she'll never want me again."

The yew trees in the churchyard were groaning with berries, their distinctive, sharp odour filling the air. Summer was still clinging on by its fingertips, but Nat knew within the next few weeks, once they were properly into November, autumn would make its presence well and truly felt.

*November.*

Nat's stomach balled.

November meant just one thing: a decision about Belfast, looming ever closer, bringing with it increasing and unwanted feelings of fear. The excitement and anticipation of starting over somewhere new had gone, to be replaced with reluctance and panic.

Only a few weeks before, Nat had been making plans, not knowing that Ash would appear just around the corner and make her question everything that had seemed so clear to her.

"It's not a surprise, you know," she said aloud. "Falling for Ash. I should have known the moment I set eyes on her again it would happen. I suppose it's not like I ever really stopped loving her." Nat sighed. "But of course nothing is ever going to happen, is it?" she said. "Between me and Ash, I mean."

Hadn't Ash made that abundantly clear at Paddington?

"So it seems moving to Belfast is the best thing I can do," Nat said, "for both of us." She thought for a moment. "Well, for Ash anyway. I'm not so sure about me." At the unwanted sharp prick of tears, Nat roughly swiped at her eyes. "Not that she cares either way."

A dog barking somewhere in the distance lifted Nat's attention away from her tears. She gazed out across the churchyard, expecting to see someone, but instead saw a pair of male blackbirds sparring with one another, each keen to hold on to his own territory.

"But I want it to, Liv." Nat turned back to the granite tablet. "I want it to matter to her." She pulled her hands through her hair. "Yes, I know I've only got myself to blame and I know it's all too late." She dusted an ant from the tablet. "But I can't stop myself from feeling how I feel, can I?"

Nat looked down, irritated to see another ant attempting to cross Livvy's tablet. She brushed it away, thinking how lovely it would be if humans could brush away their thoughts with such ease.

"You know she went home yesterday?" Nat said. She lifted her face to the waning sunshine. "And now I'm counting the hours until I see her again." Her laugh was hollow. "Even though I was thinking of making up some excuse so I wouldn't have to go down to Cornwall on Sunday." Nat glanced back at the tablet, then held up her hands. "I won't, don't worry. I'll go and I'll make it through the next week, then leave and we can both go back to living our individual lives again." She hauled herself to her feet, brushing debris from her trousers. "I'll accept the job in Belfast and all this"—she spread her arms out—"will be history." She turned to go, casting one final look down to the tablet, the heaviness in her chest returning. "Just like Ash will be."

❖

The boat was annoying Ash. The boat *never* annoyed her though. In fact, Ash often thought that Doris the fifteen-foot boat was the only thing that kept her sane—but not today.

Ash sat in her small bridge, feeling the hull rock back and forth as her passengers, aided by Gabe, stepped inside. The air inside the bridge was stale and thick with the smell of diesel, a smell which Ash could usually ignore. Today, though, it was making her feel nauseous, which only added to her displeasure. She tossed a look back over her shoulder to her passengers, a small group of eight men and two women. Perhaps it was the passengers, rather than Doris, that were irritating her. They'd never bothered her before, but then, before she'd not had so much to think about. She'd done a great job of putting Nat to the back of her mind over the past few days, forgetting everything they'd said to one another at Paddington, but now, with just a calm stretch of water in front of her and no distractions, Nat and her declarations of love were creeping back into her thoughts. Ash looked out of her side window, to beyond the harbour and out to the sea expanding endlessly towards a shimmering horizon. She sighed. Perhaps the incessant chattering was interrupting her train of thought, and that's why she was so edgy. The same train that kept storming up to London and back to Nat at a hundred miles an hour.

"All in." Gabe appeared at her side. "Harbour guys say we're good to go."

Ash nodded, throttling the engine so it gave out a roar. At Gabe's tap on her shoulder, she eased out of the harbour and made her way out between a line of bright orange buoys bobbing in the water. The chattering behind her increased now that the boat was on its way, audible even over the sound of the engine. Most of the summer tourists had now long gone, to be replaced by various groups who liked to hire the boat—and Ash and Gabe's services—for an afternoon out at sea. Today it was a photography group from the next town, hoping desperately to see an obliging seal or, even better, a whale or basking shark.

Ash and Gabe often played a game on these particular trips: pretending that sightings were rare, then enjoying seeing and hearing their passengers' reactions when a creature was spotted. The truth was, Ash knew exactly where to take her passengers for a guaranteed view, and just the right things to tell them. The passengers, grateful at the glut of sightings, were always more than generous with their tips when they eventually returned to the harbour and left the boat.

Ash smiled to herself as her boat slapped and bobbed over the waves. While the business allowed her to live comfortably, the tips afforded her the odd luxury, such as replacement parts for her battered truck. Ash looked back over her shoulder to the happy faces of her passengers. Perhaps today the seals would put on an extra-special performance and her much-needed cam belt could become a reality.

As the boat finally settled into a steady rhythm, Ash's mind slotted itself back into its familiar pattern of Nat thoughts. She heard Gabe's low voice rumbling somewhere behind her as he talked to their passengers, leaving Ash free to reflect in peace. Nat would like it here, Ash was sure. She stared out over the nodding horizon and determined that one of the first things she would do when Nat and Chloe arrived on Sunday would be to fulfil her promise of taking them out on the boat.

The familiar shadow of apprehension flickered in Ash's stomach. What would Nat really make of Ash's life down here? Her eyes automatically fell to her clothes, grubby from work, and to her hands, tanned but weather-beaten. Ash fisted her hand, then turned it over and splayed out her fingers, frowning at the obvious roughness on her palm. Nat's hands were perfect. As were her clothes. She'd only seen Ash out of context, clean, not weather-beaten, and certainly not smelling of boat diesel.

The sense of failure, never far away, shimmered under the surface.

"Nice and calm today." Gabe flopped down in the seat next to Ash. "Think we'll see Old Bruce?"

"Most definitely." Ash grinned, glad he'd interrupted her thoughts. Old Bruce was the name of one particularly grizzled bull seal who liked to droop himself over the rocks and glare at them as their boat came closer to his colony. Ash and Gabe were never sure whether he saw them as a threat to his seal harem, or whether he objected to the flash of a dozen cameras in his face. It was possibly both.

"Gabe?" Ash asked.

"Mm-hmm."

"Do I smell of diesel?" Ash whipped off her beanie and leaned closer to him.

Gabe sniffed.

"No," he said. "Why on earth would you ask me that?"

"I don't want…" Her brow furrowed. What didn't she want? For Nat to think of her differently when she saw her in her home environment? "I don't want to smell, that's all."

"Are you worried about Nat?"

Ash threw him a look. The guy was a mind reader.

"No." She paused. "Yes."

"Because despite you constantly denying it," Gabe said, "you care what she thinks."

"Only because I want her to see that I've done okay for myself," Ash replied, wishing she could tell Gabe the truth, but not knowing quite where to start. How could she tell Gabe that the woman she'd spent years alternately telling him she loved, she hated, she loved, had found herself into her heart again? Ash dipped her head to look out of the window as a seagull flew precariously close to the boat. "And I want her to know I haven't spent the last sixteen years or so pining away for her," she added.

"Even though you sort of have?"

Ash looked down at Gabe's hand on her leg.

"It's been my choice to be alone all these years," she said. "Anyway, no one would have ever wanted to be with someone who lives in a ramshackle old cottage with a stinking Labrador, and who spends half her life on a boat." She gave a light laugh, one that masked her disquiet.

"Nat will love it here." Gabe stood as the boat slowed on its approach to the rocks. "And if she doesn't," he said, "she'll have me to answer to."

"I…"

A loud caw from another passing seagull right next to the boat drew their attention away from each other briefly. They both watched it in silence as it wheeled overhead, before finally becoming a white dot in the distance.

"You think they're okay back there?" Gabe asked, looking behind him.

Ash followed his look. Her passengers were in their own worlds, snapping photographs from the side of the boat, and talking amongst themselves.

"They're fine," Ash said. "Gabe?"

"Mm?"

"You *are* right about Nat." Ash didn't meet his look.

"That you care for her?"

Ash nodded. "I can't stop thinking about her." She let out a sigh. "She told me yesterday she still loves me too."

"Ah."

"Yes. Ah."

"I'm guessing, knowing how stubborn you are, that you've not told her how you feel," Gabe said. "Even though you know how she feels about you."

"No." Ash shook her head. "I have a hard enough time admitting it to myself."

"So you're going to have to see her again," Gabe said, "knowing you like her, and she likes you, but you're not going to do anything about any of it?"

"Looks that way." Ash gazed out of her window. "Because I'm here, she's there, and it didn't work sixteen years ago, so it's not going to work now." Ash cut the engine as her boat approached a bed of seal-covered rocks. She stood, expertly negotiating the boat through the rocks towards the waiting seals. "And because, as I told her yesterday, there's a good chance she'd do to me what she did all those years ago"—the boat slowed to a stop alongside the rocks and

she moved from her wheel and placed a hand on Gabe's shoulder—
"that thought alone will be enough to keep me from ever admitting
my feelings to either of us."

"Natalie."

Nat allowed the embrace to last no more than two seconds before
she pulled away. She'd never been particularly tactile, although, she
thought with a hidden smile, it had never been a problem with Ash,
and certainly not at Paddington two days before. And Jack Greene,
the cardiologist at St. Bart's who'd taught her everything she knew,
certainly wasn't one to be too overly touchy-feely with.

"Jack. Good to see you." Nat stepped away. "How's things?"

"Never mind, how's things," Jack said. "You're supposed to
be on a sabbatical, aren't you? Before the big plunge over the Irish
Sea?"

"What can I say?" Nat sensed her confidence waver. "Couldn't
stay away." She glanced down the corridor, eager to escape to the
sanctuary of her office. After all, hadn't that been the reason she'd
come here? So she could hide away in her room on the pretext of
working? Anything had to be better than staying at home, constantly
chewing things over about Ash.

"Bloody hell, Natalie." Jack's voice boomed around her. "If
I was offered over two weeks away from this place, I'd bite their
hands off." He laughed, eliciting a forced smile from Nat.

A tightness gripped Nat's stomach. Jack was right; she'd been
lucky to have been offered so much time off—to gather her thoughts
and indulge in a little research before taking up her prospective new
post, they'd said—and in any other circumstances, she would have
done.

In any other circumstances before Ash, that was.

"I figured…" Nat's brow creased. What had she figured in the
forty-eight hours since Ash had left? That her life now had a huge
hole in it that only Ash could fill? That, overnight, Nat had begun to
think her whole life was futile? That what she did was pretty useless

if she wasn't happy? Nat's frown deepened. "I figured it would be quieter here, Jack. The noise from the traffic outside my apartment is intolerable sometimes."

"Well," Jack said, "anyone who chooses to come to this place on a Saturday afternoon deserves a coffee at the very least." He put his hand on Nat's shoulder. "Let me treat you. It'll taste like shit as usual, but at least you won't have paid for it."

Jack strode off down the corridor, Nat meekly following him. She pitched a look back over her shoulder, back down to her office, wanting to disappear in there, close the door, and make everyone leave her alone. Her feet, however, refused to obey.

The canteen was, as she expected, quiet when they arrived there. Visiting time in the hospital wasn't for another few hours, so the few people who remained at their tables were predominantly hospital staff. Nat made her way through the maze of tables, raising a hand to a few faces she recognized, the now-accustomed chill inside her at the prospect of starting over somewhere new, with new people, returning with each comforting note of familiarity at seeing her colleagues' faces.

Nat stood quietly next to Jack as he ordered coffees, then led them both to a table in the far corner. As Jack eased himself into the seat opposite her, Nat's phone hummed inside her jacket pocket. Smiling at Jack, she pulled it out, trying to demonstrate a nonchalance she certainly didn't feel. It had to be Ash. It just *had* to be. Ash hadn't contacted her since she'd left London; nothing had been said about Nat and Chloe's impending arrival the next day, almost as if it didn't matter to her. And as the hours had stretched by, and the silence from Ash had grown, that was precisely what Nat had gauged from Ash's behaviour: their visit plainly wasn't a priority for her. For Nat, though, it had been all she'd been able to think about, even before Ash had left.

While Jack spoke, showboating about a conference he'd spoken at in New York the week before, Nat glanced at her phone.

*As you've opted to receive text alerts from us, we thought you'd like to know your next bill is available to view online. Just go to www...*

"Bad news?" Jack was talking to her. Had her disappointment been that evident? "I was telling you about Donald Letterman's speech last week, but your face when you read your text..."

Nat waved him away. "Sorry, sorry." She hastily rammed her phone back into her pocket. "You were saying?"

"I was just asking you if everything was okay." Jack smiled kindly.

"Oh, just an advance notice of yet another bill." Nat picked up her coffee, wishing her hands wouldn't tremble quite so much at the prospect of a text from Ash. "That's all I seem to get these days. Bills." She rolled her eyes. "It's as if they know I'm moving."

"When's the big day?"

"Not settled yet," Nat said. "I have to ring the Royal to confirm my decision. Then I guess it'll be all systems go." Her laugh was empty.

"Richard's very pleased."

Nat's head sprang up. "Richard?" Richard had no right to feel anything about Nat. "What's it got to do with him?"

"He put in a good word about you," Jack said, "with the bigwigs over at the Royal."

Nat's insides curdled. "He shouldn't have done that."

Richard had no need to interfere, Nat thought. Yes, she'd let him help her in her early career, when she'd thought she needed him, but she'd not needed Richard for over ten years now. So just why the hell did he think she did? She picked up her coffee and frowned down into the liquid inside. There'd been a time, long ago, when she'd been lost and he'd picked her up, dusted her down, and set her on her way again. But not now. Nat hadn't needed anyone in years.

"He had absolutely no right to interfere," Nat repeated.

Jack's responding look was blithe, Nat thought.

"He knows one of the seniors over there," he said, sitting back in his chair. "Pinged an email over to him, telling him how marvellous you are."

The thought of Richard discussing her with her potential new colleague irked Nat.

"Well, I wish he hadn't." She sipped at her coffee, hoping it would take the bitter taste away from her mouth. "I rather thought I'd been offered the job off my own merits."

"You were," Jack said. "Richard just gave them a bit of encouragement."

Nat stared back down blankly into her cup. Jack's words had stirred up her anxieties over Belfast all over again, and the knowledge that Richard might—despite Jack's protestations—have had a hand in her getting the post felt like it had the potential to be a game-changer.

"They can't wait to have you on board, you know."

Nat lifted her eyes to Jack.

"Who told you that?" she asked sarcastically. "Richard?"

"Valerie Keaton. Senior Registrar over there." Jack looked at Nat, making her feel as though she were being assessed. "Despite what you think, Richard had no hand in you actually being offered the post. His email just confirmed what they already knew. That you're quite a coup for them." Jack leaned closer. "According to Valerie, you were already top of their list before Richard even contacted them."

Nat sat back, her coffee cup still cradled in her hands. Two voices were shouting loudly to be heard inside her head: one telling her Richard's interfering had tainted her new job, the other telling her to stop being so stupid because she could really make a name for herself over there if she could just get over herself. The coffee warmed her hands. She was a good surgeon, she knew that, and more than up to her new job. She'd outgrown St. Bart's years ago but had never had the courage to move on, instead preferring to dedicate her spare time to research in order to stretch herself more. Despite her reservations, she knew the Royal Victoria was going to be perfect for her; there she'd finally really show everyone—herself included—just what she could do.

"So when I said Richard was pleased," Jack said, "all I meant was, he's glad you'll finally get to do what you've been wanting to do for ages."

Nat felt her shoulders ease. Her mind had run away with her, and not for the first time. Of course Richard hadn't persuaded them to offer her the job, of course she'd got it on her own merits, and *of course* she was going to love it and make a success of it. She felt embarrassed at her own lack of confidence, and for even contemplating that the Royal Victoria would be too big for her. The truth was, if she could control her anxieties and constantly tell herself she was up to the job, it would absolutely be the making of her, the culmination of years of hard work and research. She would be the success she knew deep down she could be. The panic attacks would fade, she was sure of it. She just had to—as Callum constantly told her—have faith in her abilities and everything would slot into place.

And, really, there was nothing stopping her from going there and doing just that, was there? The thread that Nat had started to think was pulling her back from Belfast had slackened dramatically in the past forty-eight hours, because that thread was Ash, and she hadn't even bothered to contact Nat once since her return home.

While Jack talked about a paper he was researching, Nat tuned out. Heat spread across her cheeks at her own stupidity in thinking for just one second that she and Ash could rekindle something that had flickered and died, years before. Nat had been so caught up in the change of routine that Ash had brought with her to London that she'd forgotten all the promises she'd made to herself when she'd decided, months before, to leave St. Bart's and seek something more fulfilling elsewhere.

Ash had made it clear she was most definitely still nothing to her. And the sooner Nat drummed that into her head, the sooner she could get herself over the sea to Belfast and forget all about her again.

# CHAPTER FIFTEEN

The knot in Ash's stomach tightened with each move of the second hand on her bedside clock. She'd been awake for a good hour before her alarm, and had lain in bed both dreading and looking forward to the day in equal measures. Now, listening to each tick that took her closer to the hour when Nat and Chloe would arrive, each one more agonizing than the last, Ash wondered whether she'd be a nervous wreck by the time their train finally pulled into Truro Station.

Chloe had texted her the night before to tell her which train they'd both booked.

Nat had not.

It had been three days since Ash and Nat had had any contact with the other. Three days since Nat had told her she still loved her, and now Nat's silence was so prolonged, it was as though it were being pulled taut like an elastic band being stretched to its limit. So many times over the preceding days Ash had wanted to text her or call her. But each time she went to formulate a message, or scrolled down to Nat's number, something stopped her. Ash couldn't fathom what it was, though, or why she felt she had to maintain a stubborn air of indifference, when everything inside her was hurting with longing.

Ash rolled her head along the pillow and narrowed her eyes at her clock in the gloom of her bedroom, trying to focus on the hands: 5.30 a.m. She'd always had the ability to sleep like a child—

much to the envy of the insomniac Gabe—but since her return from London, her sleep had been sporadic, and she'd spent each morning doing just as she was doing now. It didn't take much figuring to understand why. In less than eight hours, Nat and Chloe would both be here, and Ash knew all her feelings—all these new, confusing feelings she had for Nat which she'd categorically denied to her in London but which were still frantically treading water just under the surface—would overwhelm her again the second their eyes met at the station. Despite hoping that time away from Nat would quell her feelings, all their separation had done was increase them tenfold, until Ash thought her head would explode from all the thoughts and anxieties that constantly eddied around inside it.

Her insomnia was testament to that.

The grey hue just behind her curtains told her it was either already raining, or just about to. Ash lay on her back and concentrated hard trying to hear it, nodding to herself in acknowledgement when she finally heard the first quiet taps on the glass. She felt cheated by the rain, annoyed that the weather couldn't have stayed nice for Nat and Chloe's arrival, whilst at the same time praying that it wouldn't rain for their entire visit, confining them to her cottage with nothing to do or say to one another.

The hardening rain began to drum a steady beat against her window. Ash locked her arms above her head and stretched, yawning loudly as she did so. The sound of her yawn elicited a thump of his tail from Widgeon, lying on the rug beside her bed, and Ash flopped an arm over, her fingers seeking his fur. She scratched at it, smiling in the dark as Widgeon let out an extended sigh, and Ash thought— and not for the first time—that her dog had always been the perfect antidote to her anxieties.

The day ahead felt like an immensely important one to Ash, and she could only assume it was because Nat would finally be in Ash's little sphere of existence, adding something extra to what should have ordinarily been a straightforward visit. It had to be perfect. It *had* to be. Ash wanted Nat to see her in her own environment, to meet her friends—well, Gabe, anyway. Perhaps the others would follow later. Despite her protestations to Gabe while she was in

London, Nat's meeting him was more important to Ash than she'd realized. Gabe was her world; she wanted him to tell her that Nat was amazing and wonderful and every other type of adjective she could think of, just so it would confirm to her what she already knew.

Ash desperately wanted Nat to experience a snapshot of this perfect life Ash had created for herself by the sea.

Ash turned over and buried her head in her pillow, groaning into it. Why did she have to still love Nat? What was it about her that was so different from anyone else? There had been a girl—quite a few years ago now, admittedly—who would have done anything to be with Ash, and yet Ash had pushed her away when she sensed things were getting serious. Ash blinked against the soft cotton of her pillow. Sophie. That had been her name, and she'd been the loveliest girl, and Ash had really liked her and had had a blast with her for the few months they'd dated.

And yet…

Ash traced a pattern on the pillow with her finger. Sophie was long gone. Fed up with waiting for a show of commitment Ash knew she'd never be able to give her. She couldn't blame her. Why would anyone wait for Ash to make up her mind, or for Ash to stop constantly stalling whenever they talked about the future?

The rain rapped harder against the window, now accompanied by a wind that whistled softly through the gaps in Ash's sash windows. Lying in bed, mulling things over and over, regretting the past whilst wishing for a future that would never happen would get Ash nowhere. With a quick tug of Widgeon's ears, Ash got up, leaving her scrambled thoughts still tangled up in the patterns on her pillow.

The train crept into Truro Station with a metallic screech of brakes that seemed to go on forever. Ash loitered in the doorway next to the ticket office, her pounding heart doing nothing to quell her apprehension, and watched as the train finally came to a standstill and its doors began to open. The previously quiet platform was instantly transformed into a hive of activity and noisy chatter as passengers spilled from the train and buzzed around her, embracing waiting friends and relatives, or pushed past her in their haste to get to the exit before anyone else.

Ash looked fretfully for the familiar faces of Nat and Chloe in amongst the sea of strangers, her brain constantly reassuring her that she had the correct train, correct station, and correct platform. Finally Nat stepped down from the train. Ash watched her as she adjusted the rucksack on her back, glanced around her, her face a picture of both worry and concentration, then stepped tentatively away from the train as she sought out either Ash or the exit. Ash looked past Nat's shoulder, watching for Chloe, but when she didn't appear, she approached Nat, winding her way against the flow of passengers.

When it was clear Nat still hadn't seen her, Ash lifted her arm high above her head and jumped slightly, smiling when Nat finally spotted her. Expecting to see Chloe just behind Nat, Ash was confused when Nat strode towards her without even a backward glance.

"You made it, then." Ash paused awkwardly, then quickly embraced Nat. She stepped away again, stuffing her hands into her trouser pockets as if she didn't know what to do with them.

"I made it." Nat laughed, slightly out of breath. "Only just though. What a morning!"

"And...Chloe?" Ash nodded over Nat's shoulder.

"She texted you."

"No she didn't." Ash pulled her phone from her pocket and looked at it. "Oh. So she did."

"Do you ever check your phone?" Nat bumped Ash's arm.

"Apparently not." *Apart from checking it every five minutes since last Thursday up until eight a.m. today, hoping you might have texted me.* "By the time I'd walked the dog this morning and tidied up"—Ash shrugged—"I just grabbed it and drove straight over here."

She looked down at Chloe's message, sent at nine thirty that morning: *Grandma's ill. High temperature, throwing up, the whole business. Ugh. Nasty! I feel torn because I soooo want to see you, but I don't feel as though I can leave Grandma. Nat says she'll come on her own and that it's totally ok. I'm so sorry* :(

"Poor Judy," Ash murmured. She put her phone back in her pocket. "Guess it's just me and you, then?"

"I wondered if I should have waited until she was better and Chloe could come," Nat said. "But these are the only two weeks I have off until I possibly have to...you know."

"The new job?" Ash asked. "It's cool. It makes sense for you not to cancel." A quiver of apprehension passed over her at the thought of spending the next four days alone with Nat. London had been a completely different ballgame; the vastness of London had allowed them both their space, and more importantly, Chloe had been their go-between—the common factor either could go to if needed. Now, it would be just Ash and Nat, and the thought of them being alone together was met by Ash with a mixture of excitement and worry. "Shall we?" She motioned to the station exit.

They walked in silence, each apparently lost in her own thoughts and slight shyness at being around the another again. It would be fine, Ash said to herself. Gabe could take the place of Chloe if necessary. Her anxiety abated. If she felt as though she was getting too cosy being alone with Nat, or so close she might do something she knew she'd regret, she'd just ask Gabe along to act as a chaperone. Simple.

"I'm parked here." Ash lifted her head to her ramshackle truck, a year's worth of mud splattered up its sides. "Can't miss it. Scruffiest thing in the car park." Her laugh masked her embarrassment, and she wished she'd thought to clean it that morning before she left.

Nat waited at the passenger door as Ash slid herself in to her driver's seat, then reached over and removed a pile of papers from the passenger seat. She flung them into the back, then nodded through the window for Nat to get in.

"Sorry about the mess," Ash said as Nat settled herself in. She fired the engine, revving it three times until she was happy that it wouldn't stall. "It's kind of my office too."

"Stop apologizing." Nat put her hand on Ash's leg. "At least you have a car. I sold mine when I moved back to London."

Ash looked down at Nat's hand on her leg. When she looked back up, Nat was staring at her.

"I'm glad I'm here at long last," Nat said. "I've…been looking forward to it. I—" She smiled then shook her head. "Never mind. Ignore me. I'm prattling on, as usual."

Ash knew Nat wanted to say more. Her face was unreadable, but Ash could sense underneath, Nat wanted to tell her something more.

"Me too," Ash said, if only to break the awkwardness that crackled between them. "And if it's as much fun as London was, then we'll have a great time."

That seemed to comfort Nat. "I'd like to think so," she said.

Nat's face was still expressionless. Her hand though, Ash noted, remained on her leg. Ash resisted the temptation to look at it or, heaven forbid, place her own hand on top of it, despite the noisiest voice she'd ever heard in her head urging her to do it. There was a time when they couldn't keep their hands off one another, where just the prospect of being alone together in a confined space like this would have been too much.

Shaking the thought from her head, Ash slammed her truck into first gear and, with a quick glance in her wing mirror, pulled out of her parking space. Nat had removed her hand from Ash's leg, leaving a small pool of cold where it had been. They didn't speak, Nat apparently preferring to stare out of her window than make idle chitchat with Ash.

Ash slipped a look to her as they rounded a corner. She wondered what Nat was thinking; perhaps she felt as uncomfortable being alone with Ash as Ash did, knowing what they both now knew, and wished that Chloe was with them to defuse the renewed clumsiness that now stood between them. Nat had seemed genuine enough though when she'd said she was glad to be there; it was just the pessimist inside Ash wanted to find a negative when there quite possibly was none.

"Did you have rain?"

Nat's question brought Ash back from her thoughts.

"Rain? Yes. Loads." Ash wondered just when she'd lost the power of speech. "It woke me up." Okay, so that was a half-truth. "I was beginning to worry that today would be a washout."

"Same at home." Nat glanced at her, then back out of the window.

Ash nodded, wishing she could think of something more to say. She couldn't.

"I meant to ask you," Nat said, "if your train home from London was okay the other day."

"Fine. Why?" Ash was surprised.

"You didn't tell me you got back okay," Nat said. "That's all."

"Don't tell me you were worried about me?" Ash stared ahead, knowing what she wanted—hoped—Nat's answer might be. Aware that Nat was looking at her, she glanced over. "Were you?"

"I was." Nat's face was serious. "And…I wanted to text you these last few days, but…"

"I guess I should have contacted you too." Ash spoke when Nat's sentence remained hanging in the air. "So maybe we're as bad as each other." She laughed, hoping it would steady the growing tension inside the car.

"Yes," Nat replied, turning her head away from Ash once more, "maybe we are."

Nat thought Ash's whitewashed cottage was like something she'd see on a box of chocolates. Or a children's book about eighteenth-century smugglers. She wasn't quite sure. It was set back from the road, down a short dirt track that Ash's truck wobbled and crunched over violently enough for Nat to have to hold on to the handle of her door. Tiny windows poked out from under a dense, thatched roof, the paint peeling from their frames a testament to their proximity to the sea, while the thick-set wooden front door with its slightly rusting cast-iron fittings proudly announced the name of the cottage: Holly Cottage.

As she slipped out of the truck and looked around her, Nat spotted the cottage's namesakes: two enormous holly bushes, the first hints of that winter's red berries beading the green foliage, stood importantly in opposite corners of Ash's garden. Ash had given a nod to the cottage's clifftop position overlooking the sea too, Nat noticed, and had given her garden a pleasing sea theme. Brightly coloured buoys peeked out from behind the bushes in her flower beds and sun-bleached shells and starfish were lined up along a wall, while pieces of driftwood, planed to a velvety smoothness by the sea, had been placed strategically around the garden.

It was, Nat thought, exactly how she'd imagined it to be. And she'd imagined it a lot over the past few days. As she followed Ash down the garden path towards the cottage, Nat's mind fell back over the days, when she'd sat in her apartment both dreading and anticipating the moment when she'd see Ash's home. Ash hadn't disappointed. Her cottage was picture perfect and Nat appreciated just how much time and effort Ash must have put into it to make it so.

She looked up, her eyes roaming over it all, finally settling on the thatched roof and its fine craftsmanship. No wonder Ash was happy down here, Nat thought as she followed Ash in through the front door. No wonder she felt so at home.

"I hope it's okay to drop off here first."

Ash's voice pulled Nat's attention back to her.

"Sure." Nat smiled at her.

"Your B and B is further down the coastal road," Ash said as she opened the front door. "It just made sense to stop off here on the way." She paused. "Besides, I thought you might be hungry. I made sandwiches."

Ash's genuineness was touching. Without thinking, Nat reached over and smoothed her hand down her arm as she passed her on her way in through the door.

"Thank you," Nat said. "I am actually *really* hungry." She followed Ash into her lounge and laughed as she spotted a large scrubbed table with three cellophane-wrapped plates, each piled high with sandwiches. "Which is just as well, bearing in mind how many sandwiches you made."

Ash looked over to the table.

"I thought Chloe was coming too." She turned back and shrugged, almost apologetically, Nat thought. It was sweet.

Nat held Ash's look. "It's sweet." She spoke her thoughts. "Seriously sweet."

"Well, don't tell everyone," Ash said. "I have a reputation to uphold."

Her unease was obvious. From Nat's continued eye contact, or from calling her sweet? Nat wasn't sure. She pulled her gaze away and wandered further into Ash's lounge, sensing Ash still watching her from behind.

"Your cottage is lovely." A feeling of comfort enveloped Nat as she looked around Ash's home, appreciating the cosy space, thanks in part to Ash's taste in colours and pictures, and the array of bright throws, cushions, and rugs scattered arbitrarily around the room. It was perfect Ash: slightly haphazard, but aching with warmth. Nat approached Ash's neat inglenook fireplace, its surround smudged with smoke, and looked at a photo. "This your dog?" She threw a look back to Ash.

"Widgeon." Ash joined her at the fireplace. "I know I'm silly having a photo of my dog, but—"

"Who said it's silly?" Nat leaned briefly against Ash, then away again. "I think that's sweet too."

"Reputation…"

Ash's rising mock-warning voice made Nat laugh.

"He's out," Ash continued. "In case you wondered. Gabe took him down with him to the boat this morning."

"I'd like to see it today," Nat said. "Your boat. If you have time."

"Sure." Ash moved away again, then stopped, looking deep in thought. "We should open Livvy's next letter first though." Her face looked etched with something that Nat couldn't put her finger on. "That's why you're here after all."

The bluntness in the delivery of Ash's statement after her previous friendliness came as a shock to Nat, draining all the cosiness from her, and she took its implications with a sinking heart.

Distance. That was what it so clearly was. For whatever reason, Ash was trying to push her away again, to remind Nat the reason she was here. Ash had just looked at her with such lifeless eyes, it was as though they were back to being strangers again. But the notion that Ash would want to push them back when Nat had thought they were creeping forward unsettled her more than she cared for; for her this whole adventure had turned out to be so much more than just the wish list, and even more so now Chloe wasn't with them. This was a chance to get to know Ash again, this time on her home turf.

Nat watched Ash, wishing that she could follow the movement of her thoughts, wishing she knew what she could do or say to keep them moving forward again. When Ash's coolness remained, Nat finally gave up trying and walked from the fireplace, Ash's distance still stinging her, the embarrassment at her sharp change in mood making her own mood darken.

"Okay," she said, trying to keep her voice level, "so let's open Livvy's letter now."

*If that's how you want to play this.*

She pulled her rucksack from her back. "Let's get this over and done with as soon as possible."

The judder of the front door, the sound of boots being kicked off and clattering across her hallway, the rapid clip of claws on her wooden floor. Another door slamming, followed by a loud curse. Only one man could make so much noise in so little time.

Ash caught Nat's attention from across her lounge and lifted her eyes heavenward as another curse rolled in from the hallway.

"Gabe," Ash said, in reply to Nat's questioning look.

Ash knew he wouldn't be able to stay away for long. So much for his, *I'll take Widgeon with me for the day so he's not under your feet when you all get back.* Ash loved Gabe dearly but sometimes he was nosier than a whole bunch of old women put together, and she knew Nat was the reason he'd brought her dog home early. Chloe too, possibly, but mainly Nat.

Not that Ash minded too much. Her sharpness towards Nat earlier had sucked the life out of the room, and she knew she was to blame for it. Now, having sat in virtual silence after reading Livvy's letter, neither wanting to be the first to start up a new conversation, Nat evidently keeping herself to herself, Ash couldn't help but be slightly thankful that Gabe had arrived to put some cheer back into the room.

She hadn't meant to be so blunt with Nat, though. But there had been something about the way Nat had been standing by her fire, gazing at her photos, that had sent Ash's insides flipping. Her resulting snappiness had been a reflex: a grouchiness at her own feelings that had taken Ash quite by surprise, immediately followed by a scratch of guilt when she'd seen Nat's face fall.

Another crash from out in the hallway made Ash frown.

"What?" Nat asked.

"Nothing." Ash shook her head, but the frown remained. "Just…I might have known Gabe wouldn't be able resist coming up here and having a nosy."

"Now I'm nervous," Nat said.

Ash looked at her. Yes, Nat *did* look nervous, endearingly so. Ash cut her glance away and concentrated on listening out for Gabe.

"We're in here," she called. "In case you were wondering."

The door opened and Gabe's face appeared.

"So you are." He grinned into the room. "Widgeon was mithering, so…"

"You brought him home." Ash tilted her head back on the sofa to see him. "Thank you." She resisted the urge to add *liar.*

"So. You're here," Gabe said.

"Gabe, Nat." Ash waved a hand. "Nat, Gabe." She watched as Gabe practically swept into the room and strode over to a visibly surprised Nat, his hand outstretched.

"Pleased to meet you," he said. "I mean, *really* pleased to meet you."

Nat hastily stood. "Likewise."

Ash watched in amusement as they awkwardly shook hands.

"You're missing one." Gabe fell into the chair next to Ash. "Chloe?"

"Livvy's mum's ill," Nat said. "So she's staying in London."

"So it's just the two of you?"

The look on Gabe's face wasn't lost on Ash.

"Just the two of us. Yes." Ash flicked a look to Nat, then away again. She looked about as uncomfortable as Ash felt.

A silence settled in the room, only punctuated by the ticking of a clock.

"How do you like Cornwall?" Gabe was the first to break the quiet. "Bit different from London, I guess?"

Stilted laughter. "I haven't seen much yet," Nat said. "Although I'm sure Livvy will have plenty for us to do in the next few days."

Ash smiled but didn't answer.

"Ash tells me you recently got offered a new job," Gabe said, "in Ireland."

"Mm." Nat moved in her chair, and Ash sensed an increase in her discomfort. "I have to confirm my acceptance, then I should be good to go next month."

"In what line?" Gabe shook his head. "Ash did tell me. I forget now."

Ash glared at Gabe. He knew full well. "Cardi—"

"—ology." Nat spoke at the same time as Ash. "Sorry."

"Sorry." Ash felt her face warm.

"It's mostly surgery." Nat flashed her a look that said, *It's okay.* "I've been doing lots of research for the last few years so I suppose the change will be good."

"Lab research?" Gabe asked.

"Lab and office." Nat nodded.

"With a bit of surgery thrown in?"

"Mm." Nat nodded. "I love the research, but I think I'll eventually get used to being back in the operating theatre more."

Ash listened quietly. Gabe was asking her all the questions she knew she should have asked Nat. Why hadn't she spoken to her about it? This new job was obviously a big deal to Nat and yet Ash had shown little or no interest in it. Ash knew just why. She'd closed her ears to it because if she did, then maybe it wouldn't happen and Nat would stay in England and…and what?

"You're excited?" Gabe asked.

"I think so." Nat laughed. "But more apprehensive."

Ash looked at her. There was that flicker of something again, passing across Nat's face. Unnoticeable to most, but to Ash? As clear as day. She knew Nat inside and out. Despite Nat's confidence—after all, it had always been Nat who'd had the fire to achieve things in life when Ash had been happy with her lot—it was nevertheless still a look she'd seen her do many times when they'd been together whenever she was stressed about something. A forthcoming exam, an argument with her parents, a tricky assignment: each resulted in a look of anguish, a slight pinch of the brows, a quick blink. The scud of a shadow across her features. Ash felt a tug in her heart, remembering how once upon a time she would have been at Nat's side at such a look. Would have gathered her in her arms and told her everything was going to be okay. Ash was there. Ash would *always* be there for her.

"Sometimes," Nat said, lifting her eyes to Ash's, "I wonder if it wouldn't be just as much fun to jack it all in and go back to just doing research." Her voice was light, but Ash knew the lightness was somewhat forced. "Or buy myself a boat and sail off into the sunset." She smiled at Ash. "But I suppose that's what an overwhelming dose of dread about picking up a major new job does for you." Nat drew her gaze from Ash and spoke quickly, as though if she didn't, she might say something else instead. The forced lightness and the wavering doubt were even more evident this time, quite in contrast to the same Nat who had oozed self-confidence about her new job at Judy's house just a few weeks before.

But that had been then. Now Ash could see Nat through different eyes and noticed the fear in the frown that she wore, heard it in the tremoring voice Nat was so keen to hide. What kind of environment did Nat work in anyway? Ash guessed Nat had needed a spine of steel to appease her parents and get where she'd got herself so far, but perhaps there was only so much steel one person had.

"So what has Livvy got up her sleeve for you next?"

Gabe's question was a welcome distraction.

"A trip on the boat." Ash's smile was broad. "Which is handy because that's what I had planned anyway." Her smile was matched by Nat's. "By the time I got the business up and running ten years ago, I never got to take Livvy out on the boat because Chloe was still too young. Livvy thought she'd wriggle so much she'd fall overboard."

"So Livvy asked Ash to take me and Chloe out on it," Nat said. "Well, just me now."

*Which is ironic,* Ash thought as she stood and went to her cabinet where Livvy's letter was propped up against some books, *considering we'd already planned a trip.* Livvy, Ash was beginning to think, was one step ahead of them. Ash pulled her letter from the cabinet and opened it up. She scanned her eyes down, and read: "*So thanks to my wriggling little fish of a daughter, my wish was never granted. Poor me.*" Ash looked up and smiled. "*Will you take her? Clo? She still wriggles as much as she did but at fourteen I should hope she'd be able to swim better if she does fall overboard (please tell her this is a joke). Nat can grumble that she doesn't have sea legs and you can all have the most marvellous time.*"

"And we will," Nat said, adding, "I do have sea legs, by the way."

"Just as well." Gabe widened his eyes. "Ash hates anyone being sick on Doris."

"Doris?"

"The boat." Ash sat back down.

"You named your boat?" Nat asked.

"I know," Gabe chipped in. "She's crazy."

"I think it's quite nice," Nat said, meeting Ash's eye. "Makes it more personal."

"See?" Ash tossed a cushion over to Gabe. "At least Nat understands me."

"Oh, I'd say Nat understands you very well," Gabe said, catching the cushion and returning it with equal force.

## Chapter Sixteen

"Her photos on the Internet don't do her justice."

Ash fell into her chair. "What?" she asked.

Gabe looked at her. "Nat," he said, "I'd not got from her photos how nice she is."

It was just gone nine p.m. Ash, recently returned from taking an exhausted Nat to her B & B and now tired herself, wasn't particularly in the mood to be discussing Nat with Gabe.

"I guess." She picked up a magazine and started flicking through it, not looking closely at either the words or pictures.

"She get to her B and B okay?"

"I took her," Ash said, "so, yes."

"You know what I mean."

Ash looked up from her magazine. "Her B and B is perfect," she said, "just as I knew it would be. That's why I chose it."

"You text her to say you're home okay?"

"Why would I?" Ash put the magazine down onto her lap.

"Because she'll be worried," Gabe said.

"Dream on."

"She'll be sitting in her cold room, waiting to hear from you."

"Stop taking the piss." Ash tossed the magazine onto the floor by her feet. "You're not even funny."

"I'm not taking the piss." Gabe leaned forward. "You should text her."

"Fine, fine." Ash launched herself over to the table next to her chair and picked up her phone. *Back home now. Everything okay with you? xxx*

"Happy?" She dropped the phone down on the chair next to her, then looked down barely seconds later as it vibrated against her leg. She flashed a look to Gabe, irritated at the amused look on his face. "That won't be her," she said. "No one texts that fast."

Ash dismissed Gabe's raised eyebrow.

"Why are you such a stubborn bugger?" he asked.

"I'm not." Ash frowned. "I'm just not the sort of person who picks up their phone the second they hear it buzz." She stole a glance at her phone, a secret smile bursting inside her when she saw the snippet of Nat's reply before her screen darkened again.

*Everything great. As was today. What time shall we…*

"Yeah, right." Gabe sat back. "Anyway, I wasn't talking about the text."

"Oh."

"I was talking about why you're fighting this thing with Nat."

"There's no *thing* with Nat." Ash air-quoted.

"But there could be," Gabe said.

Ash shook her head. "Haven't we had this conversation already?"

"Yes, but that was before I'd met her," Gabe replied. "I mean, come on. She's gorgeous."

*I know.* Ash bit at her lip.

"And you haven't seen the way she looks at you when she knows you're not looking," Gabe said. "I have." He studied her. "And you, lovely girl, can't keep your eyes off her either."

Ash didn't reply.

"You know, you're a completely different person when you're around her," Gabe continued. "This whole evening has shown that."

"I'm not."

"You really are," Gabe said. "You're the Ash I know and love. I've seen you around other people and you're never like you were this evening with Nat. Relaxed, funny, animated, chatty."

Ash frowned. "I'm always chatty."

Gabe shook his head. "Only with me, and only because you're comfortable with me. With other people you're quieter. More reserved." He looked at her. "You're yourself around Nat. It was nice to see."

"We go way back," Ash said, trying to keep her voice light. "Of course I'm going to be comfortable with her now I've become used to being around her again." She rested her head against the back of her chair. "Anyway, I'm sure when she goes on Friday, everything will go back to normal and all these feelings I've been having will probably go."

"Probably?"

"They *will* go."

"And if they don't?"

"They will. They have to."

Ash's boat was bobbing gently in the harbour, the seawater slapping at its sides with every swell.

It was the next morning, one that had brought with it a sense of anticipation for Nat of the day ahead. Now, as she followed Ash down the short cobbled slipway, she tried to decide whether the boat really did look like a Doris. Funnily enough, she thought it did.

It wasn't as small as Nat had assumed it would be, and as they neared it, she shot Ash a quick look of admiration, seeing on her face as she did so the same pleasure she saw every time Ash spoke of her boat. Doris couldn't have been cheap to buy, Nat realized, nor cheap to maintain, and it was obviously Ash's absolute pride and joy. The thought warmed her.

"So, this is her." Ash spread her arms out in front of the boat.

"Impressive." Nat's eyes roamed over the hull. "And most definitely a Doris."

"I said, didn't I?" Ash grinned. "Gabe will never get that."

Nat waited while Ash stepped on board, then accepted the hand that was held out to her. With a slight wobble and a tight grab of

Ash's hand, she silently thanked herself that she managed to get on board without making too much of a fuss.

"Grab a seat," Ash said, signalling to one of the plastic seats. "I won't be a moment." She threw Nat a towel, then hopped back onto the harbourside in one leap.

Nat put the picnic bag with their lunch in it onto the floor, then wiped a seat down with the towel, sat down, and watched as Ash busied herself with the boat's ropes, jumping on and off the boat in such a quick, casual, and practiced way that Nat couldn't help but watch her in awe.

When Ash finally had finished unfurling the ropes, she returned to the stern of the boat, slipping a wide smile and a "You okay?" to Nat as she passed her. While Ash was occupied to the front of the boat, and with the sun now nicely warming her skin, Nat sat and watched as the scene before her slowly sprang into life. People wandered up and down the harbour, a couple of teenage boys sat dangling rods from its wall, hoping to catch something—anything, and other boat owners called across the water to one another. The overnight rain had finished long before she and Ash had even left the cottage, and now the sun had resumed its position just to the south of them. A few puddles remained from the earlier downpour, shimmering in the sun, while the large, fluffy clouds that scudded across the sky brought no danger of any further rain with them. It was, Nat thought as she lifted her face and squinted against the sun, perfect weather for a day out at sea.

The invisible pull of Ash drew Nat's gaze from the sunshine back towards her, still at the helm of the boat under her canopy. She was busy at the wheel, radio in one hand. Nat was mesmerized as she watched and listened to Ash, taking in her fluid movements and the command with which she spoke her requests into her radio. The tug on Nat's heart was agony. She looked at Ash, wondering if she thought of the past as much as Nat had been just lately. Wondering if she still thought of the times they'd sneaked off to be alone, of the passion they once shared, of the connection they had that no one could have ever understood.

Now Ash was moving around at the stern. Nat let her gaze absently roam Ash's body, over her tanned skin, settling on her stomach as she saw brief glimpses of Ash's toned muscles as her top rode up when she reached above her head to collect a map from an overhead shelf. When her gaze reached Ash's face, Ash was looking back at her. Their eyes locked, the flush of embarrassment at being caught out spreading across Nat's face.

"Is she going today?" A voice called down from the harbour wall.

Nat snapped her head round to see a woman and two children looking down at her.

"I'm sorry?" Nat called back, shielding her eyes from the sun.

Why had she stared so long at Ash? Why?

"The boat. The sign says no trips today, but..." The woman gesticulated to Nat.

"Oh. No, sorry." Nat shook her head. "This is a...uh...sort of private thing. Sorry." She couldn't help the dancing feeling she felt inside as she said it. *A private thing.*

"Right. Cheers. I'll try again further down." The woman walked away.

Nat slowly turned her head back to Ash, surprised to see Ash still looking at her. Their eyes met again, encouraging the dancing in Nat's stomach to continue. It would be just Nat and Ash. At sea. All day. At that moment, Nat didn't think she'd been as happy in a very long time.

"Who was that?" Ash walked towards her.

"Somebody wanted you." Nat laughed. "Saw me and thought you were doing trips today."

"You just lost me money?" Ash gasped and clutched her chest. "I'm kidding you." She flopped down next to Nat.

"You sure?" Nat asked. "I can go and find them and—"

"Today is about me and you and...thinking about Livvy," Ash said quickly. "We'll head out to sea and raise a glass—or rather, a mug of tea—in her memory. How does that sound?"

*Today is about me and you.*

Nat couldn't think of anything nicer.

❖

A salty breeze billowed Nat's hair around her face as Ash's boat finally left the shelter of the harbour and headed out to sea. The few gulls that had followed them, hanging on the wind and calling to one another high above their heads, soon lost interest the further out they sailed and glided back towards the harbour in search of a different food source. Ahead of her, Nat could see only blue, her line of sight periodically interrupted by the odd blob of white as she spotted other boats further out at sea, their masts ticking back and forth like metronomes as they bobbed and bounced on top of the waves.

Nat stretched her arms out and rested them along the edge of the boat. Ash was occupied again up at the helm, her radio held to her mouth as she stood and steered the boat out to sea, one-handed. Nat watched her as she looked about her, talking rapidly into the radio, occasionally dipping her head to look out of her side window. Her sense of pride at watching Ash took Nat quite by surprise. She'd have never have guessed at eighteen that Ash would have been the success she so obviously was. Her pride, though, quickly faded to regret. How could she have got Ash so wrong all those years ago? How could she have had her down as being the one that would hold her back?

How could she have let Ash be the one she let get away?

Nat stared down at her feet. Ash had more integrity and grit than anyone she'd ever known, and yet she'd treated her terribly. But there was no bitterness from Ash at what Nat had done. No hate. Instead, she'd accepted her back into her life—albeit temporarily— as a friend and spoiled her and treated her just as much as she'd done when she was eighteen. Nat blinked down at the ground. Ash had always made her feel so special. Like she was everything to her, like no one else in the world mattered. Today felt just the same.

*Today is about me and you.*

Butterflies fluttered inside Nat as she thought about Ash's words, and the way she'd said them. Images on Wimbledon Common returned to her: faces inches apart, eyes locked on one another's. Skin touching skin. The urge Nat had had to kiss her that day had been overwhelming, and she was sure if her attention hadn't been drawn away by Chloe's laugh signalling her impending return, she would have done.

Nat stole another look to Ash, fighting the urge to go to her right now, circle her arms around her, and tell her just how she felt. But, like kissing her, to do that would ruin everything. Confuse everything. Change everything. Nat blinked again, harder this time, trying to hold back the vivid thought that was now trampling through her mind with such energy she drew breath from the force of it.

*Change everything.*

The panic that had left her alone since she'd arrived in Cornwall rose and fell with every breath Nat took. Her eyes darted to Ash, up at the bow of her boat, oblivious to Nat's rising anxiety. Just like at Claridge's, Nat was desperate not to let her see, but her brain was now chanting a mantra that Nat couldn't stop. Belfast was accelerating towards her at breakneck speed and she was terrified about it; she already knew that, but this panic held a distinct shift in its threat. Her life was changing and running out of control, and Nat knew the only person she trusted to calm her fears was Ash. Nat's heart pounded. But Ash would be history to her again in a few days, and then Nat would be on her own, forced to fight her demons alone again.

She didn't want to have to fight them on her own any more.

Sure, she'd been single for such a long time now, it was almost second nature to her. But just feet from her was someone she loved deeply, and who made everything in Nat's life right now so much better. When they parted again, then what? The loneliness that Nat had forced herself to accept as being normal would return and the regrets of what she did would start to haunt her again. The panic attacks would still dominate her. She was lonely in London and would be lonelier still in Belfast. Panicky in London. She'd be worse in Belfast, she just knew it. It would never end.

Nat teased at the bracelet on her wrist, seeking comfort in its soft material, and concentrated on her breathing. She sang a song in her head, and counted the now-sporadic gulls flying over the boat.

*One, two, three, four...*

Her heart began to slow and the invisible band that was pulled tight around her chest, restricting her breathing, gradually loosened its iron grip. She lifted her head to Ash, hearing her whistling to herself, and Nat smiled at the sound. Ash was happy. Ash had made this life for herself down by the sea, and she was happy. How could Nat possibly think that she hadn't confused things by telling Ash in London that she still loved her? Ash had been right; she still burned with trust issues, and Nat understood that, because she was the maker of those issues.

Nat watched Ash and shook her head. It all felt hopelessly tangled. All of it. And each time she thought she might have managed to untangle it a little, another irrational thought came along straight away that just tied it all up further still.

Nat had coped before, hadn't she? Without Ash? So if she wanted to untangle her thoughts, then she'd just have to resign herself to doing what she'd done for years once this week was over: She'd have to just manage. Alone.

In that moment, with a sinking heart but with the sound of Ash's whistling still in her ears, she knew the best thing for both of them was for her to enjoy what little time they had left together, then disappear to Ireland next month and never see Ash again.

The sunlight hitting Nat's hair brought out the beautiful tones Ash had always adored. As she sat opposite her watching Nat as she gazed out to sea, Ash thought she'd rarely seen someone look quite so resigned to something. Sure, gone was the jumpy, almost harrowed aspect she'd noticed in London, but still something about Nat's demeanour remained, and Ash knew she wanted to get to the bottom of it.

They had berthed in the shallows of St. Kerryan Cove, a beach so secluded that legend was it used to be a favourite haunt of the smugglers who once ruled the seas around the bay. But sitting on a boat on the sandbanks of an isolated beach in the autumn sunshine,

Ash thought as she stared at the sadness etched on Nat's face, should make her happy, not sad.

"What?" Nat's laugh was slight.

Ash looked away, embarrassed. How long had she been staring at her?

"Just thinking." Ash met her gaze again.

"That…?"

"You looked deep in thought."

"Did I?" Nat asked. She looked away, apparently unable or unwilling to elaborate.

"What were you thinking?" Ash pressed. "You should have no thoughts in such a place as this, other than how beautiful it all is."

"Oh, it is," Nat said. "Beautiful, I mean." She shrugged. "No, my mind is pleasantly vacant."

Ash recognized the look on Nat's face. The one that told her that what she'd said hadn't been the entire truth.

"When we were…together," Ash said, hearing a slight hesitancy in her voice, "sometimes you'd say things were okay when they weren't." She looked down at her hands. "The night we parted, for example."

Ash's mind filled with memories, all painful. Still all so painful.

"Ash, I don't want to rake up old—"

"Neither do I." Ash interrupted. "All I'm trying to say is if you want to talk, I'm here to listen."

The look on Nat's face wasn't lost on Ash.

"Talk about what?" Nat cut her glance away from Ash. When her eyes returned to Ash's, Ash noticed the sadness in them. "Yeah, maybe that would be nice. To talk."

"I know you." Ash smiled. "You must remember I know you too well."

"You know me better than anyone." Nat looked down at her hands. "Always did."

"So I know when there's something niggling at you," Ash said. "Something so bothersome it follows you from London down here." She dipped her head a little to catch Nat's eye. "And no one should be bothered when they're sitting on Doris in St. Kerryan Cove." She was gratified at the smile she'd managed to elicit from Nat. "That's better."

When Nat lifted her head, Ash saw her eyes were filmed with tears. In an instant she was at her side.

"Hey." She put her hand on Nat's arm. "No tears. They're the rules. No tears on Doris. She doesn't like it."

"Sorry, Doris." Nat's voice was barely audible.

"I didn't mean to upset you," Ash said.

"You didn't." Nat put her hand on top of Ash's. "I'm just…" She looked away. "I don't know what I am." Nat faced Ash again. "But I *am* happy being here. Don't think I'm not."

"And being happy makes you cry?" Ash tilted her head and pulled a face, making Nat smile again. "Not in my book."

"Being happy does make me cry, yes," Nat said, "when you've been unhappy for as long as I have."

Ash sat back. Nat didn't do unhappy, did she?

"Sometimes I think I've lost the ability to know what happiness is," Nat said. "But these last few days, well, this last week really— since I met you again—it's made me realize I'm not quite done yet." She looked at Ash. "So, thanks."

Ash gazed at her, her throat closing with her own tears. She fumbled in her pocket, pulled a tissue out, and handed it to Nat. "It's clean," she said. "Promise."

Ash waited while Nat wiped at her eyes, formulating her next question in her mind. A question that she hoped wouldn't bring on more tears.

"Why are you unhappy?"

Nat took a deep breath.

"All sorts of reasons," she eventually said. "Loneliness, fear of failure. Guilt." She slipped a look to Ash. "Knowing that I let the best thing to ever happen to me slip away from me." She screwed up her tissue. "Then coming down here and seeing that I didn't fuck up your life after all makes me…" Nat shook her head.

"Makes you what?"

"Makes me relieved," Nat said. "I've lived with the thought that I'd ruined your life. It's eaten away at me for years."

"But Livvy always told you I was okay," Ash said.

"Yes, but it's only by coming here and seeing it for myself that I finally believe it." Nat's voice rose. "And that in itself makes me unhappy."

"You're not happy for me?" Ash was confused.

"I am." Nat unfurled her wet tissue and blew her nose again. "I'm unhappy for myself." She turned on her seat. "Can't you see?" she asked. "I could have had all this with you too."

"Your parents would have disowned you." Ash laughed. "And hunted me down." She paused. "You've had a great life of your own." Ash captured Nat's hands again and squeezed them tight. "This is what happens in life. We take different paths. We might not be happy at the time, but then things always have a way of working out for the best."

"For you, maybe."

"And for you too," Ash stressed. "Look at you. You're fabulous! You're successful, hard-working, well-respected. You have everything you ever dreamed of having when you were eighteen."

"Everything my parents wanted as well," Nat said, "and a shitload of issues to go with it." She tugged up the cuff on her sleeve. "See this?" She pointed at her bracelet. "This is the only thing that keeps me this side of sanity. Now who's successful and well-respected?"

Ash stared at the brightly-coloured piece of material on Nat's wrist and frowned. She didn't understand anything Nat was trying to tell her. Instead of speaking, though, she touched the bracelet, running her fingers under it, feeling it, trying to understand its significance in Nat's life.

"I don't understand." Ash voiced her concerns.

"I see a therapist," Nat said. "A shrink. Once a fortnight."

"Okay…"

"Because while everyone thinks I'm successful and everything else you just said," Nat said, "underneath I'm lost. Afraid. Drowning."

Ash stared at her. No, this wasn't Nat. She'd never shown any signs of weakness in her life—not as a teenager, not at Livvy's funeral, not at Judy's house that day. And not once over the last few weeks. Except...

"That day in Claridge's when you shot off to the toilet," Ash said. "Was that...?"

"The start of a panic attack." Nat nodded. "I think you coming in and taking my mind off it eased it."

"I had no idea," Ash said. "No idea about any of it."

"I hide it well." Nat smiled. "I've had years of practice."

Ash stared out to sea, thoughts cascading through her mind like running water. All these years she'd though of Nat, swanning around her hospital, bathing in the glory of her hard work. Was the reality the opposite of that? That while Ash had made a success of her own life and was living her life to the full, enjoying every second of her cosy life in Cornwall, Nat had been up in London drowning? Were the expectations put on her as a teenager catching up with her and making her life a misery?

"Livvy never said," Ash noted. "Did you never tell her?"

"Never." Nat shook her head. "No one knows. I was embarrassed—I *am* embarrassed—to admit this image I created for myself has all been a sham."

"But you're going to be a senior consultant." Ash shook her head. "I don't understand. You've been a surgeon for years. How have you managed?"

"Just have." Nat shrugged. "It's amazing how you learn to hide your anxieties from people." She looked away. "Being here has made me feel like my old self again. How I was when I was with you." She stopped herself. "I mean, how I was when we were teenagers. Before everything changed."

Ash willed her to turn back and look at her. Instead, Nat continued to look out to sea.

"The thought of going back to London right now," Nat said, her head still turned away, "is terrifying. The thought of Belfast is even more terrifying."

"Have you told your therapist that?" Ash asked.

"Kind of." Nat shook her head. "Oh, he talks of distraction and breathing," she said, her fingers absently working at the wood on the side of the boat, "but at the end of the day, I suppose we're all flawed, aren't we?" Finally she turned and looked at Ash. "Besides," she continued, "I signed up for this life, didn't I? So I guess I'll have to just get on and deal with it."

❖

Four hours. That's how long they'd been talking. Four solid hours. By the time Nat had finished laying herself bare to Ash, the sun was slipping down over the horizon, casting a huge blood-red shimmer onto the sea.

Ash had listened mostly in silence as Nat had shared her deepest thoughts, only interjecting to contradict her or reassure her. Now, she watched Nat as she stared off out to sea and noticed, again, a slight shift in her demeanour, this time more positive. Her shoulders, too, looked lighter of load, her movements easier. If Nat had thought talking to Ash had helped, then listening to her had helped Ash just as much.

Ash's eyes fell to Nat's arm, to her bracelet hidden under her sleeve, and she wondered how she hadn't noticed Nat's anxiety. It was obvious to her now, in hindsight, that the constant fierce rebukes dished out to her by her parents—her father in particular—whenever Nat failed at anything as a teenager would eventually catch her up and have a detrimental effect on her as an adult. All the while Nat had been telling Ash her anxieties, her hand had strayed to her wrist, to tug or worry at the only thing that seemed to help her. It was a gesture Ash had seen while they'd been in London, but she'd never once imagined its significance. Watching Nat's rising unease as she spoke of her future, and seeing how much she'd relied on her bracelet as she spoke, Ash felt ashamed that she'd apparently managed to get Nat all wrong.

Nat wasn't the confident woman Ash had thought she was. Gone was the notion that Nat was selfish and self-possessed, happy to step over anyone to get what she wanted, replaced by the reality that she had been treading water all these years. In fact, while Nat had been sinking, it had been Ash who had flourished, and the truth of their respective situations now hit her like a thunderbolt.

"What are you thinking?" Nat's voice cut through the silence.

Ash turned to look at her. She looked tired, as though the strain of her confession had knocked the wind from her sails.

"Just that I've had you wrong all these years," Ash replied. "I imagined"—she paused, taking care to formulate her words—"that you were living this high life in London on the back of your success. You doing whatever it took to get where you wanted to be. You telling everyone you deserved it."

"Is that what you really thought of me?"

Ash was ashamed at the look of pain on Nat's face. Ashamed that she could have caused it.

"I didn't know, did I?" Ash said. "I didn't know for sixteen years." She looked at her hands. "All I had to go on was Livvy telling me what a success you'd made of your life. How you'd climbed the greasy pole."

"Because that was what was expected of me," Nat said. "And look where it's got me. In therapy." She looked at Ash. "I'm a mess, Ash."

"I know your parents expected a lot of you, but—"

"*I* expected a lot of me too," Nat said. "How else could I justify what I'd done to you? To us?" She gazed at Ash. "Failure wasn't an option. If I did fail, then everything I'd done would have been for nothing."

"I spent years thinking you'd just erased me out of your life," Ash said. "That you didn't care."

"I thought about you all the time," Nat said. "Thought about what I'd done to you. The best way to get over the guilt of that was to immerse myself in my work too."

"Why did you do it?" Ash held her look. "We were happy. Why did you have to change everything?"

"Because I was eighteen and stupid," Nat said, "and I've spent my life regretting it." She gave a half smile. "That probably accounts for some of the therapy too. The guilt." She drew in a deep breath and looked away. "Guilt, regret, and a fear of failure. Fatal combination."

"Sounds like you get your money's worth though," Ash joked with a glibness that she immediately regretted.

But to her surprise, Nat laughed.

"Yes, I suppose I do," she said, still laughing.

Her laughter was welcome, and so genuine and warm—quite unlike her previous superficial, unhappy laughs—that Ash felt a quiet triumph that she had been the one to finally draw it out of her. Ash stood and walked to the helm of the boat. She didn't need to turn her head to know Nat was watching her. Instead, she stared out to an unseen spot out on the horizon and listened to the sea slapping against the side of the boat, letting Nat's words sink in, knowing she should perhaps go back to her and say something.

But she couldn't.

The one thing she most wanted to say could never be said.

*Don't go to Belfast.*

Nat was adamant she wasn't up to the task. Ash thought differently. Belfast was the culmination of years of hard work—and, yes, therapy—but at the end of the day it was what Nat had always strived towards, regardless of her worries. Nat would never not go. All Ash could do now was reinforce everything she'd said to her over the last four hours, instil some confidence, and wish her all the best.

Ash gripped the boat's wheel tight, watching her knuckles blanch.

*Don't go.*

*Stay with me here.*

*I love you.*

The thought grew, snowballing through her mind. The idea of it brought about a rush of something akin to a clarity, or exhilaration, but the feelings waned as quickly as they had arrived, withering and dying as the reality of her thoughts hit Ash.

"We should make a move." Ash snapped her thoughts back, annoyed with herself for allowing them to dictate. "It's getting late."

She heard Nat's footsteps on the wooden floor of the boat.

"We have Livvy's next letter still to read," Ash said by way of explanation, sliding a look to Nat, desperate to refocus her thoughts. Nat was gazing back at her. "So we should…you know. Get back." Nat tipped her head to one side, smiled, and nodded in a gesture that made Ash's insides melt. She hastily looked back to the dashboard and flicked a switch, illuminating a line of red lights.

"Thank you." Nat's voice was quiet. Ash felt her hand on her arm and turned again to look at her.

"For what?"

"Everything." Nat's breathing was shallow. "No one's ever understood me quite like you."

Ash reached up and tucked a strand of hair behind Nat's ear. "That's because no one's ever known you quite like I have," she said.

Nat closed her hand over Ash's and held it to her face. "If I could turn back the clock…"

"Then who knows what would have happened?" Ash reluctantly pulled her hand away again. "Who on earth knows?"

## Chapter Seventeen

A sh lowered her head and looked out of her window across the fields, then up to a sky untroubled by clouds. Today, just like the previous day on the boat, would be perfect.

Nat watched her for a second then asked, "It's called Brown *what*?"

"Willy." Ash turned her attention from the window to Nat. "And you can stop that."

"Stop what?"

"Smirking. I saw you."

"Why's it called Brown Willy, for goodness' sake?" Nat asked, looking at the map that Ash had spread out on the table in front of her. "Or shouldn't I ask?"

"It'll be old Cornish, I expect." Ash joined her at the table, then traced a finger on the map. "*Brownus Willius* or something."

"That would be Latin."

"Whatever." Ash flashed Nat a grin. "They say if you live in Cornwall, it's one of the things you *have* to do. Climb to the top. It's a bit like a Londoner saying they've never seen Big Ben."

"You should work for the Cornish tourist board, you know," Nat said. "You'd have the tourists flocking here."

"I wonder why Livvy wants us to walk it." Ash cast a look to Livvy's letter, opened on her table next to the map. "Guess it's something else she'll never get to do." She walked back to the window and resumed gazing out at the fields outside.

"She'll be with us in spirit though."

"Well, I have to say, it's the perfect day for climbing it. Sunny, not too hot." Ash smiled back over her shoulder to Nat. "What do you think?"

Nat joined her.

"Looks good to me," she said. She cast her a sideways glance, almost feeling the excitement radiating from her. "Livvy sure knew what she was doing when she put the Cornwall list together."

Ash turned from the window. "What do you mean?" she asked.

"I'd say London was my type of things," Nat replied. "Theatre and afternoon teas. I have a feeling Cornwall is going to be more your thing."

"Do you mind?"

"Did you mind the theatre and Claridge's and having to trawl round the Tate?"

Ash thought for a moment then smiled. "No," she eventually said. "I didn't mind at all."

"Then I don't mind walking mountains with you, and goodness knows what else Livvy has up her sleeve," Nat said.

*I don't mind doing anything, as long as it's with you.*

Nat focused on looking at a bird in Ash's garden, hoping Ash hadn't been able to read the expression on her face which she was sure gave away the thoughts in her head.

"Then I guess we'd better pull on our boots," Ash said. She stepped away. "You're cool with Widgeon coming?" she asked. "I couldn't possibly even think about walking up there without him coming along too."

Nat looked towards the door where Widgeon stood, his eyes fixed firmly on Ash, his tail half wagging in hope.

"Totally cool." Nat smiled. "He can pull me up there if I get too tired."

Ash's boots sent scree tumbling behind her as she scrambled up the north face of the hill. They had been walking for nearly half an hour, the last ten minutes of that up the steeper climb that would take them to the summit. The ache in Ash's thighs told her it had been too long since she last climbed Brown Willy, and as the burning intensified with each step, she resolved to make more of an effort in the future to visit it. Ahead of her, Widgeon was investigating a particularly interesting rock, his tail beating a rapid rhythm as his interest increased with each sniff. Behind her, she could hear Nat's heavy breathing as she clambered up the path. Ash stopped walking, savouring the warmth flooding her leg muscles as her blood pulsed rapidly under her skin with each heartbeat, then gradually slowed as her breathing eased.

"You okay?" She called down to Nat, laughing when Nat lifted her middle finger in response. "Too much for you?" she half laughed and half shouted.

"You know, I've been going to my local gym three times a week since I was thirty," Nat said, her breath coming in gasps, "but I've never done a workout like this." She arrived at Ash's side, turned, and bent over, her hands gripping her thighs. "Jeez, and I thought I was fit." Nat looked up at Ash and laughed.

"Guess you can't walk up over a thousand feet without it making your lungs hurt just a little bit," Ash said.

She stepped aside as Nat straightened up and adjusted her footing on the loose scree. She could sense Nat staring out and stole a look to her. Nat's face was pleasantly flushed from the walk, her lips redder than she'd noticed them ever being before. A few strands of hair escaped from her beanie and flapped gently in the breeze that wrapped itself around them, so that Nat persistently brushed them away from the corners of her mouth. Ash studied her profile, wishing—not for the first time—that things could have worked out differently between them. She was so beautiful, Ash thought, the sun teasing out the soft tones of her skin, highlighting the smoothness of her cheeks, and intensifying the clarity of her eyes.

"It's stunning up here."

"I told you," Ash said, but she wasn't sure if she meant Nat or the moors. "Worth the climb." She knew wishing for something that hadn't happened was pointless. Regretting it was more pointless still. Nat was here now, and that was all that mattered at that moment. She should just enjoy the day and think about regrets—if she had to—another time. "Only about another half-hour climb and we'll be at the top." She shoulder-bumped Nat at Nat's mock-grumbling. "Come on. Widgeon can lead the way."

Walking trousers suited Ash, Nat thought. As did the boots, the jacket, and the beanie. In fact, the whole ensemble looked as though it had been made just for her. And she looked stunning in it.

They had resumed their climb to the summit and, just as before, after walking together for the first ten minutes or so, Ash had gradually increased her step and moved ahead of Nat. Not that Nat minded. Her concentration alternated between making sure her boots gripped the gravel underfoot and admiring her perfect view of Ash.

Just as at Richmond Park the week before, Ash was in her element out here on the hill. Nat could feel her enthusiasm—could almost grasp it in her hands—as Ash cherished the environment around her. Her enthusiasm was infectious, Nat thought, as Ash periodically pointed out something of interest in the far distance, or a bird or plant that had caught her eye on their ascent.

And Nat realized just how much she thrived on Ash's passion. It made her feel alive—far more alive than she ever felt in London. It was as though Ash was opening her eyes to a whole world that she never knew existed: Ash's world.

And Nat loved it.

"My dog is trying to tell you something."

Nat snapped her head up. Ash was standing in front of her, hands on her hips, impish look on her face. Nat peered over Ash's shoulder to see Widgeon on his back, rubbing himself against the grass, his legs flailing in the air, his tongue hanging like a large piece of pink ribbon from the side of his mouth.

"He's trying to tell you to hurry up." Ash winked. Nat grabbed the hand that was offered to her, allowing herself to be pulled up the last two steps. She stood next to Ash, watching Widgeon as he continued his rolling, oblivious to his audience.

"Is that what he does?"

"Always," Ash replied. "Usually when I'm being slow on his walks." She frowned. "Either that or he's found something delicious to roll in. I'm hoping it's the former."

Nat pulled a tissue from her pocket and blew her nose into it, the exertion of the climb combined with the chilly hill air turning her nose into a dripping tap.

"Your dog is as barmy as you," she said, stuffing her tissue back into her pocket. She pulled her beanie off and tousled her hair, savouring the cool air blowing through it. "That the summit?" Nat lifted her chin ahead of her, to a small crop of rocks. "Or is it an illusion?"

Ash laughed. "It's the summit, I promise you."

"Can you imagine if we'd brought Chloe up here?" Nat said. "Imagine the grumbling."

"Livvy probably thought it would have been character-building for her." Ash rolled her eyes.

"I miss her," Nat said suddenly. "Livvy."

"Me too."

"Do you ever wish you could turn the clock back?" Nat asked, not meeting Ash's eye.

"Sometimes."

"I don't just mean about...me and you." Finally Nat looked at Ash. "I mean about everything."

"But does anything ever stay the same?" Ash asked.

"We were so happy," Nat said, not answering Ash's question. "You, me, and Livvy." Her gaze grew distant again. "Sometimes I remember the stuff we did at school, and that's when I wish I could turn the clock back."

"It was all a long time ago now."

Nat felt Ash's hand on her arm and looked down. Sensing Ash looking at her, she raised her eyes to meet hers. "Yes, but sometimes I wish..." Nat began.

"You wish?"

"Nothing." Nat smiled. She shook herself, as if to shake the thought from her. "Shall we press on? I'm getting hungry."

❖

The summit of Brown Willy was worth the burning thighs, the breathless lungs, and the sweat that now trickled slowly down into the small of Ash's back.

As she sat on a rock, Nat's unanswered wish still lodged in her mind, Ash gazed out around her, indulging herself in the beauty of the moors. Dark streams cut a swathe through the desolate moorland, which was dotted with rocky outcrops and granite boulders. The evocative sound of curlews calling to one another in distant marshes and estuaries echoed in the air, and intrigued, Ash shrugged her rucksack from her back, opened it, and pulled out her binoculars.

She felt Nat sit down beside her but didn't pull her binoculars from her eyes, instead choosing to concentrate on the small flock of lapwings skimming and diving across a distant boggy field. Just like on the boat, Ash sensed a disquiet from Nat and knew she probably wanted to finish what she'd started further down the hill. But for now, Ash was happy for her mind to be free of thoughts and for the silence—only punctured by the distant wail of the curlews—to remain.

Finally, once the lapwings had settled and the curlews remained elusive, Ash put down her binoculars.

"Anything interesting?" Nat asked.

"Few birds. A boat out on the River Fowey." Ash shrugged and placed the binoculars at her feet. "And lots of moorland." She threw a grin to Nat. "*Lots* of moorland."

"Hungry?"

The emptiness in Ash's stomach suddenly made itself heard. "Guess that answers that," Ash said. She brought her knees up to her chest, embarrassed at her rumbling stomach. "Talk about timing."

"Mine usually rumbles during meetings," Nat said. "And always at the quietest moments."

"Why do they always do that?" Ash accepted the foil-wrapped sandwich that was handed to her. "Good thing about my line of work is no one can hear when I'm hungry over the sound of the boat's engine." She laughed.

"I remember years ago, during my finals..." Nat stopped.

"Go on."

"Just...thinking my concentration was going to be ruined thanks to my noisy stomach."

Nat's discomfort at her words was palpable.

"You *can* talk about your time at medical school, you know." Ash unwrapped her sandwich but avoided eye contact with Nat. "It won't kill me."

"It's not important." Nat cleared her voice. "It was a stupid story anyway."

"But you still sailed through your finals," Ash said, "despite your annoying anatomy." Unexpectedly she wanted to know. Why, though, knowing Nat was uneasy about it? To make her squirm? No, that wasn't it. Ash bit into her sandwich. She wanted to know, to find out how Nat's life had panned out compared to hers. Gaps needed to be filled.

"Yeah, I did okay," Nat replied.

"The letters after your name tell me you did more than okay," Ash said.

"Funny how being up here, far from London, makes all those letters seem so immaterial," Nat said.

Ash turned her head slightly, watching as Nat stared out ahead of her, soaking up the view.

"Belfast will be nicer than London, though," Ash said. The words sounded forced, almost as though she didn't want to speak them. Didn't want them to be true. "Can't get much greener than Ireland."

"I guess." Nat unwrapped her sandwich, then hesitated. "No, Belfast's going to be great." She shot a smile to Ash. "I'm going to give it some of that positivity you talked to me about on the boat yesterday."

Ash felt a stab of disappointment, immediately followed by shame at her hypocrisy. What made her think she could dish out advice to Nat, then be frustrated when Nat acted on it?

"Back there on the hill," Nat said, breaking Ash's train of thought, "I told you I wished something."

"You did." Ash narrowed her eyes and peered out in front of her. She wouldn't prompt, or question. She would just let Nat tell her what she so obviously felt she needed to tell her.

"I wish things had turned out differently." Nat's brow creased. "That...we'd stuck together. If I'd known at eighteen that I'd lose my two best friends before I'd reached forty then I'd have—"

"Thought more about your actions?" Ash offered.

Nat pulled her gaze to Widgeon, weaving his way round the rocks to the side of them.

"I'd have tried to think more about the repercussions," Nat replied. "I lost you, and my friendship with Livvy was never the same either."

"Seriously?" Ash twisted her body round to face Nat better. "You and Livvy?"

"Oh, it wasn't really anything like that."

Nat was backtracking, Ash could tell.

"She couldn't understand what had happened," Nat said, "or that I'd never tell her."

"Did you two fall out?" Ash was astonished. She'd had no idea. Sure, she knew Livvy was upset at what she'd perceived as a major falling out between Ash and Nat, but she'd never told Ash any more than that.

"For a while," Nat said. "That's why I ended up going to uni in Edinburgh." She looked at Ash. "Oh, we made up. It was all a storm in a teacup."

"I'd hardly call you finishing with me a storm in a—"

"I didn't mean me and you."

The severity in Nat's voice surprised Ash. Her own knee-jerk sharpness back to Nat surprised her further.

"Well it was a big deal to me." Ash tossed the remains of her sandwich to one side, no longer hungry.

"Me and you," Nat said, "is a whole different ball game." Now she'd finally spoken again, her tone was gentler. She paused, and not for the first time over the past five minutes, Ash wished she could read her mind. "One which maybe we ought to talk about again," she offered. "We do still need to talk about us, I think."

"Did you know the name of this hill comes from the Cornish for *hill of swallows?*" Ash screwed up her foil and put it into her pocket. "No swallows today, though."

"You're changing the subject."

"I know." Ash jumped up, brushing breadcrumbs from her trousers. "Guess I'm not in the mood for talking right now." She hastened away from Nat and clambered over a pile of small rocks, whistling sharply to Widgeon as she did so.

She headed towards a man-made rock pile, savouring the hill air that buffed around her, occasionally making her jacket billow. Blowing Nat's words away from her. She crouched at the base of the rock pile, studying the myriad rocks that other climbers had placed there over the years, each one of whom probably had their own stories to tell. Ash picked up a small rock and studied it. What had Livvy said to Nat all those years ago? She'd never told Ash any of it, had never even given a hint that the pair of them had fallen out, even if their falling out had only been brief. Ash turned the rock over in her hands, half expecting Nat to join her. She didn't. The rock was smooth. A good size. Perfect. Had Livvy guessed it had been more than just two friends drifting apart? This rock would nestle nicely with the others in the cairn. Just another rock from another person on the hill with another story to tell. Now Nat wanted to tell Ash her own story, but Ash wasn't sure she wanted to hear it.

She leaned closer, placing her rock in a convenient small crevice, then wiggled it a little until it settled into its space. She slipped a look back down to Nat, still sitting on her rock, still eating her sandwich. Ash watched her for a while, secretly wanting her to come up and join her, whilst at the same time wanting to be alone so she could process her thoughts which were scrolling through her mind at a hundred miles an hour.

Ash picked up another stone and rubbed her thumb over it. And what about her and Nat's future now?

*We still need to talk about us.*

"We do." Ash murmured, wiping the dirt from the stone. "We don't." She watched as the lumps of mud fell in small clumps from it.

There was no *us*, even though Ash had liked the way Nat's words had set off a clatter of confusion inside her. Had loved the way in which Nat had said it had muddied her mind with a bewildering mixture of excitement and disquiet.

Ash stood, dusting the dirt from her hands.

Could there ever be an us? Only she, Ash thought, as she took one final look back down to Nat, could answer that particular question.

## Chapter Eighteen

Nat felt the first drops of rain just as she swallowed the last of her sandwich. She scrunched up her foil wrapping, stuffed it into her rucksack, then glanced up to the heavy purple sky, blinking as raindrops, fatter now, fell onto her face.

"We need to go."

Ash's breathless voice sounded somewhere behind her. Nat turned just in time to see her hurrying back down the hill towards her, sending gravel tumbling down in her haste.

"What were you doing up there all that time anyway?" Nat asked as she stood.

"Adding to the cairn."

Nat followed Ash's gaze back up the hill.

"All this time?" Nat asked.

"All this time." Ash grabbed her rucksack. "We really need to go."

The rain was falling faster now, drumming against the rocks with increased fervour, sending water spraying out with each hit. Nat shouldered her rucksack, shuddering as water from it trickled down her neck, and followed Ash, already four or five steps ahead of her. Lightning flashed in the distance, the sky now darkening with alarming speed, the thrashing rain greasing the already precarious rocks and familiar gravel path. To her side, the dark mass of the forest which they'd walked through on their way up quivered as the thunder grumbled in reply to the lightning, already much closer than it was before.

"Does the weather always change this quickly up here?" Nat fell into step beside Ash, casting a worried look behind her as the dark clouds continued to chase them back down the hill.

"Always." Ash laughed. She batted the rain from her face, then flicked it from her fingers. "Bodmin Moor isn't for the faint-hearted." She flashed a grin at Nat.

Nat glanced at her, surprised to see the glee in her face. Nat, her wet trousers plastered to her cold legs, her red hands so frozen she could no longer feel her fingers, felt anything but gleeful.

"You're mad." Nat shook her head, then hunched her shoulders as another roll of thunder swept over their heads, this time accompanied by an immediate and fleeting burst of lightning.

They scrambled back down the hill, their silence only punctured by the hammering rain which drummed against their waterproof jackets and the rocks. An occasional sharp whistle from Ash to Widgeon kept him from straying too far, but the dog seemed as keen as Nat to get back to the safety of Ash's truck which was still too far away for Nat's liking.

"My mother always said"—Ash called out to be heard over the sound of the rain—"that there's no such thing as bad weather. Only insufficient clothing."

Nat looked down at her sodden trousers.

"I always thought your mother was eccentric," she said. "Eccentric but—"

It all happened in a heartbeat. In amongst the chaos of the rain, the thunder, Widgeon running between them, and the glassy granite rocks, Nat didn't see exactly what happened, but the shriek from Ash was enough to tell her that whatever had happened was bad.

She was at Ash's side in a heartbeat, stumbling over tufts of wet grass and crawling the last few inches on her hands and knees to get to her. Ash had slipped and tumbled away from her, coming to rest further down the hill. She was lying in the foetal position, cradling her arm against her chest, and as Nat scrabbled over to her, she could see her face was twisted tight in pain. Nat wasn't sure what was worse: Ash's look of utter anguish, or the rain continuing to pound relentlessly onto her blanched face, insensitive to her obvious agony.

"Ash." Nat knelt next to Ash and wiped the wet from her eyes, still screwed up tight against her pain. "What happened?" The dislocation of her shoulder was obvious; less clear were any other injuries. Instinct kicked in, and Nat knew she had decisions to make. She looked down the hill, calculating the amount of time it would take them to return to Ash's truck, then back to Ash. When Ash's answer was too hoarse with pain to be heard, Nat leaned over her and scanned around her, frantically looking for any rocks nearby that Ash could have hit her head on. She could see nothing obvious, except for the slab of shiny, wet granite Ash had evidently slipped on, further up the hill. Relief flooded Nat's senses.

"Did you hit your head on anything on the way down? Ash? Ash? This is important." Nat's fingers moved expertly up and down Ash's spine and neck. "Can you feel this? And your toes?" She gently pushed Widgeon away as he leaned against her, intrigued at his owner's apparent new game.

"Shoulder. It's…"

Ash moved and winced.

"I know. Don't move."

"I can feel you touching me," Ash whispered. "And I can feel my legs and toes. I didn't bang my head. It's all good." She gingerly straightened her legs and rolled onto her back, still cradling her arm against her, then turned her head to one side, blinking the rain away from her eyes. "It's just my shoulder. It's gone again."

"I said don't move," Nat chastised. She hunkered over Ash, her body sheltering Ash's face from the rain, and again started feeling her way up and down her neck. "And that's all okay? Can I move your arm a little so I can see your shoulder better?"

Rain continued to drench them, and Nat angrily blinked away the raindrops that dripped from her hat and down her forehead, blurring her vision. She gently moved Ash, apologizing when she cried out.

"You've dislocated it before, right?"

"Twice." Ash's face creased. "But not for a few years now."

Nat shifted her position. She smoothed away a stray strand of wet hair that had escaped from Ash's hat and gazed down at her, her mind in chaos. Sure, she'd done reductions before, but not for many years. And certainly not on the side of a rain-lashed hill.

"The answer's yes." Ash's eyes met hers. "Because I know what you're about to say. You're going to put it back in, right? So the answer's yes. Do it."

Nat shot a look back down the hill, imagining Holly Cottage, a hopelessly long distance away, remembering the bog they'd both struggled through at the start of their walk. The weather, the quagmire at the entrance to the car park, and the terrain all made it impossible for Nat to even contemplate guiding Ash back down with a dislocated shoulder. She angrily swiped away a raindrop from the end of her nose and gazed back down at Ash. What choice did she have?

"It'll be quick," she said softly to Ash, "I promise you."

"Okay." Ash blinked slowly, whatever colour was left in her face quickly draining away. "I remember last time it was only mildly agonizing." She gave a faint smile.

"Who's the doctor here?" Nat returned her smile. She scrambled to her feet, cursing as her foot slipped on the wet grass, and unzipped her soaking jacket. "You'll not feel a thing this time, I guarantee it."

"Hmm."

Nat raised an eyebrow to Ash, then swiftly pulled her hat off, followed by her long-sleeved shirt. Her T-shirt underneath immediately began to dampen in the driving rain, and she hastily shrugged her jacket back on, zipping it back up.

"Ta-da." Nat held up her long-sleeved shirt. "Sling. It'll allow your muscles to relax after I've popped you back in."

"Nice colour." Ash's eyes rolled in her head. "I think I'm delirious."

"No," Nat said, pulling the arms taut on her makeshift sling, "you're just plain daft." She fell to her knees again and scooted her wet beanie back onto her head, grimacing at the sensation of the cold material against her warm head. "I'm going to slowly rotate your arm," she said, concentrating on the task at hand. "It should go back in easily." Nat gazed down at Ash. "I'm very good."

"I hope so."

"Trust me." Nat smoothed her hands up and down Ash's arm and held her gaze. "So where did you have your last reduction done?"

"Local A and E. Gabe took me."

"Did it hurt?" Nat extended Ash's arm, rotating it slowly, her eyes never leaving Ash's.

"Not much. But then I had gas and air there."

"Did it take long?" Nat asked, noticing the flicker of panic on Ash's face.

"No, it was...that's a bit uncomfortable." Ash's face twisted and she rolled her head away from Nat's gaze, her eyes closing.

"I'm sorry, I'm sorry." Nat stopped what she was doing and smoothed Ash's hair again. "It'll be over soon, I promise."

At Ash's nod, Nat flexed Ash's shoulder again, hearing the noise she'd been waiting for, then drew her hand slowly down it until their fingers were interlocked.

"Better?" she asked, smiling when she saw Ash look at her arm. "Pain all gone?"

"It's done?"

"I told you I was good." Nat draped Ash's arm over Ash's chest and looked down at their entwined hands, Ash's cold and damp in hers. She closed her other hand over it and squeezed, gratified when she felt the merest hint of warmth peeking through. "Want to try and sit up?"

Ash nodded.

"Careful." Nat reached over and placed her hands behind Ash's shoulders, gently helping her sit up. She watched, relieved, as Ash's face, previously blanched a sickly shade of white, gradually grew pinker as her blood pulsed.

"Feels good." Ash waggled her fingers.

"You'll need this." Nat picked up her shirt and placed it around Ash's neck, tying the arms together to make her makeshift sling, then carefully placed Ash's arm into it. "Still okay?"

"Fine."

"No pins and needles?" Nat asked. "No numbness?"

Ash shook her head.

Relieved, Nat sat back and hugged her knees. Widgeon joined her, pressing his warm but soaked body up against her side. Nat scratched at the fur on his head, smiling as he emitted a long, deep sigh.

"I think he likes you," Ash said.

"So he should," Nat replied. "I just fixed his owner." She looked at Ash. "We should get you in the dry. You don't want to add pneumonia to your list of ills."

"Is it even still raining?" Ash lifted her eyes to the sky and blinked. "I hadn't noticed."

"Well, you've been preoccupied throwing yourself down hills." Nat softly pulled on Widgeon's velvety ear, then stood. She held out a hand to Ash.

"Ready?" she asked.

"As I'll ever be." Ash reached up and took Nat's hand.

"Steady," Nat said. "You'll be a bit light-headed."

She carefully pulled, guiding Ash to her feet, then instantly drew Ash to her as Ash stumbled.

"Okay?" Nat's arms were gentle around Ash, their cheeks touching. She could hear Ash's shallow breaths, feel her shivering slightly against her body. "You're shaking."

"I'm cold." Ash's breath was warm against Nat's skin. "And dizzy."

"I said you would be."

Nat closed her eyes, enjoying the feel of Ash against her. Just like at Paddington Station the week before, Nat was surprised to feel that Ash's body felt the same as she'd done all those years before. No, perhaps not *quite* the same. Now Ash was more toned. Less squidgy than she was at eighteen. Nat smiled against Ash's hair at that thought, then frowned as a past image flashed in her mind. A woodland drenched in summer rain. A hug, just like this one. Heads buried in necks. Hair tickling cheeks. Then a long kiss. The sweetest, longest kiss Nat had ever had.

Nat pulled back. She was aware her breathing had deepened, so she turned away, afraid that Ash would notice. She stared out in front of her, trying to see through the grey clouds, trying to focus her mind.

Belfast.

Her familiar mantra chanted in her head. Time to think of Belfast. This time next month she could be there. She *had* to be. All she had to do was make one quick phone call, and…

Nat turned to see Ash staring at her. There was a look in her eyes that Nat hadn't seen before. It was a look of hope.

❖

"Jeez, you go out for a ramble on the hills and come back looking like this."

Ash forced a smile at Gabe's fussing. She allowed herself to be steered to her sofa, grumbling all the while that she wasn't an invalid, then gratefully sank down into it, ignoring the fact she was caked in mud and now, in all probability, so was her sofa.

Gabe and Nat stood in front of her and stared down.

"Do you like my makeshift sling?" Ash ran her hand over it. "It's Nat's."

"Nice colour." Gabe nodded in approval.

"That's what I said." Ash gingerly moved her arm and nestled it tenderly against her chest. "Although I was delirious at the time."

"You should get out of your wet clothes," Nat said, Ash shifting slightly as she sat down next to her.

"Still feel okay?" Nat asked, smoothing a hand over her shoulder. "Absolutely sure there's no numbness in your arm or fingers?"

"It's all right," Ash replied. "Just stiff."

"Don't forget to take the painkillers like I told you, okay?"

Ash nodded, aware at just how much her body had tensed at Nat's proximity and touch. Her nerve endings tingled as if on high alert, as if the next touch from Nat would set off a chain reaction throughout her body. Her breathing was hollow, every fibre twitching.

"You'll have stretched your muscles," Nat said, resting back into the sofa, "so it's important to keep the sling on." She looked at Ash, their eyes meeting. "You'll need to rest it," she said, "and when I say rest, I mean *rest*."

"Yes, Doctor."

"Seriously. So that means if you need help with anything for the next twenty-four hours," Nat continued, "you call either me or Gabe, okay?"

"Okay."

"Then I'll show you some exercises to strengthen it." Nat smiled at her. "I'll get you sorted again, I promise."

"Thank you." Ash held Nat's look, grateful for everything she'd done.

"I'll go for now," Nat said, pulling her gaze away and getting to her feet. "So I can get changed." She signalled towards Ash. "You really should change out of those wet clothes too."

"You could use my shower," Ash said. Despite her pain, she wasn't ready for the day to end. Not just yet. Not like this. "Borrow some clothes. We're about the same size." She coughed slightly. Images of Nat that had threatened for days, certainly since Wimbledon Common, trampled through her mind. Now, a shower image had just been added to the list. Ash cleared her throat again. "If you want, that is."

"No, I'll head off." Nat paused slightly, then nodded, as if her mind was finally made up. "It's getting dark. I can be back at my B and B in fifteen minutes."

"I'll drive you." Gabe picked up his woollen hat from the sofa, then crammed it messily onto his head. "You'll be okay?" he asked Ash.

"I'll be fine." Ash made to stand, accepting the hand from Gabe that was offered to her. "I'll send Widgeon out with a note round his neck if I pass out," she said, adding, "Joke!" when she saw the look on Nat's face.

"I'll be back in half an hour," Gabe said, his concern touching Ash.

She walked with Nat and Gabe to the door, feeling the adrenaline of the day begin to dwindle to exhaustion. All Ash wanted now was a hot shower, PJs, dinner, and bed. In that order. Nat too, she thought, looked shattered, and the thought pricked at her heart. Perhaps she should try harder to make Nat stay? The idea of Nat going back to her B & B on her own was awful.

"Won't you stay?" The words were out before Ash knew it. "Please?"

Nat turned to look at her, and Ash could see the mixture of emotions on her face: tiredness mixed in with the confusion over what she really wanted to do.

"I…" Nat began.

*Stay.* Ash held her eye.

"…should really go."

The heaviness in Ash's chest at Nat's reply was compounded by the conviction with which Nat had said it. Ash immediately felt foolish. Cheated, even. Of course Nat would want to go—why wouldn't she? She was cold and wet, and more than likely already fed up with Ash's company for the day.

"Of course." Ash smiled tightly in an attempt to mask her disappointment. "I'm sorry. Of course you need to get home and dry as soon as possible." She walked to the door, ignoring Gabe's look, and opened it. "Shall I text you in the morning?"

The expression on Nat's face was tangible.

"Sure," Nat eventually said. "In the morning." She reached out and took Ash's hand. "You should get some sleep."

Ash nodded. Nat moved away slowly, letting her hand remain in contact with Ash's until the very last moment possible. Ash lowered her eyes, feeling drawn by her touch. Pulled to her. With a quick smile to Gabe, and an assurance to him that she'd be fine on her own, she closed the door behind them and stood, listening to their footsteps as they receded down the path outside.

The silence of the empty room filled her ears. Ash rested her forehead against the cool wood of her door frame, feeling her cheeks dampen with tears she didn't even know were coming. Banging her palm angrily against the frame, she shoved herself away and strode to the bathroom, hoping the hot shower would be just what she needed to clear her mind.

❖

Gabe was talking boats. In fact, Gabe had been talking boats from the minute they'd got in his car, and Nat still didn't have a clue what he was talking about. His words vacillated around her as she looked out of the passenger window, watching the countryside smudge past her in the fading light.

She should have stayed. She wanted to stay, but of course Ash might have just been being polite in asking her to. She'd looked exhausted, and no wonder. The last thing Ash would have wanted was for Nat to accept and for her to have to play host for the next few hours.

She stared straight out of the windscreen in front of her. She'd made the right decision, she knew; if only her heart would understand that and cease its increasing heaviness with each bit of distance Gabe was now putting between her and Ash.

"Does this mean the end of Livvy's wish list for you and Ash?"

"I'm sorry?"

Gabe was talking. Nat rubbed at her eyes.

"I'm sorry," she repeated. "I was miles away. I'm really tired." She smiled over to him.

"Sea and mountain air does that to you." Gabe laughed. "The list? Will Ash be able to do the rest of it now her shoulder's crocked?"

"She'll need to rest it, that's for sure." Nat's body tensed as she muffled a yawn. "Otherwise it'll keep popping out."

"Nice." Gabe pulled a face.

"Although Ash never really was one for resting."

"You remember her well." Gabe laughed loudly. "Trying to get Ash to rest is like trying to keep a puppy from wriggling. Impossible."

"She loves her life here, doesn't she?" Nat said. "Her boat and the sea and everything."

Gabe shot her a quick look. "She does," he said. "Very much."

"I could sense in London she was desperate to get back here." Nat looked back out of the passenger window. "I can kind of see why."

"It gets you like that," Gabe said. "It's a very stress-free place to live. Why do you think so many Londoners have houses down here?"

"Mm." Nat had no answer to that. Her mind had drifted, again, apparently to resume its search of answers to the questions it was persistently finding.

Two days. That was all she had left, and the sadness that thought stirred up in her was almost painful. In three days she'd be back in London. In a few more, possibly Belfast. The pain intensified.

"We only have two wishes left," Nat suddenly said, voicing her thoughts, "so it's not as if we totally failed Livvy."

"You've done well." Gabe looked impressed. "I'd say Livvy would be very happy if she were here now."

Dusk had inched into darkness by the time Gabe pulled his car up outside Nat's B & B. She thanked Gabe, thanking him further for his offer to collect her again in the morning, then got out of the car. She stood in front of the B & B and gazed at the front door, listening to the diminishing sound of Gabe's engine as he disappeared into the night. Back to St. Kerryan. Back to Ash.

With a deep breath, Nat hitched her bag onto her shoulder and wandered wearily to the door.

❖

Ash held a hand to the running water, allowing it to trickle through her fingers and scurry down her bare arm until it dripped from her elbow. Once she was satisfied with the temperature, she stepped cautiously into the shower cubicle, anticipating some discomfort in her shoulder when she pushed against the wall opposite her to steady herself, relieved when there was none.

The hot water felt good, even if it did nothing to soothe the ache behind her eyes. Ash lifted her face to it, enjoying the feeling, then stepped fully under the flow. Hot needles pricked at her skin, inviting a brief whole-body shiver until she became used to the feeling of warmth and allowed the water to soak her. The citrus blast from her shower gel uplifted her senses, making her feel more energized than she had been moments before, and as she scrubbed at her skin, a hunger that had been missing since she'd fallen on the hillside hours before suddenly appeared.

Remembering, Ash looked down at her shoulder. She warily ran her fingertips over it, pressing lightly at her bone. Nat had been awesome on the hill. No, more than awesome. Her hero. Ash smiled down to the swirling water at her feet. Nat had been her hero. She hadn't flapped, hadn't panicked. She'd just done what she'd had to do, and Ash hadn't felt a thing. And all the attention she'd given her afterwards? Ash's smile deepened. That had been equally awesome.

Nat had guided Ash back down the hill as though Ash were a fine piece of china. On the way home, too, she'd taken care of her, asking every five minutes if she was okay, whether she was in pain. Nat had been so lovely. Nat had *cared*. Sure, Ash was certain she was lovely with all her patients, but there was something more that afternoon, even if Ash couldn't quite fathom what it was. There was…genuine worry and affection.

Ash switched her shower off and stood, watching the gurgling plughole as the soapy water hiccuped and bubbled and finally disappeared. Images of the whole day came and went, immediately and absurdly followed by those of Nat and a man—whom she assumed to be Richard—together. She slipped a towel from its rail and rubbed at her face, trying to erase the images, angry with herself for allowing her brain to dictate her thoughts without doing anything to try and stop it.

Ash pulled the towel from her face and caught sight of herself unexpectedly in her mirror. She peered into her own face, almost for reassurance from her own reflection, tilting her head first to the left, then to the right, and searched her own eyes, wondering what Nat thought—if she thought anything at all—when she looked her. Ash knew she didn't have the overt prettiness of some other women, but what she did possess were strong features that had become more striking with maturity, and which she knew other women envied, from their comments over the years.

She bent her head closer to the mirror, her breath leaving small opaque circles on it. Was that how Nat saw her too? Her thoughts returned by their own will to Richard. Ash knew she shouldn't care that Nat had been married, but she did. The thought of her being with someone else cut her deeply, and even though she appreciated the marriage hadn't lasted, there was also an overwhelming feeling of sadness that after they'd parted Nat had been able to have a relationship of sorts when Ash had festered in her own misery, unable to hold down any kind of anything, even if her arresting good looks *were* appreciated by other women.

Ash lifted a brow and smiled at her own reflection at the irony.

But she knew that her sadness was purely selfish. Regret for herself that she'd never been able to give herself to anyone other than Nat. The sadness was compounded by the stark realization that she would *never* be able to give herself to anyone other than Nat in the future either. How could she, when all she wanted now was to be near Nat again, to share her space, and hear her breathe, just like before?

Ash rubbed harder at her skin, enjoying the feeling of the rough towel against her. She'd fought so hard over the last week to ignore her growing feelings, but no matter how much she put her fingers in her ears, those feelings just shouted louder to be heard until, finally, they could no longer be dismissed.

The shudder of the front door downstairs told her Gabe had returned.

"That you?" she called out from the bathroom.

"'Tis me." Gabe's gravelly voice shouted back up to her.

Ash carefully pulled on her pyjamas, warm from the radiator, and went back downstairs. Gabe was already sitting in his favoured chair by the window, Widgeon on his back at his feet.

"You didn't have to come back, you know." Ash eased herself into her chair. "I'll be fine."

"I know." Gabe threw a blue package over to her. "Nat told me to get this sling for you. I picked it up at the pharmacy on the way back."

Ash stole a look to Nat's shirt, draped over the back of the sofa.

"I kind of liked using her top as a sling," Ash found herself saying. She looked back to Gabe. "It smelled of her." She sensed her face growing hot.

"And Nat smells lovely." Gabe smiled. "That girl uses some expensive perfume, you know."

Ash gazed down to Widgeon on the floor, his barrelled chest now being rubbed by Gabe's socked foot.

"I think…" She frowned, rethought her words, then continued. "I want…" The words wouldn't come. Ash scratched at her hair, annoyed with herself. "I don't want her to go."

"So you have to tell her that."

"How can I?" Ash lifted her eyes to his. "When I know she'll be leaving in a few weeks' time?"

"Maybe if you told her how you feel," Gabe said, "and knowing how she feels about you, things could change."

"Do you think?" Ash held his gaze. "Do you think any of this could change?"

"Only you two can decide that," Gabe said, getting to his feet. "Only you two can decide both your futures."

## CHAPTER NINETEEN

The sea smelt good.

Nat pulled her jacket tight around her and closed her eyes, letting the light sea breeze toss her hair around her face. The step she was sitting on was cold and damp, but Nat didn't care. She was too busy tasting the sea, just as Ash said she liked to do.

It was eight a.m. A night interrupted by endless thoughts of Ash, London, and Belfast had meant Nat had been awake since six, up since seven, and walking on the beach ever since. She'd watched the sun rise over the line of the sea, a shimmering jelly of orange slowly peeking up over the horizon, and had imagined Ash, in her cottage further down the coast, fast asleep.

Too many times already that morning she'd wanted to ring Ash, telling herself she just wanted to know how she was, and whether her shoulder was holding out. The reality of it, though, was she simply wanted to hear her voice. Now, sitting on the steps that led down to the beach, the sun now slowly creeping up higher into the sky, Nat desperately tried to focus her mind on the day ahead.

If only it was that simple.

Everything inside her wanted to jump into a taxi and go to Ash's cottage right now. And yet, a voice inside her head told her she couldn't. She shouldn't. To rush over there, desperate to see Ash again would just confirm everything she already knew: she loved her.

A force, quite unlike anything she'd felt since she'd first fallen for Ash as a naive fourteen-year-old, had marched in from the sidelines and was now threatening to overwhelm her. Nat stared down at the pebbles, the tiredness that had nothing to do with her lack of sleep making her limbs feel weighted down, and wondered exactly when it had all happened. Even though they'd not been alone much in London, she'd sensed the tension between them whenever their eyes met. Whenever she closed her eyes, she could see her, smell her, remember the taste of her, and now the overwhelming strength of her feelings for Ash was beautiful and terrifying in equal measures.

Nat returned her gaze to the sea. It sparkled, crystal clear, as though her renewed love for Ash had instantly made everything else in her life clearer. Noises were louder. Lines were sharper. The air was cleaner, and Nat felt a clarity and honesty for the first time in years.

"Nice morning."

The call from just in front of her caught Nat's attention. A man, walking his dogs, waving. Nat smiled. "Isn't it just?"

"Bit chilly." The man rubbed his hands up and down his arms and returned Nat's smile.

"It is. Yes."

The man carried on.

The breeze returned, stronger now. Nat closed her eyes to it and took her mind back sixteen years, seeing her and Ash as teenagers. She'd loved her then and she loved her now. So why was the happiness she felt at her own admission of love combined with a sense of deep disquiet? She drew in a long breath, then bent over, picking up a small pebble and tossing it a few feet from her, listening in satisfaction at the pleasing *crack* when it landed in amongst some other pebbles.

Because Ash had made it clear to her that loving her was pointless. Ash had already told her she couldn't love her, so why had Nat allowed herself to fall for her all over again?

Nat blinked the wind from her eyes. She should never have let Ash back into her heart, and she knew with certainty Ash would never let her back in. Nat jumped up from her step, wiping at her wind-stung eyes. A discreet rumble from her empty stomach told her she'd skipped breakfast one too many times over the past few days, and as she made her way back to her B & B, her mind was already on what she was going to eat.

It was either that, or drown in her thoughts of Ash.

❖

"You opened your letter."

Ash looked up as Gabe leaned over her shoulder and peered down at the letter on her lap.

"I did," Ash said, folding it back up. "How else am I supposed to find out what's next?"

"You won't be doing a next," Gabe replied.

"Who says?"

"Me."

"You're a doctor now, are you?" Ash said as she watched Gabe fall into the chair next to her.

"No, but Nat is," Gabe said, "and she'll tell you exactly the same thing."

"She can try. Anyway, why are you here?" She glanced at her watch. "You said after nine."

"So I'm early."

"A whole hour early."

"I wanted to make sure you were okay." Gabe frowned. "Isn't that allowed?" He lifted his chin to the letter. "So, what's next?"

"Sea fishing." Ash gave a hollow laugh. "Like that's going to happen now." She adjusted her Polysling, grimacing a little.

"It still hurts?"

"Just a bit tender." Ash rested her head back. "I guess some tendons got twanged."

"You should call Nat," Gabe said. "I'll bet she's sitting over in Trevelyan right now, wondering how you are." He paused. "Besides, you'll need some company here today."

"You can be my company too." Even Ash knew she didn't sound convincing. "You, me, and Nat can all out somewhere together."

"You know I'm taking the boat out today," Gabe said. "The wildlife group?"

Ash groaned. A group of amateur wildlife photographers had chartered the boat for the day. Gabe was skippering, and the money was way too good for him to turn down just so Ash wouldn't have to spend time alone with Nat.

"Sure," she said. "I totally forgot."

"Anyway, Nat will be expecting to come over," Gabe said reasonably. "I'm sure she'll enjoy nursing you until I get back."

Even Ash was impressed with the speed with which he dodged her thrown cushion.

Nat answered on the second ring.

"Hey."

"Hey."

Within that split second of their greeting, Ash's thought process spun, absorbing the sound of her voice, imagining with vivid precision Nat sitting in her room. She thought about what she was wearing, how she was sitting, what she was feeling right now. Hair up or down? Ash loved it when she wore it up. Had she eaten? When would she be coming over? Did she even *want* to come over?

"How's your shoulder?" Nat asked, breaking Ash's train of thoughts. "Did Gabe buy you the Polysling like I told him? Have you taken your painkillers today? And you *so* better be resting it like I told you to, missy."

A warmth spread about Ash. When Gabe fussed about her she found herself getting irritated with him. With Nat it was perfect and lovely, and made her feel as though she was wrapping a cosy blanket about her.

"It's okay," Ash replied. "I have the sling, and yes, I've taken two painkillers already this morning, and yes, I've been resting it."

"Good." Nat paused. "Now maybe I can stop worrying about you."

"You didn't need to worry about me." Ash couldn't stop the smile that spread across her face.

"Yes, I did," Nat replied softly.

A silence skimmed between them.

"So…" Ash looked up at the ceiling. "About today."

"Well you can forget about fishing for a start."

Ash laughed. "You opened your letter too, huh?"

"I could…just come over and hang out with you instead," Nat said slowly.

Ash's stomach twinged.

"You could," she said, "unless you'd rather do something on your own, now we've had to abandon the wish list? I don't know. Sightseeing, or…?" Her words hung in the air.

"There's nothing else I'd rather be doing," Nat said, "than spending the day with you."

"Good." Ash's breathing slowed. "Me neither."

"If I get a taxi over for, say, midday?"

"You could make it earlier." Ash swallowed. "If you want."

"Ten-ish?"

"But only if you want."

"I want." Nat laughed. "Trust me, Ash. I want."

Nat looked at the leather bracelet on her wrist. The skin around it looked different. Less angry. She pushed her sleeve back down over it, concealing the bracelet again, and returned her gaze to the bedroom window. She would tell Callum on her return to London, Nat decided, that just a few days in the countryside had abated her anxieties. He'd be pleased, maybe even cut her a bit of slack for a while. Perhaps—and this would be a first—she could even skip a session. Nat smiled to herself at the thought.

The ring of her phone brought with it the usual split-second skip of her heart and hope that it would be Ash's name waiting for her, even though she'd only spoken to her five minutes before. Nat turned from the window and snatched her phone up from her bedside cabinet, her hope melting into delight when she saw Chloe's name instead of Ash's.

"Hey, you," she said when she answered. "How's your grandma?"

"She's better," Chloe said. "Well, she's eaten something this morning, so she says she's well on the way."

"That's a relief." Nat walked from her bed and unhooked her jacket from the back of her door. "Does she still have a fever?"

"She says no."

Nat sensed Chloe pause, so waited.

"Nat?" Chloe asked.

"Mm-hmm?" Nat shook her jacket out straighter, then laid it out on the bed.

"Can I come down?"

"Here?"

"Yeah. I'm gutted I'm not with you guys right now."

A myriad of emotions hit Nat at Chloe's words. She wanted to see her, of course she did, yet at the same time…

"Of course you can come down." Nat shook the thought away. "Ash will be so happy for you to come and hang out with us."

Nat stared at the wall. Would Ash be happy? Or would she be thinking the same as Nat—that they only had one more day together before Nat had to return to London, and it would be perfect if they could spend it alone?

"Come down." Nat shook the thought away. She was being selfish, she knew. Of course Chloe should come and be with them, even if it was only for twenty-four hours.

"Awesome." Chloe sounded breathless. "I'm kind of packed already, so—"

"You can come down today." Nat finished her sentence for her.

"If that's cool?" Chloe asked. "I figured you were due back tomorrow anyway, so we could travel back to London together."

"Sounds good." Nat held back a sigh. How could her time in Cornwall be nearly over already?

"There's a train at eight forty-five," Chloe said, "so I could be with you by half past one."

Nat's head felt muddied by the unexpected change of plans. She would be with Ash by ten; that would give them three and a half hours' alone time before Chloe arrived, and then everything went back to how it had been in London. The cocoon they'd created for themselves would be no more, and then they'd have to emerge back into the real world.

Nat frowned. She could do it. *They* could do it.

"We'll see you at Truro at one thirty then," she said. "Well, it'll be us and Gabe. Ash can't drive. Long story."

"Ash can't drive?"

"I'll explain when I see you."

Widgeon was sunning himself in the garden, having snagged a tiny pocket of morning sunshine next to the shed, when her taxi finally pulled up outside the cottage. Nat thumbed a note from her purse and handed it to her taxi driver, declining his half-hearted offer of change, and got out. The thump of Widgeon's tail on the grass told her he'd seen her, but the sun was evidently proving too irresistible for him to get up and meet her. Instead, his eyes followed her journey up the front path and straight to Ash's front door, before closing against the sun again.

Nat rang the doorbell, looking over her shoulder to see the taxi bumping its way back down the track and out of sight. A tinge of nervousness at the prospect of spending the entire day with Ash again flickered and immediately extinguished inside her the second Ash opened the door and their eyes met, to be replaced instead with an overwhelming feeling of contentment.

"You look tired." Nat studied Ash's face. Her eyes, clouded underneath, looked leaden. "Is it your shoulder?"

"A bit."

Nat stepped into the cottage.

"It was okay first thing," Ash said, motioning for Nat to head into the lounge. "Feels a bit stiff now though."

"It will do for a while yet." Nat sat down, watching as Ash sat down in the chair opposite her. "But you've taken some painkillers, haven't you?"

"Yes, Doctor." Ash saluted with her good arm.

Nat focused on Ash's Polysling, the protective feelings that had overwhelmed her on the hill the day before returning to her, stronger than ever.

"Force of habit." Nat settled back.

"Is your bedside manner like this with all your patients?" Ash caught her eye.

"Not all." Nat held her look long enough for Ash to look away first.

They were silent for a while as the seconds ticked past, their eyes meeting briefly, accompanied by a smile, then looking away again, only to come back together a few seconds later.

"We'll have company this afternoon, by the way." Nat was the first to speak. "Arriving on the one-thirty train."

"Oh?"

"Chloe," Nat said.

"She's coming here?"

Nat studied Ash's face. Had she imagined the look that had flickered across it?

"Judy's feeling a bit better," Nat said, "so Chloe wants to spend the day with us, then travel back with me tomorrow."

"That's sweet," Ash replied. She paused. "Although…"

Nat raised her eyebrows. "Although?"

A smile spread across Ash's face. "This is going to sound terribly selfish," she said, "but I suppose I've kind of liked it being just the two of us." Ash held up her hands. "Not that I didn't enjoy London with her, but…you know."

"I know exactly." Nat's smile mirrored Ash's. "It's been good, hasn't it? Just the two of us."

Their gazes parted.

"How about a walk before Chloe gets here?" Finally Ash spoke. "A walk on the dunes might be nice this morning."

"I'm up for it."

"We can walk from here," Ash said, "along the coastal path."

Nat nodded as Ash continued to tell her about the dunes. Nat was no longer listening closely though. Instead, as Ash spoke, Nat's gaze absently travelled her face, her eyes, seeing Ash's range of expressions as she enthused about the beauty of the dunes, whilst at the same time apologizing for not being able to do anything more exciting than walking now she was injured. Nat didn't care. Ash had just voiced her own thoughts; that she'd enjoyed the time they'd spent alone just as much as she had. Now, with each word, look, and gesture from Ash, the invisible pull gathered her ever closer to her. Nat craved her, letting images of them together—images she'd managed to block out for years—filter into her mind. Images of the two of them together, aching for one another's touch. Of the intensity between them, of the heat and the passion they'd once shared.

In that moment, sitting in Ash's front room, Nat thought she'd never loved her more, or wanted her more. Ash, she was sure, needed her too, and the innate protection Nat felt for her surged as she realized she wanted to care for Ash for the rest of her life. She loved that Ash had needed her the day before. With an internal smile, Nat knew Ash was the least vulnerable person she knew, but she also knew that right now all she wanted in her life was to care for Ash and keep her safe.

"So?" Ash asked. "Sound good?"

Nat's eyes fluttered open, meeting Ash's.

"Sounds perfect."

## Chapter Twenty

A sh grimaced as her jacket infuriatingly refused to go on first time. Her shoulder ached, despite the painkillers she'd had at breakfast, and now the effort of even trying to shrug on her jacket seemed beyond her. Finally, never being the most patient of people, she flung it to the floor, adding a curse for good measure.

"Last time I heard a swearword like that it was from a sailor."

Ash turned to see Nat leaning against the door frame to her front room, her arms crossed against her chest.

"Stupid jacket wouldn't go on." Even to Ash's own ears she sounded childish, and she couldn't help the smile that tugged at her lips.

"Where's your sling?" Nat pointed to Ash's arm.

"There." Ash threw a look down to her sofa.

"You need to wear it." Nat pushed herself away from the door frame and came over to Ash. "Put your jacket over it."

Ash stood, feeling every inch the naughty child, as Nat retrieved first the sling from the sofa, then Ash's jacket from the floor. She watched Nat as she adjusted the sling, seeing a hint of a frown cross her face, then waited for her to return to her.

"Here." Nat stood in front of Ash and looped the sling over her head. "Give me your arm."

Ash did as she was told, offering her arm to Nat's outstretched hand. Nat took Ash's wrist and eased her arm into the sling, her hand gentle against Ash's skin. Ash stared at Nat's hand touching her, her skin soft on hers. She met Nat's gaze.

They didn't speak, choosing instead to search each other's eyes. Ash wondered if Nat was seeking answers to the same questions Ash was secretly harbouring. Time seemed to stand still, neither willing to break their gaze or move away.

"Ash…" Finally Nat spoke, then slowly, tentatively, lifted her hand and traced her finger across Ash's cheek. Her touch set Ash's skin on fire and she felt herself melting into Nat's touch as she watched Nat's skin flush, her eyes darken. She'd spent so many years thinking she hated Nat, had wasted so much time asking herself over and over why Nat'd done what she'd done. But she didn't hate her. She loved her.

Their faces were inches apart, lips just a second away from colliding. It would be so easy to give in to it, to lose herself in Nat again. To let Nat back into her life.

Ash blinked then stepped back. The room closed in around her, the walls crushing her, deepening her breathing, making her heart pound. When her eyes found Nat's again, she saw the obvious desire in them. Ash turned away, snatching her jacket from the back of her sofa.

"We should go"—she cleared her throat—"while it's still sunny."

Not daring to chance seeing the look on Nat's face again, she brushed past her and hastened from the room.

The golden dunes of St. Kerryan beach beckoned as they walked in silence along the cliff path heading away from Holly Cottage. Nat's mind was in turmoil. She knew she'd instigated the moment, making the first move by touching Ash's face, but the truth was, she'd been unable to help herself. There had been something about the way Ash had been struggling with her jacket, her face a picture of pain and frustration, that had brought all Nat's protective instincts to the fore again. They would have kissed too, Nat was sure of it, and she'd never wanted anything more in her life. The ache that had been left on her lips told her that.

But Ash had pulled away. Nat slid a look to her as she walked beside her, her head turned towards Widgeon who was running some way to the side of them.

Ash had felt it too, Nat was sure. She'd seen it in her eyes. Why hadn't she been able to give in to it, like Nat knew she would have done? The tension had grown steadily between them over the last two weeks, the barriers that had initially been up had slowly come down. Yet Ash still was unable to give herself to Nat.

She sensed Ash slowing as she watched out for Widgeon who had run across the dunes in pursuit of an invisible rabbit. Nat walked on, alone with her thoughts, the wind buffing around her stirring up more thoughts. Their carefree teenage years returned to her as her feet sank into the soft sand, vivid and beautiful memories of whispered declarations of love, of the passion they'd once shared. Now, though, they were adults, still able to ignite the same fire they had when they were teenagers. Still able to weaken the other just by a touch or a look.

Nat slowed and looked back to Ash. She knew Ash had been staring at her and she stopped and held her gaze, as though she were trying to find out what Ash was thinking. If only she could read her mind right now. Ash's face as she approached her gave nothing away, but her eyes told a different story, speaking to Nat of confusion and hope.

Ash pulled her gaze away from Nat's as she got ever closer to her, tuning instead into Widgeon in an attempt to distract herself from Nat's intense stare. Her mind twisted and turned as she tried to make sense of what had happened back at her cottage. What had *nearly* happened.

She'd come so close to giving in. She felt close to defeat, but while her mind felt fuzzy with confusion over her feelings for Nat, her heart was clear in what it wanted. It would have been so easy just to give in, Ash thought, to the desires that had grown in intensity over the last week. So easy…until she remembered that, this time tomorrow, Nat would be gone.

Ash looked up. Nat was waiting for her. As Ash picked up her pace, Nat started walking again, slowly enough to allow Ash to fall into step with her. They walked, side by side again, their footsteps crunching on the hard sand of the path, drowning out the thoughts in Ash's head.

"This way." Ash's words broke the silence between them.

She veered off to her right, her shoes immediately sinking into the softer sand of the dunes, her steps becoming more unsteady on the undulating ground. Tufts of grass poked out from the sand, their strands waving like lustrous hair in the breeze, while further down on the beach, lines of people and dogs dotted the sea's edge.

They stumbled further along the dunes, the drag of the sand pulling on Ash's muscles enough to make her want to stop and catch her breath for a while.

"Shall we sit down?" She stopped and bent over, leaning one hand on her leg. "This is killing me."

"Your shoulder?" Nat's hand rested on Ash's arm.

"Legs." Ash shook her head and laughed. "I think I'm getting old."

"You know, yesterday will have taken it out of you too." Nat guided Ash down onto the sand. "But, yes, you're probably getting old too." She flopped down beside Ash. "I mean, come on. You *will* be thirty-six in February. You're ancient." She gently bumped her arm.

"You remember my birthday?"

"Of course I do," Nat replied. "You were born on the fourth of February in Guildford Hospital at around"—she raised her eyes— "ten a.m., I think your parents said. Oh, and on a Tuesday, which makes you full of grace."

"And you were born on a Sunday, if I remember correctly," Ash said, "which makes you good and gay."

"Correct on both counts."

They laughed together, their eyes meeting as they did so.

"Your favourite meal is lasagna," Nat continued, "your favourite colour is blue, you hate reggae, and you prefer dogs to cats although it's a close-run thing because you're pretty potty about cats too, even though you can't have one because they make you sneeze too much."

"Very good." Ash nodded. "Well remembered."

"I remember everything about you, Ash," Nat said. "Everything." She looked away, then back to her. "You've never left me."

Ash stared out to sea. There was so much she wanted to say to Nat, so much she wanted her to know.

"That last day at school," Ash said. She dug her heels down into the sand, enjoying the sharp stretch on her calf muscles. "If I'd known that would be the last time I saw you, I'd have tried to remember your face." She looked at her. "So I could have carried your image with me everywhere I went, in here." She tapped the side of her head. "No one ever came close to you, Nat. No one." She drew in a deep breath and looked away, knowing she was tired of trying to fight it any more.

"I never wanted to end things with you, Ash," Nat said. "You have to believe me. I was…in a bad place. I felt everything was out of control." She laughed through her nose, her laugh sounding bitter. "No change there, then."

"You feel out of control now?" Ash asked.

"Everything's happening too fast." Nat paused, then hastily added, "Ireland, I mean." She frowned. "I want to slow time down. Make the time I've got left here last forever."

Her eyes fluttered open, finding Ash's, their gazes locking in an expression of mutual longing.

"But it *is* happening, isn't it?" Ash said quietly. "And neither of us can slow any of it down."

When Nat didn't answer, Ash turned her head away, scanning the dunes for Widgeon, desperate to break the tension that now crackled between them. When she turned back and saw the expectation in Nat's eyes, the pain was almost unbearable.

By the time they returned from the dunes, the clock had already stretched well past midday and was rapidly heading towards one.

With Widgeon racing ahead of them up towards Holly Cottage, Ash's thoughts turned to Chloe, now just half an hour away from them, and she stopped suddenly in the middle of the path.

"The truck," she said, shaking her head. "How can I fetch Chloe in it?"

"I'm already on it." Nat spoke back over her shoulder to her. "I told her Gabe would collect her. He won't mind, will he?"

"No, he won't mind," Ash said, falling into step beside Nat, "except for the fact right now he's about two miles out into the English Channel with a group of wildlife photographers."

She sensed Nat slow her pace.

"Ash, I'm so sorry," Nat said. "I just didn't think. I assumed he'd be here, and I told Chloe—"

"Chill." Ash put her hand on Nat's arm. "Truro's only a few miles from here. I'll just drive one-handed."

"You won't."

The chiding tone in Nat's voice made Ash smile.

"I'll drive," Nat said. "I was the one that made the mistake, so I'll drive us."

"In my truck?" Ash asked.

"No, in a tractor I'll steal from a local farmer," Nat said. "Of course in your truck."

"When did you last drive?" Ash asked. "You don't have a car any more. You told me that when we were in London."

"Hmm…when did I last drive?" Nat appeared deep in thought. "Let me think…"

"You see, that doesn't really instil much confidence in me," Ash said.

"It's like riding a bike, isn't it?" Nat said. "You never forget."

"Didn't you have trouble on the bikes in Hyde Park last week?" Ash bumped Nat's arm, then clutched her own arm as her shoulder jarred.

Nat stopped walking.

"Do you ever learn?" she asked, shaking her head.

A grin spread across Ash's face. "Nope."

❖

"So, reverse is lift and up to the left." Ash closed her hand over Nat's on the gear stick, lifted it with her, and engaged reverse gear. "Got it?"

"Yes, ma'am."

"Ignition stick is in the usual place," Ash said, leaning across Nat, "and headlights are here, if you need them."

"Are you expecting a blackout?" Nat asked. "Armageddon? The end of the world?"

"Sorry?"

"Why would I need the headlights at one o'clock in the afternoon?" Nat asked.

"You never know." The look on Nat's face made Ash smile. "Okay, fair point. But you know where everything else is, yes?"

"Yes."

"Then I guess we should go," Ash said. "End of the lane, take a right."

"Is this going to be like a driving test?" Nat asked, releasing the hand brake. "Will you pass or fail me?"

"I'll let you know at Truro."

The truck crunched over the gravel on the track leading from Holly Cottage and slid out onto the lane. Ash sat back in her seat and watched the hedges that lined the lane blur as Nat picked up her speed and headed out towards the main road leading out of St. Kerryan. As the miles sped past and they drove ever closer to the station, her mind tumbled back over the last forty-eight hours: To their time on the boat when they'd just talked and talked. To the walk up Brown Willy. To their companionship, and the feeling of comfort she felt around Nat.

She rolled her head and stole a look to her. Nat was concentrating hard on driving, and Ash knew she was, in all probability, terrified at driving her truck, despite all her bravado back at the cottage. Ash's thoughts raced ahead of her, to arriving at the station and seeing Chloe again. Would Chloe being back with them change the dynamics between her and Nat? Would the chemistry, that had been so evident just lately, disappear as if it had never existed?

"Take the next exit," Ash said, returning her gaze to the road. "Then a right off the roundabout."

From the corner of her eye she saw Nat nod, but she didn't answer.

Equally, Ash wondered as Nat pulled the truck off the main road, would Chloe notice a difference in them? The girl was switched on, tuned, it seemed in London, to every look and word. Ash now wondered if what was so blindingly obvious to her would be as obvious to Chloe.

"Next left?" Nat's voice cut through Ash's thoughts. "It says Truro Station parking, but is there a pickup and drop-off point somewhere else?"

"No, go down there," Ash said, pointing left. "The pickup point is next to the car park. We'll just park up and wait." Her eyes fell onto the clock on the truck's dash. "It's half past one now, so we won't have long to wait."

Nat swung the truck into the station's forecourt and pulled up next to the car park. As she killed the engine, Ash peered out of her window, expecting to see a train at the platform. While she looked out, she heard Nat rustle next to her, then heard a beep from her phone. She turned to see Nat scrutinizing her phone, her brow creased.

"Look like it's delayed," Nat murmured. "Twenty minutes."

Ash crossed her arms and settled back further in her seat.

"We'll have to play I Spy," she said, nestling her head against the headrest.

"We could talk," Nat suggested.

Ash looked at her.

"I figure once Chloe arrives, we won't get any time alone," Nat continued. "To…talk. Like we have been." Nat held Ash's look. "It's been nice."

Ash unbuckled her seat belt and moved in her seat. "It has," she agreed. "Being with you alone down here, even just for a few days, has been awesome."

"Like it used to be?" Nat offered. "All those years ago?"

Ash moved again. "No." Her voice faltered. "Different to how it used to be."

The truck's cabin suddenly felt smaller than it had on the journey over. Nat's leg felt closer to Ash's, her arm seemed to brush hers with every small movement.

"Does it feel better than it used to?" Nat asked. "Because for me it does." Nat's eyes didn't leave hers. "Getting to know you all over again makes it feel better. I like the adult you've become. I like how we've become."

The low sun filtering in through the truck's windows warmed Ash's skin. Her proximity to Nat, in the confines of the cabin, warmed her further, and while Nat still spoke, she felt herself drifting ever closer to her.

"I like that we're so comfortable with one another," Nat said. "And when I think how awkward everything was between us, even just last week, I can't believe how far we've come."

Ash stared at her, uncomfortable at the direction of their conversation, and equally uneasy at the intensity of feeling she knew was increasing with every look and movement inside the truck.

"Don't you feel it?" Nat asked. "Ash? Don't you feel there's something?"

"I still think we should play I Spy." Ash knew she was taking the coward's way out. She looked out of the side window. "We've got a little bit to wait yet."

As Ash stared out of the window, she was aware of Nat breathing softly next to her.

"Okay," Nat finally answered. "You still don't want to talk, right?"

"Chloe will be here any minute." Ash shrugged, but didn't look back to Nat.

"Ash. I…"

"Something beginning with *T*." Still Ash didn't look at her.

"Fine." Nat sighed, then was silent for a moment. "Tree."

"That was too easy, wasn't it?" Ash flashed her a smile.

"Just a bit."

Another silence returned, this time punctuated by another sigh from Nat.

When the silence became too much, Ash said to her side window, "I have to say, when I saw you again at Livvy's funeral, I never imagined that weeks later I'd be sitting in my truck playing crap I Spy with you."

"So you did see me at the funeral," Nat said.

Ash turned nodded. "I didn't want to talk to you," she said. "I was so stupid."

"I think we both were." Nat smiled, and as she began to speak again, a cargo train slowly rumbled past them on the tracks, drowning out the last of her words. Once it had passed, she said, "You could have had *train* just now if your timing had been better."

They both watched as the train disappeared from view.

"What do you suppose was on it?" Nat murmured.

Ash crossed her arms again and sank down further in her seat, already bored of I Spy. "I don't know," she said. "Hundreds and hundreds and hundreds of..." She let her words hang in the air until Nat nudged her.

"Of what?" Nat asked.

"Elephants."

"Stop it."

"Saucepans."

"You're nuts."

"Chocolate teapots."

"Mad as a hatter."

Ash slowly turned her head to look at Nat. "And you know it."

Nat met her gaze. "Yeah, I know it," she said.

As they looked at one another, the energy that had surrounded them, but which had then lifted slightly during their all too brief attempt at I Spy, returned. It was insane, Ash thought, sitting in her truck with Nat, too scared to move in case they touched one another, so nervous at the knowledge that was the one thing she really wanted to do right now. Their game forgotten, and knowing she shouldn't, Ash slowly placed her right hand on Nat's leg. When Nat didn't object, Ash traced her finger lightly up and down the material of her jeans. Glimpses from the past ebbed and flowed in Ash's mind, of moments just like these: the two of them entwined, so comfortable in one another's company, lost in one another's gaze. Snapshots that were so stark, Ash felt the hot spread of tears threatening the backs of her eyes.

"We shouldn't," Nat said.

"Do you mean that?" Ash asked, a shiver pulsing through her when she saw the look on Nat's face.

Ash heard Nat's breaths deepening, turning almost to sighs, and reluctantly slid her hand from Nat's leg, desperate to touch her again, but afraid of what she was doing. Knowing where it might end. Nat reached over and took her hand, bringing it back over to her leg. To Ash's surprise, Nat wrapped her hand round Ash's and guided it lightly up and down her thigh, imitating what Ash had just been doing.

"I've been thinking all day about us," Nat said, her voice so quiet Ash could barely hear it. "About how we used to be."

"And?" Ash could hear her own heart hammering in her ears.

When Nat didn't answer her question, Ash resumed her stroking, trailing her fingers back and forth across Nat's jeans. Finally, Nat moved her leg slightly and Ash, assuming she'd had enough, stopped stroking. Instead of moving away from her, though, Nat reached over, lightly tracing a finger across Ash's cheek. Ash felt hot fire scorch across her skin, her nerves set alight from Nat's touch.

"I miss you," Nat said quietly. "I miss *us*."

She scooted closer to Ash, frowning at the seat belt impeding her, unbuckled it and slowly leaned over. The immediate feel of Nat's lips meeting her skin, nuzzling against her neck, kissing along her jawline, took Ash by surprise, sending her senses into spasms. Ash closed her eyes, thinking she ought to stop, that none of this was fair to either of them, but Nat's immediacy, her soft lips kissing their way up and down her neck, searing her skin, the tip of her tongue teasing her while she kissed her, rendered her helpless.

*Stop.*

*Don't stop.*

The words drummed a relentless beat in Ash's brain.

But she couldn't stop.

Nat shifted her position again and sighed as she reached over and gently turned Ash's face towards her, Ash's senses spiralling as she opened her eyes and saw Nat's eyes darken as their lips finally met. Their kiss was soft at first—tentative, even—but slowly deepened as tongues clashed and hands were lost in hair, Ash aching with the weeks of pent-up longing which were finally exploding with a passion she felt unable to stop. She murmured against Nat's lips as she felt her suck on her tongue, her hands creeping under her top to seek bare skin. Everywhere Nat touched her burned like fire. She felt drunk from Nat's touch, as though her layers of skin were being stripped away as every nerve in her body tingled, every inch of her set alight. Ash was lost in their kiss, unaware of anything other than her and Nat, their moans mingling as their kisses grew more urgent.

Only the low rumble of a train, accompanied by the metallic squeal of brakes broke their kiss.

"Chloe," Ash murmured against Nat's lips. "She'll be here any moment…"

Nat pulled away, her eyes still on Ash's, and Ash knew it was only the sound of the train doors opening and slamming, and Chloe's impending arrival that stopped them from kissing again.

## Chapter Twenty-one

A nd she was all over him, and I was, like, it's too gross."
Chloe was holding court in the back of the truck. "I sent a photo to Amanda and even she thought it was gross, and let me tell you, there's *nothing* that grosses Amanda out."

Nat stole a look to her in her rear-view mirror as she drove back towards Holly Cottage. "And they were sitting opposite you?" she asked.

"Across the aisle." Chloe made eye contact in the reflection. "But, still. Four hours. *Four hours* of making out on a train. Insane."

"And gross, apparently." Nat stole a glimpse at Ash, their smiles matching.

Just the way Ash looked at her now brought their kiss back to Nat. Her gaze fell onto Ash's lips, remembering how it had felt, just a few minutes before, to be kissing her. The shudder that extended right down her body at the memory was both unexpected and intense.

They hadn't spoken after they'd kissed. Instead, Ash had stumbled from the truck, saying something about Chloe's train which hadn't reached Nat's ears because Ash had slammed the truck door and strode across towards the platform, leaving Nat still in the driver's seat, her heart still pounding in her chest. Nat hadn't cared. They'd kissed, and it had been the best feeling in the world. It hadn't felt like it had all those years before; it was better. More passionate. Less the fumbling of eager teenagers, more the care, softness, and attention of adults.

Nat shivered again. Gone were the kids they had been. Gone was their silliness, their pettiness, their immaturity. She knew, with an absolute certainty, that she now loved the woman Ash had become just as much as she'd loved the teenager she'd been.

"So what have you guys been up to?" Chloe's voice broke Nat's reverie.

"This and that." She spoke up to Chloe's reflection, careful to avoid eye contact with Ash.

"A sling doesn't suggest this and that," Chloe said, leaning forward in her seat and tapping Ash on her shoulder.

"Long story," Ash said.

"Funny," Chloe said, "that's what Nat said too." She sat back. "Want to explain?"

This time, Nat did catch Ash's eye. "Maybe," she laughed.

By the time every tiny detail of Ash's fall on Brown Willy had been recounted, Ash was starving, although, considering it was by then well past two fifteen, that wasn't much of a surprise. A detour via a beachside café that she knew, and which she declared did the best lattes in the whole county, was decided, and by two thirty, lunch was finally a distinct possibility.

The sun was just starting its descent again, bathing the café in a low golden glow, by the time they arrived. They chose to sit outside, keen to make the most of the unusual but welcome continued warm October weather and finally, to Ash's relief, ordered lunch.

"I could get used to this." Ash rested her chin in her palm, the sun warm on her back. "And letting Gabe take charge for once is always good." She smiled across the table to Nat.

"You'll have to get injured more often." Nat returned her smile.

"But next time I won't have you to take care of me, will I?" Ash said, leaning back into her chair as their food and lattes were brought out to them. She hadn't meant to say it, hadn't meant for Nat to hear the tinge in her voice, triggered by the reality that soon Nat would go again.

"No," Nat said, her smile fading in front of Ash's eyes, "I don't suppose I will."

"And it actually popped out?" Chloe said, reaching across to snag her panini. "Your shoulder?"

"It dislocated," Nat corrected, "not popped out."

"Same thing," Chloe said. "And still totally sick."

"And still totally painful." Ash smiled.

"Is it hurting you?" Nat reached across the table and touched Ash's arm. "You know I have painkillers on me if you—"

"It's fine." Ash closed her hand over Nat's. "Stop stressing."

"Ash is as tough *as*," Chloe said. "I'm thinking a popped shoulder is nothing to her. Am I right?" She looked at Ash.

"Well, I've had better experiences." Ash pulled her hand from Nat's and laughed. When she looked over, Nat mouthed, *You sure?* and she nodded, mouthing back, *I'm sure.*

"So," Chloe said, picking up her panini from her plate, "bummer about Mum's letters, right?"

"Completely," Ash said. "Thanks to my falling halfway down a hill, we ran out of time to finish them all."

That was one of her biggest regrets, Ash thought as she glanced over to Nat—the chance to honour all eight of Livvy's letters hadn't materialized.

"I thought we did okay," Nat said, "considering everything."

"I thought we did more than okay." Ash smiled back at her. She picked up her panini, its melted cheese oozing out of its sides, scooped some of the cheese out with her finger, grimacing at its heat against her skin, then plopped a globule of it into her mouth. "I thought we did better than either of us could have expected."

"Mum said you would." Chloe spoke through a mouthful of panini. "She was always right."

"You knew?" Ash's own panini paused halfway to her mouth. "What your mum was planning?"

Chloe nodded. "She told me." Her voice sounded thick with food. "She wanted me to do it. The way she spoke to me about it... it was like it was the most important thing in the world to her." She glanced at Ash. "Knowing you guys actually did it would have made her so happy."

Ash slipped a look to Nat.

"And knowing how well you both got on would make her even happier. You want that?" Chloe pointed to Ash's uneaten slices of red onion, then forked three up when Ash shook her head.

"Well, I'm glad," Ash said, swallowing down the tightness in her throat. "And now it's up to us to make your one and only day here the best ever."

"And then, back to London." Nat's voice was quiet, and as Ash felt Nat's level gaze, she sensed another utterance on the tip of her tongue. Instead, Nat remained quiet.

"Do you have lots to do when you get back?" Ash didn't want to speak the words. Didn't want to think about it. "Ready for your move?"

"Yes," Nat said, her voice clearer and more firm this time, "I suppose it'll be all systems go."

Ash bit into her panini and studied Nat as she concentrated on slicing her own panini in half. Her mind travelled back. They were seventeen, eating in a café such as this, about to part again whilst Nat took her three weeks in France with her parents. Happiness at being together in the sun—just like now—had been stained with sadness at their impending goodbyes. Just like now. Only back then, Ash always knew she'd see Nat again. Now? She just didn't know.

"But you two are totally going to stay in touch, aren't you?" Chloe asked, apparently reading Ash's mind.

Ash looked over to Nat, seeking answers in her expression, but seeing none.

"Are we?" she finally asked. "Can we?"

"Ireland's not far, is it?" Nat's smile, Ash thought, masked the same unease that Ash herself felt.

"No." Ash forced the smile onto her lips. "I guess it's not far at all."

"I mean, they have airports there and flights there, right?" Chloe said. "You should *so* go and see Nat once she's over there."

Chloe, Ash thought, was doing a fine job.

"Once I'm settled," Nat said, "you must come and stay."

"Yes," Ash said, "I should." She paused. "I will. I'd really like that."

Nat held her gaze. "I'd really like that too."

❖

Nat wasn't sure how she'd managed to get back to London without breaking down. She remembered nothing of her and Ash's parting, except for their embrace, which had gone on for the longest time, neither of them apparently wanting it to end. She'd pushed to the back of her mind the look of longing and confusion that had been on Ash's face, refused to even think about it each time it threatened to return to her. Instead, she'd relied on Chloe's company to keep her thoughts from straying back to Cornwall, grateful for her incessant chattering and observations that took her mind off Ash and her desire to get off at each station and return to her.

Nat put the key in the door of her apartment, pushed it open, then closed it behind her with her foot. She dropped her rucksack at her feet and stared out at the yawning space of her lounge. From her kitchen, her refrigerator hummed a low tune, whilst from outside came the muffled drone of traffic on the road. Other than that, the silence of her apartment consumed her. Nat wandered further into her apartment, her eye caught by the red flashing light on her answer machine, telling her eight people had left her messages in the few days she'd been away. The post, brought in by the same neighbour who had been feeding Smudge, piled up on a table that was already spilling over with the previous week's unanswered mail.

Nat sank down into her chair by the fire, kicked off her shoes, and curled her legs up under her. It was, she thought miserably, as though everyone wanted a piece of her when all she wanted was to be left in peace so she could be alone with her thoughts of Ash.

She rested her head back against her chair and closed her eyes, tiredness setting in. Every time she closed her eyes, though, her brain chose to replay her kissing Ash, and her longing came back stronger each time. She opened her eyes again and the images fled, allowing her to focus instead on a small crack on her wall which she'd thought for years looked like a spider. Nat knew she'd instigated their kiss in the truck the day before, and she hadn't been able to help herself. There had been something there, an intimacy between them that had grown slowly over the days, that had left her unable to resist Ash. The tension, every time their eyes had met, had been palpable, so Nat couldn't be blamed for giving in to it, could she? Each glance they'd shared had pulled Nat closer to her, each touch had set Nat on fire.

There was still something there. A spark. She knew Ash had felt it too, had seen the look in her eyes. There had been a heat in her eyes, a craving. A look of need and desire that had driven her crazy. Nat hadn't mistaken it.

The tiredness enveloped her again. The train journey home, the Tube from Paddington, the long slog down the street to her apartment had all exhausted her. London exhausted her. Since when had that happened? She hated it, hated everything about it: the traffic, the noise, the people. For years she'd endured the daily grind of life in the capital, but being in Cornwall had given her a glimpse of what her life could be like. Nat opened her eyes and stared up at the ceiling. Belfast would be no different to this, she knew.

Maddie was right: Nat had everything in the palm of her hand. An awesome job waiting for her with an inflated salary. So why wasn't she happy? Because she knew she'd committed the cardinal sin. Thanks to Ash, Nat had experienced time away from her chaotic life and found she'd actually liked it, and then she'd let her mind run away with her, letting it take her to a place where traffic didn't drone outside the window, where no one felt the need to contact her every five minutes, and where she could finally be herself.

But she thrived on chaos, didn't she? Or was that the old Nat? The one that used to throw herself into her work and London life as a way to forget just how lonely she was?

Nat looked down as she heard soft feet shuffling on the carpet and saw Smudge blinking back at her. Just for a few days, she'd taken herself away from the bedlam that was her life and transported herself to a place of calm, and of wide open spaces where even pet rabbits didn't need to be confined to a fourth-floor apartment with no hope of ever experiencing fresh air.

She'd taken herself to Cornwall. To Ash.

Nat reached over and stroked Smudge's ears flat against his head.

She'd given herself a snippet of what life could be like, and she'd loved it.

"I've done a daft thing," she said to him. "And I'm about to do an even dafter one."

Smudge's ears pinged back up.

"Want me to tell you all about it?" she asked.

Ash crouched at the water's edge and picked up a pebble. She turned it over in her hands, smoothing her fingers across it, then skimmed it out to sea. She watched it bounce once, twice, three times, then disappear under a circle of foam with an audible plop.

Watching Nat leave had been agony. Not even being able to drive her to the station had been agony too. Ash had had to watch Nat and Chloe leave her cottage, knowing they'd be going straight back to the B & B, then on to the station without her. Their embrace at her cottage had felt so different to the one they'd shared at Paddington the week before. There had been an understanding in it, a maturity that hadn't been there before, but one which Ash was glad existed.

Ash stared into the green depths of the water. She tilted her head to one side. Could she even call it green? Unthinking, she brought her hand to her lips and brushed her fingers across them. Her brain let her think she could still taste Nat on them, could still feel her lips on hers. What was blue-green called? Jade. No, the water wasn't jade. Ash stared harder, driving the memory of kissing Nat from her mind. Concentrate. What was the colour of the sea? Teal. Too fancy. She frowned. Why had she let Nat kiss her neck like that? Why had she then given in to her?

Sea green. That was what it was. Ash jumped up, then kicked a mound of pebbles into the shallow water by her feet. Nat was gone. Ash had let her go, with promises of staying in touch, but without even trying to tell her how she felt about her, so now it was pointless staring into the dimpling waters thinking about their kiss or trying to make sense of anything any more. She turned, whistling for Widgeon, and began walking along the shoreline. She knew soon Nat would be away, off to her fabulous new life in Ireland, and all her dreams would be realized. Years of hard work would come to fruition, and their brief rekindling of whatever it was that had been rekindled over the past few weeks would be just a distant speck in her memory because Ash knew deep down that despite everything they'd said in the café the day before, she'd probably never see her again. Nat would be too busy in her new job to even give Ash or Cornwall a second thought. That was the way things happened, wasn't it? Promises, promises.

As Widgeon sidled up at her side, her hand automatically fell to stroke his head, her fingers raking his fur. Ash picked up her pace, eager to get home before the rain which had threatened all morning decided to break. It was pointless, she knew, thinking things over and over any more; Nat had a new life waiting for her, and it was pointless, Ash constantly looking at her phone, waiting for the call she knew would never come. Pointless expecting the invite over to Ireland she knew would never materialize.

Ash glanced up at the brooding clouds and quickened her stride some more. She and Nat would soon be forgotten to one another again, and the sooner Ash managed to understand that, the sooner she too could move on.

## Chapter Twenty-two

The log pile that Ash had spent the last half an hour making was growing larger. Which was just as well because with each hurl of a log, the ache in her shoulder amplified. But Ash carried on, her sling tossed to one side, the pain acting as a useful distraction.

Nat had been gone over forty-eight hours. Ash stood and extended her back, hearing a satisfying crack somewhere low down in her spine. Forty-eight hours and not a word. Not that Ash was surprised. Right now, she figured, Nat would be knee-deep in boxes and suitcases, busy getting ready to move. That's how it was. Ash nudged a log back up against the pile with her boot. That's how it was always going to be before they'd met up again. Nat was always going to go to Ireland, no matter what. Destiny and all that.

Ash bent and picked up the next log, ignoring her complaining shoulder. Nat would be horrified, she thought with a wry smile. Nat would have, by now, bundled her back into her lounge, fussing and cursing Ash's stupidity. Nat would have taken care of her. Ash looked about her. Nat would have worried. She flung the log onto the pile, then watched as it bumped its way back down, shifting a few others on the way, before coming to a rest at the base of the pile.

"Stupid son of a…" She kicked the log, then hopped back hastily as four or five others crashed down.

Defeated by the logs, the ache in her shoulder, and the even bigger ache in her heart, Ash decided to give up. With a click of her fingers to a patiently waiting Widgeon, she left her back garden and rounded the corner of her cottage just in time to see Gabe walking up the garden path towards her front door.

"Morning, loveliness." Gabe waited on the path. "Harbour master says it's too windy to take Doris out today, so I've come up here to play instead."

"Did you tell this afternoon's group?" Ash's second click of her fingers finally had her dog at her side. "Can we reschedule them?"

"All done. Panic not." Gabe came to her and put his hand on her shoulder. "You appear to be slingless, by the way."

"It's in the back garden." Ash tossed a look over her shoulder. "It was getting in the way."

"Of?"

"Nothing." Ash opened her front door. "Coffee?" She stood to one side to let Gabe in first. "You can make it. You know you always make it much better than I do."

She followed Gabe to the kitchen, trying to ignore the pans and crockery she'd allowed to stack up over the past few days. While Gabe busied himself filling her coffee maker, Ash rested against her kitchen counter watching him.

"Nat told me two weeks." Gabe spoke without looking up.

"Two weeks what?"

"Keeping the sling on." He looked over to Ash. "She wouldn't be happy if she knew."

"Well, considering *a*, she's not here, and *b*, I won't be seeing her again," Ash said, "I'd say it doesn't matter." Her shoulder gave a twinge at that moment to remind her that it did matter.

"You've still not contacted her?" Gabe asked.

Ash shook her head.

"Even though she's crazy about you and you're crazy about her?" Gabe asked.

"Gabe, this time next week she'll be standing in an operating theatre with a scalpel in her hand not even giving me a second thought." She looked at him. "We've been over this a thousand times."

"Well it seems a shame," Gabe said. "All of it. You, Nat, the letters." He snapped the lid down on the coffee maker. "And you've definitely lost your spark since Nat's been gone."

"No, I haven't."

"Yes, Ash." Gabe walked over to her. "You have." He took her hands. "Why are you being so stubborn?"

Ash opened her mouth to speak then closed it again. She had no answer to Gabe's question.

"You want to hear my opinion?" Gabe asked.

"No," Ash said, "but you're going to give it to me anyway, aren't you?"

"Sure am." Gabe smiled and squeezed her hands.

Ash looked up at him.

"I think it's time you grew up," Gabe said.

"Thanks." Ash stared at a point just to the left of Gabe's shoulder.

"You and Nat aren't teenagers any more," Gabe continued. "The relationship you *could* have now is a million miles away from the one you had at school."

"Do you think so?" Ash asked, looking back up at him.

"You have to forget everything that happened years ago," Gabe said, "and see Nat for what she is now, not what she was then." He gestured with his hands. "Equally, you need to see what your relationship with her could be like now, rather than constantly harking back to what happened."

Gabe's words made Ash feel as if she'd been struck by lightning. She knew exactly what Nat was now: the adorable, funny, beautiful woman that she always knew, even back then, she would turn into. Ash looked at Gabe, thinking, not for the first time since she'd known him, just how awesome he was. She knew he was right, too; for as much as Ash desperately missed what she and Nat had once had, she knew she was missing more what they could have right now. Perhaps it really was time to see their relationship through an adult's eyes, rather than persisting in still seeing them through a teenager's.

"You really do have to stop thinking about the past," Gabe continued, taking the thoughts from her head, "if you're to have any kind of future with her." He looked her straight in the eye. "It's got to be worth a try, don't you think?" he asked. "You and her?"

Ash held his gaze and slowly nodded.

"It's not like Ireland's so very far away," Gabe said, a smile spreading across his face.

"That's what Nat said," Ash said.

"Then listen to what she's saying to you," Gabe said. "Sure, it's not ideal, but if it's meant to be between you two, then you can make it ideal, can't you? You can make it into whatever you want it to be."

"I've never been to Ireland." Ash smiled ruefully down at the floor. "Guess it wouldn't hurt to see what it's like."

"So it's time to stop keeping her at arm's length," Gabe said, "isn't it?" He returned to the coffee maker and pulled two mugs down from a shelf. "And don't forget, you both still have Livvy's letter to think about."

"What about Livvy's letter?"

"Well aren't you curious what she had planned for the pair of you as her last wish?" Gabe asked. "The last wish that the pair of you should have done together while Nat was still down here?"

The coffee boiled. Ash slipped a look through the kitchen door to her front room and to Livvy's letter, feeling a stain of guilt. She'd delayed opening the final letter, somehow fearing what would be inside it. Knowing that the last letter would cut her final link with both Livvy and Nat. That the adventure—the one she'd both dreaded and loved—would finally be over. That the thread that had pulled her through the last two weeks, closer to them both, would at last be severed and everything Ash had hoped wasn't true would be: Livvy really was dead and Nat was never coming back into her life ever again.

"It'll mean the end." Ash spoke her thoughts. "The end of the journey."

"Or the gateway to a new one," Gabe said. "Have you thought of that?"

❖

The music was too loud, the bass too reverbing. If the rapid, pounding beat was supposed to inspire the gym users, it merely served to give Nat a headache. Enough. She slowed her pace on the bike and called over to Maddie.

"I'm done."

She reached over and turned her machine off, then stepped away. She wrapped her towel round her neck, wiping at her eyes and her hairline.

"You're done already?" Maddie called over from her bike.

"I can't concentrate." Nat swirled a hand around her head. "Too loud."

If only it was the music stopping her concentration. She walked across the gym and sank down onto a chair. The unscheduled visit to the gym had been Maddie's idea—*a distraction from your thoughts*. It hadn't worked. Instead, Nat had found herself deeper and deeper in thought the longer she cycled, imagining her bike taking her out and away from the gym, out of London, and straight back to Cornwall.

"Now I *definitely* know you're getting old." Maddie sat next to her. "Music too loud indeed." She looked at her. "You're still in Cornwall, aren't you? In here." She tapped her temple.

"There's no point in wishing I was somewhere I'm not, though," Nat said.

She stared around her, at the starkness of the gym. She missed St. Kerryan and everything about it: waking up to the sound of the sea, the suck and swish of the waves against the pebbles on the beach, and the crying of the gulls overhead. The way the air smelt clean and fresh, quite unlike the choking pollution of London. Going to bed happy but exhausted from a day walking along the coast, excited knowing she'd see Ash again the next day.

Having something, for the first time in years, to look forward to.

"I can't believe she let you go," Maddie said, "bearing in mind what you just told me you're prepared to do for her."

"I'm doing it for me too." Nat rested her head against the wall. "I'll finally be doing what I do best, but I'll be free of my responsibilities." She rolled her head against the wall and looked at Maddie. "And free of my therapist." She laughed. "Free of mind."

"It's a shame you never got to finish your friend's wishes though."

"Livvy's?" Nat frowned. "We had a pretty good crack at them though," she said. "Six out of eight." Her smile returned. "That was six more than I thought we'd do when I read her letters at Judy's house."

*When I was scared stiff of seeing Ash again.*

Nat stared at the wall opposite her. That all felt like such a long time ago now.

"And Ash?" Maddie asked. "Do you think she ever thought you'd have gone as far?"

"We came a long way," Nat replied. "Further than either of us imagined." She wasn't sure whether she was talking about the wish list or their feelings for one another.

"But you're back up here and she's still down there," Maddie said. "So perhaps not as far as you'd hoped."

"No." Nat stood. "Not nearly as far as I'd hoped."

## CHAPTER TWENTY-THREE

L ivvy's final letter to Ash remained unopened on her coffee table. Gabe had left an hour ago, just before dusk, leaving Ash with nothing else to do but stare at the letter and try to summon up the courage to read it.

She sat in her chair, her mind tumbling back over the years. To the first time she met Livvy and Nat, as clear to her today as it was then. Three nervous year sevens arriving at school at the same time, standing together in the corridor exchanging worried glances, too scared to speak to one another. Then the delight at finding they would be in the same class together, familiar faces in amongst a sea of strangers.

Then, as year nines, bolder. Firm friends with a familiarity that none of them could have ever dreamed possible. Regularly in and out of one another's houses, weekends and holidays spent hanging out in central London, directing tourists the wrong way and trying to make the guards at Buckingham Palace laugh.

There was always so much laughter. Ash smiled in the fading gloom of her lounge.

It had been true what Lisa Turner had said to Ash at Livvy's funeral. They'd been The Untouchables: invincible, their friendship impenetrable, much to the envy of the other girls at the school.

Her eyes fell to the letter again. Could she salvage what was left of her and Nat? Could she do it for Livvy? Ash scooted over to the table and picked the letter up. Inside, she knew, would be the end. She slipped her index finger under the flap and shook the letter out.

Dearest Flash,
So here we are at our final letter. My last wish and now the end of the road, as it were.

Ash looked away, focusing on a tree branch waving in the breeze outside her window. *Our final letter.* She drew in a deep breath and returned to it.

Did you manage to do the whole list? Did Chloe behave herself? (Did you?) And did you all have an absolute blast doing each thing? I really do hope so, because I have a tiny confession to make; they all served a really important purpose.

Now you're confused, aren't you? Yes, I know you *knew* they served a purpose: to show Chloe some of the wonderful stuff I experienced in my oh-so-brief life, and to help her in her grieving for me. And you are correct, and I thank you from the bottom of my heart for agreeing to do it. I'm sure Chloe loved having her two favourite non-aunties back in her life again, if only for a short while.

But...my letters were also designed for another purpose, and that purpose involved you and Crackles.

I knew about you and Nat, you see. All along. And while I always wanted you both to tell me you were together, I suppose I understood why you'd want to keep it to yourselves, but...My God! You two were *so* good together, you know that? Okay, I know what she did to you was awful and terrible and I'm sure you dreamed of so many different ways to kill her slowly after she left you (joke) but, oh, Flash! It's Nat! It's you and Nat! It's Nat and you, and you two were always meant to be together, you know?

Ash squeezed her eyes tight shut, forcing the tears from them. Livvy knew. Livvy had always known. She opened her eyes and gazed upward. Of course she'd known. Beautiful, clever Livvy. Ash looked back to the letter.

Now, I know at this point you'll be shaking your head at all this, so I need to tell you something, because I'm sure Nat never told you, even though you should have just spent the last two weeks together talking about stuff.

She tried to find you. Her parents tried to make her spend that last summer studying (you know what they were like) but she ignored them because she realized what a terrible thing it was she'd done to you and she wanted to go and find you, beg you to forgive her. Take her back. She went over to France, into Spain, nearly into Portugal before she finally gave up, knowing it was futile. Europe's a big place, Flash. But you have to believe me when I tell you she was distraught when she knew she'd lost you for good. Distraught and guilt-ridden.

You know, our friendship was never the same after that. Mine and Nat's. She retreated into herself, shot off up to Edinburgh as soon as she could so she could get as far away as possible from London and her parents, and threw herself into her studies up there. She knew she'd made the biggest mistake of her life, Flash. More than that, she knew that what she'd done had broken up our threesome forever.

Ash let the letter fall to her lap. Why hadn't Nat told her more about that? If Ash had known, just for a second, that Nat had actually come looking for her, she would have gone to her. Instead, as the weeks and months passed, she'd had to endure the belief that Nat never thought of her, her spirit dying just a little bit more with the realization that Nat didn't care a thing for her.

Hot tears rested in Ash's eyes. She wiped them away with her sleeve and picked up Livvy's letter again.

The years passed. You came back and built up your stonking business from scratch, Nat became this super doctor, I became the best bloody lawyer this side of the Thames, and I saw the pair of you individually. But the three of us were never a trio ever again, Nat was a shadow of her former self, and you still couldn't even bring yourself to say Nat's name out loud.

Let me tell you some home truths. You never got over her, she never got over you, and do you know how many times over the years I just wanted to bang your heads together and say, for goodness' sake, *talk* to each other. But you never did.

Bet you're talking now though.

In case you haven't guessed by now, I wanted my letters to also be a way to get you two talking to each other again. I don't know if you can ever get back what you once had, but talking could be a start, hey?

She loves you, Flash. Categorically, unequivocally, head over heels. Always has done, always will do, and she knows she messed up big time with you.

A table for two has your name on it at The Fisherman. You know the place you took me when I came down to visit you one summer and Chloe was teething and screeched the place down? I always thought it was lovely, and just the sort of place for the perfect tête-à-tête. But without a squawking, ruddy-faced baby, obviously.

I Googled it, and it's still there.

Take Nat there. Talk some more. Lay some ghosts to rest and maybe, just maybe…

And that, dear Flash, is my last wish for both of you. Be happy. You were made for each other.

So now this is where I sign off. Eighth letter, over and out, and all that.

I miss you, and I want you to know that the time when I knew you was the best of my life (well, apart from having Chloe, obviously). I'm just sorry you, me, and Nat never got to grow old together. But I guess c'est la vie, even if that is the shittiest thing ever.

Enjoy life. Have no regrets. It really is too short, Flash.

Love you loads.

Livvy xxx

Ash pulled the letter to her chest, the ache inside almost unbearable. She held the letter, reading it over again, picking out the bits that made her happy and made her sad. A smile passed over her lips as she read Livvy's words, hearing her voice, the smile fading as she realized that Livvy would never get to have her final wish, and that if she'd thought her letters would bring Ash and Nat together again, then she'd been mistaken. That thought hurt more than anything else.

Ash's eyes roamed over the last few paragraphs. She remembered her visit to The Fisherman, trying to appease the teething Chloe. They'd sat outside, Ash recalled, and had been pleased to find a table down by the river as far away from everyone else that they could find. Livvy had made a joke to the waiter about her daughter not liking the food there and the waiter not laughing, but Ash nearly choking with laughter over it. It had all been in Livvy's deadpan delivery, Ash remembered now, the crushing feeling in her chest returning as she held back the tears.

How could she honour this last wish, after everything that had happened? How could she expect Nat to come back down to Cornwall and have one last dinner with her when Ash had been stupid enough to let her leave without telling her how she felt about her? More than that, Ash knew she'd never be able to sit opposite Nat, having to hear about her new life in Belfast, knowing she'd never be a part of it. It would all be just too painful.

Ash's hand dropped to her side as Widgeon leaned against her leg. She pulled his ear though her hand, her mind turning over. Six out of eight wishes wasn't bad. Livvy would totally understand. Ash looked to the table again, her phone close by. But what if…?

Her heart started to pound. Would Nat want to do the last wish? Maybe she could put the ball in Nat's court, and then leave it to her to decide whether she wanted to fulfil this last wish before she left for Ireland. Ash lurched forward in her chair, sending Widgeon stumbling back, and snagged her phone from the table. Her fingers trembling at the prospect of seeing Nat again, Ash dialled her number, her adrenaline rapidly dwindling down to a trickle of disappointment when she heard Nat's automated voicemail. She killed the call, then sat brooding. Now she'd implanted the seed, Ash knew she needed an answer. She opened up her emails, found Nat's email address at St. Bart's, and wrote:

Hey Nat,
    Hope you're okay.

Ash's face pinched. Would Nat be okay? She deleted the words and instead wrote:

    Just opened Livvy's last letter. It was way more painful than I could have ever imagined. Did you read it yet? If you haven't, read it soon and tell me what you want to do. I desperately want to honour her last ever wish, and I hope you do too.
    Let me know your decision.
    Ash.

Kisses? Ash's frown deepened further. No kisses.

She hit send and switched off her phone, holding it in her hand and tapping it against her lip, deep in thought, pleased she'd thought to leave the decision to Nat. It was up to her now. If Nat didn't want to see her again, then fine. If she did? The tapping slowed. Then Ash would deal with that, if and when.

Her phone buzzed against her hand. Ash pulled it from her lip and swept her thumb across the screen, bringing up her emails.

Auto reply.

The email address Natalie.Braithwaite@stb.nhs.org is no longer active. All emails to this address have been automatically forwarded to Jack.Greene@stb.nhs.org. If you have any queries, please contact the hospital on...

Ash stared at the email. So, there she had it. Nat had left St. Bart's and gone to Belfast already. Couldn't wait to get out of London. Ash was sure Nat had told her the post wouldn't be available until November, and that she wouldn't be ready to leave for another week yet, but she must have left early. Ash's hand flopped to her side. Nat really was gone. Her mind thick with confusion, Ash picked her phone back up and drew up Google. She frowned. What was the name of the hospital in Belfast again? Royal something. There it was: Royal Victoria. With a sinking heart, Ash found the phone number for the hospital and dialled out.

The hospital's main reception answered on the fourth ring.

"Hi." Ash's throat was dry. "I don't know if you can help me, but I need to find an email address for one of your new cardiology consultants, please? Her name's Natalie Braithwaite."

## Chapter Twenty-four

A light drizzle was falling against the window, blurring Nat's view outside. Faces down on the street became distorted, cars and buses melted as one. She braced her shoulder against the cold wooden frame of the window and stared out, unseeing, trying to pass off the persistent hot tears that needled the backs of her eyes as just tiredness. There was nothing more she could do, and even though her heart was begging her to keep trying, her head told her it was pointless.

Ash's prolonged silence had made her feelings to Nat perfectly clear, and even though she had clung to the faint hope for the past week that Ash might find a way to let go of the past and give her another chance, this had finally convinced Nat her fight was over. She shoved herself away from the window and wandered back into her lounge, kicking a discarded sock out of the way. It was all over. Her, Ash, Cornwall. The only faint pinprick of hope was the knowledge that she wouldn't have to endure Belfast after all. The formal letter she had written to her supervisor explaining her decision had been surprisingly easy, bringing with it a profound sense of relief.

Nat's gaze rested on the pile of books stacked up on her table. The calmness which always accompanied the prospect of an afternoon delving into her reference books returned. Since her return from Cornwall, she had plunged herself into some research as a way to stop herself from fermenting in her own abject misery. It had been a godsend too, pulling her mind away from her unhappiness and offering her a new focus. A message from *The Lancet* had been one of the many messages left on her phone while she'd been away; a new research opportunity—just the sort she could really get her teeth into—had been put to her, and she'd jumped at the chance. Working from home would be just what she needed now, allowing her the flexibility to work as much or as little as she wanted, and offering her the chance to study just where she wanted too.

And Nat knew exactly where she wanted that studying to be.

She sat in her chair and closed her eyes. A brief lull in the traffic outside brought a quietness, instantly transporting her back to the peace of St. Kerryan. Her mind took itself on a journey to the harbour, where Doris bobbed patiently waiting for her passengers. To the coarse pebble beach by Holly Cottage, where the water lapped quietly at the shore's edge, and then on to Widgeon, no doubt somewhere at Ash's side. And what of Ash? Would she be thinking of her right now? A sigh left Nat's lips. Somehow she doubted it.

Not wanting to, but unable to help herself, Nat pulled her phone from her pocket and found a photo of her and Ash, taken the morning on the dunes before they'd kissed in Ash's truck. She stared, seeing everything she ever wanted in a person in the eyes that gazed into hers, and knew that even if she never saw Ash again, she'd never forget the way she'd looked at her that day. Nat ran a finger gently across the screen of her phone, over Ash's face. Kissing Ash had just released all the pent-up emotions that walk on the beach had manifested. Ash had felt it too, Nat was sure of it. In the way she'd looked at her, a flicker of a reminder of something they once used to have.

Nat glanced at the letter on the table next to her, from the Royal Victoria. They'd been more than understanding, Nat knew. She put her phone down and picked the letter up.

Dear Dr. Braithwaite,
    We are sorry to hear of your decision not to take up the offer of the post of…

Jack Greene had been horrified. Nat had heard on the grapevine too that Richard had been disappointed, but all Nat had felt was the burden lifting from her shoulders and floating far away from her the second she'd written the words that she'd wanted to write for weeks.

Nat looked away. A shimmer of insecurity returned at the thought of what her future now held. Would she move somewhere else? *Could* she? Her apartment, spacious and bare at the best of times, suddenly felt cavernous. Nat pulled at the cuff on her sleeve, looking down at the leather band on her wrist, and pulled on it, twisting it round her wrist, warding off the stab of panic that she knew was just one more thought away. If she stayed in London, her life would remain unfulfilled. Nat concentrated on her breathing, making a mental note to endeavour to find something outside the city boundaries. Something smaller, more personal. Perhaps not even an apartment, more of a house. Or a cottage, maybe. Not that it could ever be like Holly Cottage. Her breathing quickened.

This was no time to be thinking of Holly Cottage again.

Nat sprang to her feet and walked over to her books. She needed a distraction from her thoughts that constantly tugged her back down to Cornwall, taunting her, needling at her insides, teasing with what her life could have been like. She sat at her desk and opened up the first book where she'd left off the night before, then picked up her pen. She read, her eyes not seeing the words, and tapped the pen against her lip.

The buzz of her intercom, piercing through the quietness of her apartment, startled Nat. She looked to her door, her pen dangling between her fingers. It would be Jack, or Maddie, or—heaven forbid—Richard, come to try and make her see sense about Belfast. She could hear their voices now: *You were made for this job. It's everything you ever wanted, isn't it?*

Nat looked back down at her book. Well they could stay right there, outside her door. None of them truly knew her, and none of them would ever be able to convince her to change her mind.

The intercom buzzed again, longer this time. More urgent.

Whoever it was, Nat was determined they'd not sway her. Sighing, she put her book down and rose, stuffing her pen into her pocket as she wandered to the door. She lifted the receiver, not getting the chance to speak before she heard her voice.

"It's me," Ash said. "I really need to see you."

❖

Nat's heart hammered in her neck at the sound of Ash's voice. Ash was in Cornwall. With Widgeon. And Gabe and… She wasn't here. How could she be?

"Please let me up." Ash's voice sounded breathless. "Please. I need to see you."

Blindly, Nat pressed the intercom and stepped away. She unlocked the door and pulled it ajar, then wandered back into her lounge. Her mind raced, scenarios and conversations coursing through her brain as she paced the floor, dizzying her.

Ash was in Cornwall. Ash wasn't here.

She turned at the squeak of her door.

Ash was here.

Nat looked at her, standing in the doorway, looking so adorably lost. Nat watched as she came further in, shutting the door behind her, and stood, unsure where to stand or what to do with her hands. Nat knew she should go to her, put her at her ease, but her feet refused to move.

Because Ash was here.

"I got the train." Ash shook her head. "I mean. You know." Her face coloured. "To talk to you." She looked down then back up to Nat. "I need to talk to you because ever since you left the other day, I've been wishing I'd talked to you more." She lifted out her arms. "So here I am."

Nat couldn't speak. Ash had travelled five hours on a train because they hadn't talked enough? She looked questioningly at her, seeking answers in her eyes, then stood, dumbly, as Ash came closer to her. Nat watched her as she looked around the room, knowing she should say something—anything—to her, but no words would formulate.

"Drink?" Finally she managed something coherent.

Ash shook her head. "I've been really stupid," Ash said. "I mean, *really* stupid."

Nat didn't answer.

"I rang Belfast," Ash said. "They told me you turned the job down."

"How could I go?" Nat asked. "When it would mean leaving England...and you?" She looked at Ash. "If I stayed, then I thought maybe we'd have a better chance of something..."

"You can't not accept it." Ash shook her head. "You just can't."

"I can, and I have," Nat said. "There are plenty of research jobs out there. Do you know," she said, "now I've made the decision not to accept it, I feel as though a weight has been lifted." She blinked. "For months I've been suffocated by it all. But I made the decision the minute I had to leave you in Cornwall," Nat said smiling, "and it was like a light-bulb moment."

"You'd change everything for us?" Ash asked. "Everything you've worked so hard for?"

"Don't you see?" Nat said. "I *want* to give it up. I'm tired, Ash. Tired of being this person everyone expects me to be." She smiled. "All I ever wanted was to do research, but that was never enough for my father, or for Richard," Nat said. "A quiet medical research job where I could just be left alone." She looked at Ash. "You know he got me the job, don't you?"

"Your father?"

Nat shook her head. "Richard."

"Richard?" A look, sharp and swift, which Nat hoped might be jealousy crossed Ash's face.

"He put in a word for me, although no doubt ably encouraged by my father to do so." Nat frowned. "I felt railroaded into going for the interview," she continued, "just as I've felt railroaded all my life." She met Ash's gaze. "But no more."

"But I can't believe you'd actually sacrifice Belfast for me," Ash said.

"Belfast isn't a sacrifice," Nat said. "Belfast was something I thought I wanted when I didn't have anything better in my life. Then you came along and you were way better than anything else in the world." She reached out and took Ash's hands in hers. "You were more fulfilling and more rewarding than anything I could ever imagine, and at the end of the day I wanted you more than I wanted the job."

"Wanted?"

"*Want.*" Nat pulled her hand from Ash's and brushed a finger lightly across her collarbone. "I want you so much, Ash. Everything I want in my life is standing in front of me right now," she said. "Everything else is immaterial." She threw a look to the letter from the Royal, still on her chair where she'd left it. "It was easy telling them"—Nat smiled—"because I'd rather be with you."

Ash didn't speak.

"I'd do anything for you." Nat took Ash's hand again and kissed it. "I was stupid enough to let you go once," she said, "but I'm never letting you go again." She gazed at her. "It's always been you, Ash. No one but you."

Nat paused.

"What is it?" Ash asked.

"But do you want this?" Nat asked. "Do you want me?"

Ash looked at her in a silent reply then leaned closer, cupping Nat's face in her hands. Nat closed her eyes as she heard Ash whisper her name, shivered as she felt the first feather-light sweep of Ash's lips on hers, her light touches igniting something deep inside her. Nat went to pull away, but Ash's lips found hers again, drawing her back. Nat deepened the kiss, feeling the contact she so desperately craved, and smiled into Ash's lips when she heard a soft moan escape from Ash. Their lips still together, Nat was out of control and completely at Ash's mercy. She put her hands on Ash's chest and pushed her slowly back to a waiting chair, then eased Ash down, finally releasing her from the kiss. She looked down at Ash, noting with satisfaction her ragged breaths, and quickly straddled her, feeling the heat radiating from her.

"Don't stop," Ash whispered. "Kiss me again."

Without another word, their lips collided, days of yearning sending a surge of electricity through Nat's body as she felt Ash's tongue devour her, her heart hammering in her chest as her desire consumed her.

Finally, reluctantly, they parted, their foreheads resting on one another's, their chests rising and falling in a deep rhythm.

"Does that answer your question?" Ash asked. She looked up at Nat. "I love you, Nat." She held her gaze. "I thought when you left me all those years ago"—she hushed Nat as Nat protested—"that I'd had all the love wrung from my heart." Ash reached up and brushed Nat's hair from her flushed face. "But it's full again. Full of love for you."

"I love you too." Nat traced a finger across Ash's face then leaned to place butterfly kisses over her lips, down her neck. "I'll never stop loving you."

❖

Nat was in her arms. Ash opened an eye and looked down at her sleeping body, her arm casually flung across Ash, their legs tangled together. Ash rubbed her foot against Nat's, smiling when she grumbled and burrowed her head further into Ash's neck.

On the floor next to the bed were letters from the Royal Victoria, shredded and scattered about the room like confetti. Nat wanted her. Ash pulled her arms around her tighter and sighed out a deep, satisfied sigh. Nat meant everything she'd said to her in Cornwall, and Ash couldn't be happier. All her insecurities had disappeared the second Nat had stood in front of her and ripped up her letters, thrown the keys to her apartment over her shoulder, and told Ash she loved her over and over until they fell into one another's arms again. All Ash's doubts and questions had scattered around the room like the pieces of Nat's letters, to be replaced by security and a hope for the future when Nat had told her she couldn't be without her.

Ash moved her arm as she felt Nat stir against her.

"What are you thinking?" Nat asked.

"Just how amazing you are." Ash bent her head and kissed her neck, trailing kisses along her jaw, knowing all the right spots to linger over.

"Almost as amazing as you," Nat offered.

"Almost." She traced a finger over Nat's ribs, teasing her skin and smiling when she felt her squirm at the sensitive spots.

"You always used to do that." Nat murmured against Ash's shoulder. "Hit that tickly bit."

"Is that right?" Ash's finger drew a circle just above the spot, feeling the goosebumps rise on Nat's skin.

"And that." Nat bit her lip.

"You used to like it." Ash stopped tickling and pulled Nat to her, their kisses now slower, her fingers back on Nat's ribs, smoothing down her side, to her hip, and back again.

"Still do," Nat answered, her lips still against Ash's. She paused. "Ash?"

"Mm-hmm?"

"Can we date?" she asked. "Can we get to know one another all over again?" She looked into her eyes and read the meaning in them.

Ash pulled Nat closer. "I think I'd like that very much," she said.

"Starting with dinner?" Nat asked. "Livvy's letter said—"

"I read it." Ash smiled. "The Fisherman has a table with our name on it."

"Somehow I think Livvy might be with us in spirit when we go there," Nat said.

"And that would make things perfect, wouldn't you say?"

Ash kissed Nat's hair. "More than perfect," she said with a smile.

# EPILOGUE

A thin spiral of smoke was rising from the chimney of Holly Cottage as Ash made her way back up from the boat. She stopped for a moment and stared up at it, watching it twist and turn in the breeze before disappearing into the night sky. Ash flipped her collar up higher against the bitter November wind and clicked her fingers to Widgeon, who immediately fell into step beside her.

The smell of cooking from inside the cottage when she opened the front door instantly made her feel hungry. Kicking off her dirty boots, she made her way into the kitchen to investigate. A simmering pan on the stove brought the smells closer to her, and she wandered over to it, then lifted the lid to see what was inside.

Feeling arms encircling her from behind, she leaned into the embrace, savouring the warmth of the body that was now pressed up against her.

"How was your day?" Nat's hair tickled Ash's ear.

"Busy." Ash turned around and looped her arms over Nat's shoulders. "Two trips either side of lunch. Not bad for mid-November." She kissed her gently. "Yours?" she asked when she pulled away again.

"I've nearly finished the paper," Nat said.

"The piece for *The Lancet*?"

"The very same." Nat smiled. "Something about the peace and quiet here agrees with my studies."

"And you had time to cook too." Ash threw a look towards the stove. "I could get used to this."

"Good." Nat kissed Ash's forehead. "You should."

"I wanted to show you something." Ash released herself from Nat's embrace and took her hand. "Come on." She pulled her towards the door.

They stepped outside and stood on Ash's doorstep, looking up into the endless night sky.

"Stars just like beads," Ash said, wrapping her arms around Nat. "Exactly like I told you all those weeks ago in London."

Ash saw the look of happiness spread across Nat's face as she gazed up at the stars.

"I'd like to think Livvy's looking down on us right now," Nat said. "If only so we can tell her how much her letters have helped." She looked at Ash. "Do you think she knows?"

"Oh, she knows." Ash pulled Nat closer to her and smiled up at the stars. "She definitely knows."

# About the Author

KE Payne was born in Bath, the English city, not the tub, and after leaving school, she worked for the British government for fifteen years, which probably sounds a lot more exciting than it really was.

Fed up with spending her days moving paperwork around her desk and making models of the Taj Mahal out of paperclips, she packed it all in to go to university in Bristol and graduated as a mature student in 2006 with a degree in linguistics and history.

After graduating, she worked at a university in the Midlands for a while, again moving all that paperwork around, before finally leaving to embark on her dream career as a writer.

She moved to the idyllic English countryside in 2007 where she now lives and works happily surrounded by dogs and guinea pigs.

# Books Available from Bold Strokes Books

**24/7** by Yolanda Wallace. When the trip of a lifetime becomes a pitched battle between life and death, will anyone survive? (978-1-62639-6-197)

**A Return to Arms** by Sheree Greer. When a police shooting makes national headlines, activists Folami and Toya struggle to balance their relationship and political allegiances, a struggle intensified after a fiery young artist enters their lives. (978-1-62639-6-814)

**After the Fire** by Emily Smith. Paramedic Connor Haus is convinced her time for love has come and gone, but when firefighter Logan Curtis comes into town, she learns it may not be too late after all. (978-1-62639-6-524)

**Dian's Ghost** by Justine Saracen. The road to genocide is paved with good intentions. (978-1-62639-5-947)

**Fortunate Sum** by M. Ullrich. Financial advisor Catherine Carter lives a calculated life, but after a collision with spunky Imogene Harris (her latest client) and unsolicited predictions, Catherine finds herself facing an unexpected variable: Love. (978-1-62639-5-305)

**Soul to Keep** by Rebekah Weatherspoon. What *won't* a vampire do for love… (978-1-62639-6-166)

**When I Knew You** by KE Payne. Eight letters, three friends, two lovers, one secret. Can the past ever be forgiven? (978-1-62639-5-626)

**Wild Shores** by Radclyffe. Can two women on opposite sides of an oil spill find a way to save both a wildlife sanctuary and their hearts? (978-1-62639-6-456)

**Love on Tap** by Karis Walsh. Beer and romance are brewing for Tace Lomond when archaeologist Berit Katsaros comes into her life. (987-1-162639-564-0)

**Love on the Red Rocks** by Lisa Moreau. An unexpected romance at a lesbian resort forces Malley to face her greatest fears where she must choose between playing it safe or taking a chance at true happiness. (987-1-162639-660-9)

**Tracker and the Spy** by D. Jackson Leigh. There are lessons for all when Captain Tanisha is assigned untried pyro Kyle and a lovesick dragon horse for a mission to track the leader of a dangerous cult. (987-1-162639-448-3)

**Whirlwind Romance** by Kris Bryant. Will chasing the girl break Tristan's heart or give her something she's never had before? (987-1-162639-581-7)

**Whiskey Sunrise** by Missouri Vaun. Culture and religion collide when Lovey Porter, daughter of a local Baptist minister, falls for the handsome thrill-seeking moonshine runner, Royal Duval. (987-1-162639-519-0)

**Dyre: By Moon's Light** by Rachel E. Bailey. A young werewolf, Des, guards the aging leader of all the Packs: the Dyre. Stable employment—nice work, if you can get it…at least until silver bullets start to fly. (978-1-62639-6-623)

**Fragile Wings** by Rebecca S. Buck. In Roaring Twenties London, can Evelyn Hopkins find love with Jos Singleton or will the scars of the Great War crush her dreams? (978-1-62639-5-466)

**Live and Love Again** by Jan Gayle. Jessica Whitney could be Sarah Jarret's second chance at love, but their differences and Sarah's grief continue to come between their budding relationship. (978-1-62639-5-176)

**Starstruck** by Lesley Davis. Actress Cassidy Hayes and writer Aiden Darrow find out the hard way not all life-threatening drama is confined to the TV screen or the pages of a manuscript. (978-1-62639-5-237)

**Stealing Sunshine** by Tina Michele. Under the Central Florida sun, two women struggle between fear and love as a dangerous plot of deception and revenge threatens to steal priceless art and lives. (978-1-62639-4-452)

**The Fifth Gospel** by Michelle Grubb. Hiding a Vatican secret is dangerous—sharing the secret suicidal—can Felicity survive a perilous book tour, and will her PR specialist, Anna, be there when it's all over? (978-1-62639-4-476)

**Cold to the Touch** by Cari Hunter. A drug addict's murder is the start of a dangerous investigation for Detective Sanne Jensen and Dr. Meg Fielding, as they try to stop a killer with no conscience. (978-1-62639-526-8)

**Forsaken** by Laydin Michaels. The hunt for a killer teaches one woman that she must overcome her fear in order to love, and another that success is meaningless without happiness. (978-1-62639-481-0)

**Infiltration** by Jackie D. When a CIA breach is imminent, a Marine instructor must stop the attack while protecting her heart from being disarmed by a recruit. (978-1-62639-521-3)

**Midnight at the Orpheus** by Alyssa Linn Palmer. Two women desperate to make their way in the world, a man hell-bent on revenge, and a cop risking his career: all in a day's work in Capone's Chicago. (978-1-62639-607-4)

**Spirit of the Dance** by Mardi Alexander. Major Sorla Reardon's return to her family farm to heal threatens Riley Johnson's safe life when small-town secrets are revealed, and love may not conquer all. (978-1-62639-583-1)

**Sweet Hearts** by Melissa Brayden, Rachel Spangler, and Karis Walsh. Do you ever wonder *Whatever happened to...*? Find out when you reconnect with your favorite characters from Melissa Brayden's *Heart Block*, Rachel Spangler's *LoveLife*, and Karis Walsh's *Worth the Risk*. (978-1-62639-475-9)

**Totally Worth It** by Maggie Cummings. Who knew there's an all-lesbian condo community in the NYC suburbs? Join twentysomething BFFs Meg and Lexi at Bay West as they navigate friendships, love, and everything in between. (978-1-62639-512-1)

**Illicit Artifacts** by Stevie Mikayne. Her foster mother's death cracked open a secret world Jil never wanted to see…and now she has to pick up the stolen pieces. (978-1-62639-472-8)

**Pathfinder** by Gun Brooke. Heading for their new homeworld, Exodus's chief engineer Adina Vantressa and nurse Briar Lindemay carry game-changing secrets that may well cause them to lose everything when disaster strikes. (978-1-62639-444-5)

**Prescription for Love** by Radclyffe. Dr. Flannery Rivers finds herself attracted to the new ER chief, city girl Abigail Remy, and the incendiary mix of city and country, fire and ice, tradition and change is combustible. (978-1-62639-570-1)

**Ready or Not** by Melissa Brayden. Uptight Mallory Spencer finds relinquishing control to bartender Hope Sanders too tall an order in fast-paced New York City. (978-1-62639-443-8)

**Summer Passion** by MJ Williamz. Women loving women is forbidden in 1946 Hollywood, yet Jean and Maggie strive to keep their love alive and away from prying eyes. (978-1-62639-540-4)

**The Princess and the Prix** by Nell Stark. "Ugly duckling" Princess Alix of Monaco was resigned to loneliness until she met racecar driver Thalia d'Angelis. (978-1-62639-474-2)

**Winter's Harbor** by Aurora Rey. Lia Brooks isn't looking for love in Provincetown, but when she discovers chocolate croissants and pastry chef Alex McKinnon, her winter retreat quickly starts heating up. (978-1-62639-498-8)

**The Time Before Now** by Missouri Vaun. Vivian flees a disastrous affair, embarking on an epic, transformative journey to escape her past, until destiny introduces her to Ida, who helps her rediscover trust, love, and hope. (978-1-62639-446-9)

**Twisted Whispers** by Sheri Lewis Wohl. Betrayal, lies, and secrets—whispers of a friend lost to darkness. Can a reluctant psychic set things right or will an evil soul destroy those she loves? (978-1-62639-439-1)

**The Courage to Try** by C.A. Popovich. Finding love is worth getting past the fear of trying. (978-1-62639-528-2)

**Break Point** by Yolanda Wallace. In a world readying for war, can love find a way? (978-1-62639-568-8)

**Countdown** by Julie Cannon. Can two strong-willed, powerful women overcome their differences to save the lives of seven others and begin a life they never imagined together? (978-1-62639-471-1)

**Keep Hold** by Michelle Grubb. Claire knew some things should be left alone and some rules should never be broken, but the most forbidden, well, they are the most tempting. (978-1-62639-502-2)

**Deadly Medicine** by Jaime Maddox. Dr. Ward Thrasher's life is in turmoil. Her partner Jess left her, and her job puts her in the path of a murderous physician who has Jess in his sights. (978-1-62639-424-7)

**New Beginnings** by KC Richardson. Can the connection and attraction between Jordan Roberts and Kirsten Murphy be enough for Jordan to trust Kirsten with her heart? (978-1-62639-450-6)